THE TEMUJIN MURDERS

A Hank Tower Novel

By Charlie Horn

Curst greed of gold, what crimes
thy tyrant power has caused.
...Virgil

This book is a work of fiction. Names, characters and incidents are products of the author's imagination. Names of places, if real, are used fictitiously. Any resemblance to actual events, or people, living or dead, is entirely coincidental.

© Charles Horn 2012. All rights reserved.
ISBN-13: 978-1480056725
ISBN-10: 1480056723

**Published by
Calco Inc.**

For the entertainment
of family, friends and fans.

**OTHER HANK TOWER NOVELS
BY CHARLIE HORN**

Wall Street Killers
The Bennington Murders
The Death Chip

See www.charliehornfiction.com for previews.

THE TEMUJIN MURDERS

PROLOGUE

Even a psychopath can be self conscious. If he had raised the small tea cup by pinching its delicate side handle, someone might have noticed his disproportionately long fifth finger spike into the air like a crooked baton. It was an inch and a half longer than his middle finger. He never shook hands because of it; nor did he dress flamboyantly, speak too softly or too loudly, or let his hair or whiskers grow too long. Anonymity was essential in his trade.

He returned the cup to its saucer and casually turned a device that resembled an iPhone toward the back wall of the Palm Court, an Old World tea spot on the lobby floor of New York's Plaza hotel. A well-dressed, handsome man with perfectly coiffed hair streaked with touches of gray and a stunningly beautiful woman were seating themselves at a table for two in front of the back wall's floor-to-ceiling mirror. The man wore a dark Armani suit over his lean, muscular frame; she was wrapped in a clinging, magenta Dior dress with a narrow slit in its front from neck to waist. Both had flawless skin and expensive tans.

He watched their flirtatious nibbling of the canapés until, as he expected, the man whispered a room number. She squeezed his hand and took a plastic key card from him and put it in her small, bejeweled purse.

The man with the long finger took the room number off his listening device and drifted casually to the elevators. At room 716, he put what resembled an EZ-Pass under the doorknob. The door clicked open. He entered and hid inside a large closet and waited.

She came into the room ten minutes later and immediately tossed the mountain of pillows stacked at the head of the bed on the floor and pulled down the spread. She undressed and slipped between the cool sheets. The excitement of her first adventure with the handsome Italian had her heart racing. Ten minutes later he arrived. He stood at the foot of the bed in front of her and removed his clothes in a slow, teasing way, taking excessive care to hang his jacket, tie and trousers just so over the back of a wing chair. Naked, he went to the end of the bed and with a predatory grin pulled at the sheet she was pressing to her chin in mock modesty. They were afire. She let go of the sheet, exposing herself, and leaned forward. With wild eyes she locked her hands behind his neck and started to pull down his head.

The man with the long finger stepped out of the closet and went to the bottom of the bed. His hand was holding a gun with a silencer attached to its muzzle. The first pop from the 9-millimeter sent a bullet into her forehead; the second pop sent one into the back of her lover's head.

He checked his work, turned to leave – and stopped. The lock on the door had clicked. He flattened himself against the wall behind it. A man entered the room, paused a second, then stepped forward, holding a camera. He fell face down. The killer observed him thoughtfully while he detached the silencer, then turned and opened the door. He saw the hallway was empty and walked quickly to the elevator, leaving Hank Tower behind, bleeding on the floor.

CHAPTER 1

I became a root-and-branch New Yorker the day after I graduated from business school and started spying for the government. After working fifteen years for the Headmaster, as our gang of fifty called him, I left and started my own firm, Hank Tower and Associates, Private Investigators, LLC. Business was good the first two years. I even won the favor of highly placed New Yorkers, including the Mayor; but a dry spell had arrived and was now in its third month. It's the true and honest reason why I took an assignment I would have otherwise refused.

It was a freezing cold day in February when he strode into my modest, two-room office on East Fifty-sixth Street. He looked like an overfed aristocrat out of *Doctor Zhivago* inside a massive fur coat trimmed with an expensive sable collar. A round fur hat sat atop his head like a bird nest. He would have been a dead-ringer for a Siberian bear, but for the rosy cheeks and red nose. He had burst through my outer office past a protesting, but helpless, sixty-three-year-old Lydia Larson, my receptionist and office manager.

The man's first words were…

"It's hot in here!"

It was. The old, leaky building kept the radiators working at full throttle. He tossed his tent-size coat onto my new faux-leather couch, blanketing most of it, followed up with his hat and, grimacing, squeezed his bulk between the arms of the shiny black chair in front of my desk. If he had chosen my couch, it might have taken a crane to get him back on his feet.

He released a gust of air, paused to be sure he had my attention and with a hard stare asked,

"Do you break legs?" I said it wasn't my line.

"How about pistol whipping?" I demurred again.

"Too bad. I need someone beat to near-death and I can't do it myself." I wondered why. He looked like he could pin a gorilla.

"I would be an easy suspect," he explained, reading my thought. "He's my partner."

"And why do you want him beat up, Mr....?"

"Santori, Phillip Santori – because the bastard stole from me. He's been in my pockets for weeks. If it weren't for the damned vacations Janet insists we take – Aspen, Bermuda, Barcelona, I think she throws a dart at a globe and then gets the tickets – I would have caught him sooner."

"Mr. Santori, before we continue, a short marketing survey. How did you find me?"

"A friend in the media. I use a lot of media."

"A name?"

"No."

"Okay, let's move on." I asked, "Do you know where the stolen money is, Mr. Santori?"

"In our Gross Domestic Product, that's where it is! Spent! Blown! Irretrievable! That's why I want his legs broken." I repeated my policy, and added...

"There are loosely organized firms in the city that can accommodate you, but I am not affiliated with any of them. They also have a way of returning unexpectedly for a favor from those they accommodate, a favor you might not want to provide."

"I understand," he said, disappointed.

"Tell me how your partner stole the money." This was a dead end, but my professional curiosity had taken charge, and his partner's scheme might be useful to know. A while back I had worked with some IRS agents for a year, helping them pump details out of a catch to improve their future effectiveness.

"TV, that's how, snaky bastard, as if I wouldn't find out. It was all those trips." He was still struggling to fit himself comfortably in the chair.

"He stole your TV?"

"No, no. Infomercial TV, the kind you see late at night, pushing diet products, wrinkle removers, exercise machines, that kind of TV."

"He stole an infomercial?"

"He did indeed. A damned good infomercial. It was doing a six to one…"

"A six to one?"

"Right. Unheard of in the business. That means for every dollar spent on advertising you get back six in sales. At six to one the money rolls in."

"What was the product?"

His leaned forward, excited.

"What a product! Tested, proven and guaranteed, to quote the infomercial. We have done many infomercials over the years, but this one out-pulled them all. It came as close to printing money as you can get without a press. If Janet hadn't hauled me off to Moscow, it would still be printing." His face reddened. I asked about the product.

As if it weren't important, "The product? It's a vibration belt you wear around your waist while you sleep to reduce belly fat. Actually helps you sleep, too. We have a clinical on that. But sleep was a secondary claim. We had tons of testimonials, a couple from celebrities, and it sold for only two easy payments of $19.95 each. A fantastic deal! People are desperate for slimmer waists; they'll pay hundreds, thousands.

"We had twenty-foot containers full of belts coming in from China. We called it *Sleep and Slim*, trademarked of course, but we couldn't get a patent. God, what a product!" he finished with a heavy sigh.

Innocently, "It sounds like there was a sizable profit."

"Sizable? We were bringing in two-hundred-and-fifty-thousand dollars a week in profit, Mr. Tower, not sales, profit! And then it started dropping."

"That's where your partner came in."

"It all happened while Janet had me gallivanting around over there in commie land. The bastard placed the show on other stations behind my back, stations he thought I didn't know about. Idiot! He set up a separate fulfillment house with belts he shipped – stole! – out of our warehouse and diverted the money to himself, money we should have shared. It was a well-oiled sister operation, all his – not his and mine – one hundred percent his, the greedy s.o.b. And he stole it while Janet was pumping up the Russian economy with my dollars. Did he think I wouldn't check out such a large drop in sales? If he had been less greedy, siphoned off the sales gradually, I might have written it off to natural attrition."

"How much profit do you think he diverted to himself?" Here was a whole new world.

"Best I can tell, he was at it for about six weeks before I was able to stop it. That's a million and a half in profit, seven-hundred-and-fifty of it mine, money I could use right now!"

"Money you say you can't retrieve. Didn't you have a contract?"

"Contracts are rare in the direct response TV business. If you wait for a contract that everyone agrees on before you launch, the word can get out and someone else gets the cream."

"So you want his legs broken."

He drooped down in the chair, belly and legs extended, his large pepperoni face crestfallen.

"Yes, but you have talked me out of that. But I know another way to get even – and make no mistake, Tower, I want to get even – and if you can't help me do it, I will find someone who can."

"What is the other way?"

"His wife. I am almost certain she is cheating on him and if she is, I want to shove it in his face from New York to the Coast. I want enough proof to run a full-page ad in the *Wall Street Journal, The New York Times* and *U.S.A. Today*, maybe a thirty-second spot on the Super Bowl. I want the world to know he's a cuckold and a thief. I want him *persona non grata* to anyone in the infomercial business, any business. Now, I can prove the theft part, but I need proof for the cheating-wife part. Since you have talked me out of the broken leg solution, which I still prefer, I want you to get me the proof."

Frankly, in this day and age, I never thought a spy-on-my-spouse case would walk in my door and I had no interest, if one did. But this situation had intriguing angles to it. I decided to consider it a theft case instead of a divorce assignment and smiled at the rationale for the real reason, i.e., the dry spell.

"My fee is one-thousand a day, three-day minimum, plus an advance on expenses of five-hundred dollars."

"It's a deal. Get me the proof I need in three days and I'll double those charges," and then falling into the vernacular of his trade, added, "No questions asked."

He leaned forward awkwardly to the edge of my desk and wrote two checks for thirty-five-hundred dollars. "I'll gladly give you the second one three days from now, if I have proof."

This needed no rationale to accept. The company had adequate funds, but I treated them conservatively to be sure salaries, rent and other fixed costs were always covered during long, client-less periods. More important, an extra thirty-five-hundred dollars would let Carol and me get out of cold New York for warmer climes.

I picked up the check. "Deal. Now, I need names. Start with your partner's."

"Paul Santori." He said the name slowly with an emphasis on all the syllables.

I hesitated. "Your partner is related?"

"We're identical twins. Same size, same voice, same handwriting, same mannerisms. Look here. See this ugly mole on my neck?" He loosened his collar.

"Paul doesn't have one. It may be the only way you can tell the difference between us, if you ever have to. Paul lives in a co-op on Fifth Avenue across from the Metropolitan Museum of Art. A posh three-bedroom spread, probably worth ten-to-fifteen million today." He paused and smiled satanically.

"The building's Board of Directors will be the first to throw him out. Scandal is not their thing."

"Wife's name?"

"Eleanor. She's probably twenty years his junior, thirty-three or so, don't know for sure. They have been married three years. I must give the bastard credit. She's a real looker. He, on the other hand, is not. If you need proof, look at me."

"Meaning other men might be interested."

"And vice versa. She uses her looks to mess up male minds, toys with them, gets thrills out of it, I think. Here's an example. The two of you are at a cocktail party, you interest her, she wants to meet you. She doesn't just put out her hand; she walks right up to you, almost touching her front to yours and gushes out 'I'm Eleanor. No need for last names,' and arranges her face somewhere between a sexy pout and an inviting smile. Just when she senses you want to haul her in, she backs away and looks over her shoulder as if to say, 'Not now, but stay in touch'. I've seen her do it a dozen times."

"Do you have a picture?"

"Three of them, in winter clothes, summer clothes and a bikini."

I looked at them carefully, memorizing the tilt of the chin, her stance, the way she posed her arms and held her hands, her hair styles and other nuances. You can tell a lot from candid shots, if you analyze them. These said she was clearly a flirt – and gorgeous. She could easily "mess up male minds." I said,

"She's movie-star quality." I walked around to the front of my desk and leaned against it.

"OK, Phillip Santori, next step is for me to get on her tail, figuratively. It's almost eleven. Do you know where she lunches, shops, walks, anything? Does she have a dog?"

He stood up. He was under my six-one, but he outweighed my

one-hundred-and-eighty pounds by fifty or sixty.

"An English bulldog, probably one of the ugliest of the world's uglier breeds, walks it back and forth in front of her building on Fifth. Any insight there, Tower? I'll give you mine.

"The animal's rugged appearance attracts males, the shy ones who are intimidated by her looks. A woman wouldn't look at the damned thing if she could avoid it. While the unsuspecting fish makes chatter about the dog as an opener, she's sizing him up, getting his business and availability, deciding whether to set the hook or wait for a more promising fish. I saw this more than once from the apartment window."

"Give me your cell number. I'll let it ring twice, hang up and call again, so you know it's me and can find privacy."

"I like that. The dog's name is Chaucer. She lunches wherever her fancy says, but I would try the Palm Court in the Plaza hotel. It's touristy and less likely for someone to recognize her."

I helped him don his two-tons of fur and led him past a scowling Lydia Larson to the door. I promised he would soon know if Eleanor was cheating on his thieving, mole-less twin, Paul; and if she were, he would have the proof. His returned stare triggered a danger beep from my inner voice, but it was too weak to remember.

CHAPTER 2

The Plaza is the grand dame of New York hotels. At Fifty-ninth Street and Fifth Avenue it dominates the southeast end of Central Park and looms mightily over the Grand Army Plaza with its statue of a triumphant General Sherman riding high on his horse. Stand on the distant side of the Plaza, look up at the grand old dame, its windows and the mansard roof, and it seems to say "I will not judge you. I have seen it all over my ninety years of service." If such a statistic existed, I would wager that it would prove the Plaza has hosted more affairs than any other hotel in New York.

It was a cold twenty-minute walk from my office west to Fifth Avenue, then north to Fifty-ninth and finally up the hotel's front steps into the warmth and bustle of its beautiful, redecorated lobby. Ahead of me, centered in the middle of the main lobby was the Palm Court, perhaps a little tired now, but once Manhattan's ultimate tea spot. It comes with a maitre d' and dozens of tables for two. I don't know if this is where Vincent Youmans got inspiration for his wonderful song, but the Court's designer definitely had tea-for-two in mind.

People of all shapes and languages were entering, but Eleanor was not among them. I took up station to the right of the Court's entrance where I could see the arrivals without being seen.

At 12:45 she walked in through the revolving doors and turned left toward the lobby bar, then turned back toward the Palm Court. Every healthy male eye took a look. A few moments later, a tall elegant man with graying sideburns, dressed in a perfectly tailored Italian suit emerged from the lobby bar and greeted her with a kiss on both cheeks. She checked her fur coat and they were seated at a discreet table near the back wall.

I took a table about twenty feet from them and aimed the camera Bill Sanchez, a friend and former fellow employee of the Headmaster who now works for the National Security Agency, gave me when I started out on my own. It was the size and shape of a small cell phone; but it could pick up a pimple and a whisper at thirty feet. The Italian suit took a chair at a table for two and Eleanor pulled hers close enough for hip contact. Their voices were too soft for my ear, but not for the recorder's.

I ordered a glass of pinot noir, slightly chilled, which was delivered graciously along with a small plate of puffy, creamy things. I opened up the *Wall Street Journal*, nibbled at the puffy, creamy things and watched the two of them perform. A ten-year-old, make that a six-year-old, could tell these folks had something going. After about forty-five minutes of giggles and chatter he slid a key card across the tablecloth into Eleanor's hand and asked for the check. I laid down some cash, strolled out into the lobby and started planning where to spend that thirty-five-hundred-dollar bonus: Naples, Florida, St Bart's in the Caribbean? Picture-taking wasn't my *modus operandi*, but it was certainly easy cash.

She left the table for the elevator bank. I waited while he dallied for ten minutes or so and followed him onto the same elevator. We both exited on the seventh floor. He stopped in front of what, based on the room numbers on my left and right, would be 716. I walked around a turn in the corridor out of sight, waited about fifteen minutes for the two of them to get comfortable, then backtracked. A *Do Not Disturb* sign dangled from the door knob.

It was "B" movie time – fifties "B" movie, but the picture of beautiful sirens, including my own Carol, rising out of a warm and transparent Caribbean Sea, dressed in topless bikinis overrode my "B" movie prejudice. Just this once...

I waited another couple of minutes, then quietly slid another gift of Bill Sanchez's, a key card that could open virtually any hotel room door in the nation, through the slot, turned the door knob quietly and with camera in hand stepped inside the room just long enough to see two naked bodies on a large bed, one on top of the other, both with a bullet hole in the head, before I spiraled down into a kaleidoscope of bursting stars and suns and blackness.

I struggled awake about twenty minutes later. Blood was running down my neck from a head that felt like an NBA guard was dribbling it. My camera was gone, but the bodies were still there, one staring at the ceiling, the other staring at a dead Eleanor's chest. It was professional. The shots were perfectly placed and, thankfully, all I got was an "I wasn't paid to kill you" blow to the back of my head. I doubted there was a suspicious fingerprint in the room.

I let the phone ring twice, cleared it, then called again.

"Santori!" came blaring back.

"I'm in room 716 in the Plaza with your proof, but you won't need to advertise it. It will be in all the papers tomorrow, free. Eleanor is dead and her lover, or one of her lovers, name unknown, is lying on top of her equally dead. Both shot in the head, both *au natural*. This is a heads up, Phillip. My next call is to the police."

"My God. What should I do?"

"It looks like a professional killer. Get your alibi nailed down. This happened about a half hour ago, and get ready for the cops. They will first inform husband Paul and then question you. If you are truly twins, the *Post* and *Daily News* are going to have you both on page one with a 'Which one did it?' headline. Get out your best suit and tie."

From the other end came what a sick turkey coughing up gravel might sound like.

I hit Captain Holden's button on my cell. Recently captain, I should add. When we met he was a lieutenant. We shared the solving of a case that could have had devastating consequences to the City of New York. A grateful mayor awarded me financially and Tom with a promotion. His Honor implied it was largely on my recommendation. I doubted that, but I did my best to have Tom believe it. He answered.

"Tom, I have a double murder at the Plaza Hotel, room 716."

A thoughtful pause. "Hank, I appreciate your concern for my job, but you can stop with the murders. I have plenty to do without your help." An attractive client of mine only weeks ago was killed by a poisonous gas released from a pendant given to her by an unappreciative lover.

"These two look professional, two perfectly placed shots from about ten feet. The killer was in the room when I barged in and hit me just hard enough to put me down without killing me. I'll be here."

"You'd better be. I'm sending a patrol car now to secure the scene. Don't touch anything"

"Tom!"

"Right. I'll call the Medical Examiner. I'm on my way."

The curtain had fallen on my thirty-five-hundred-dollar bonus and with it my Caribbean fantasy. Now, I worried about the first thirty-five-hundred and chided myself for not banking it immediately. I had walked right by a branch of my bank on my way to the Plaza. On the other hand, Phillip *Sleep and Slim* might need me now more that ever. I could at least vouch for his presence until 11:00 this morning.

Considering the length of my dallying in the corridor waiting for the two lovebirds to lock in, I figured I was knocked down about one-fifteen. That meant Phillip Santori had two hours and fifteen minutes to account for prior to the murder. His best alibi was that getting into the room ahead of the victims was beyond his capacity. How the pro got in didn't matter. He got in, waited, and when his victims' attention was fully occupied, fired two well-aimed shots. He was probably sitting near me in the Palm Court.

Two uniformed officers showed up at the door almost instantly and blocked off the area; then Captain Tom Holden came in with two more officers and a fingerprint woman who was soon followed by the M. E. and an assistant. I explained to Tom how I happened to be there, how I got in, and acknowledged that the whole affair wasn't my finest hour. Phillip Santori's name and request were not revealed. The M. E. examined my head, cleaned it and applied as discreet a bandage as possible while praising the person who clobbered me for picking the exact spot on my skull for a quick and safe knockout, all the while bragging that I was lucky he still carried gauzes and sterilizers in his bag. His patients were usually dead. All this took about an hour after which I went down to ground level into the Plaza's lobby bar for something to drink.

It was only 2:30, less than five hours after my fur-coated, *Sleep and Slim* hawker swaggered into my lair looking for a leg-breaker. Life moves. I took a seat in a high-sided, rattan chair that backed up to a wall so my bandage was not easily noticed and ordered a Remy XO cognac.

Carol would notice it, of course, and that would lead to unpleasantness. I put that out of my mind and started to reminisce. This was where I first saw her. Then, as now, my attention was on other events. But the pre-Adam male eye – no matter how distracted – will pick up on things it is programmed to notice, among them long and lustrous brunette hair, high cheek bones, a fair complexion, a shapely chest and terrific legs. There were many other seats I could have chosen that day, but despite my fog, I chose to sit in one close to hers.

She had been stood up at the last minute.

"A friend and I," she had said, "were to meet in the Food Hall downstairs about one o'clock." She had given up waiting and came into the quieter lobby bar to make some calls.

I had just suffered a blow to the head then, too, but this one was worse. I took a sip of the cognac and closed my eyes to thwart whoever was banging pots and pans behind my forehead.

We had made eye contact, smiled at each other and started talking about nonsense things, which led to what she did, what I did and, finally, what Nature does took over. Carol said she had just taken a job as a crime reporter for the *New York Daily News* after a stint with a smaller paper in the Midwest.

That was nearly two years ago. Now, we live together in her apartment in Greenwich Village and I have been with her to St. Louis, her hometown, to meet her uncle Jack. Jack is the stand-in for her deceased parents. Since that visit she has switched jobs to the *New York Post* and made a name for herself by creating a web site to help find missing persons and solve cold cases. It's called solve-it-ny.com. News Corp promotes it with ads in its newspaper, the *New York Post*, and there are a few ads on the site itself, including one of mine. Since moving in together she has suffered heartache when I come home with knife wounds, bruises, lumps on the head and other battle scars, as I will tonight.

She wants a child badly; I don't. She had a miscarriage after consciously or unconsciously forgetting her birth control pills.

It all started ten feet from where I sat now in the Plaza Hotel's lobby bar. I savored that memory, hoping it would overcome the tension I foresaw when once again I would present myself to her, bandaged and smelling like an ER. But for the rigid economics of a professional killer, I would be dead. That fact once again reinforced my belief that my line of work doesn't allow for the responsibility of a child. She counters that policemen, soldiers and fireman are fathers. I have no meaningful rebuttal, so I retreat and we fall asleep empty armed.

I let the call ring twice, hung up and called back. The "Santori" response had lost its boom. I said with force,

"We need to talk Phillip. Meet me at my office in one hour."

I wanted more time for my cognac and a small snack.

On the way to my office I stopped at the bank and deposited the first thirty-five-hundred. The elevator was out again, forcing a climb up the two flights. My office door was ajar. This is not a good sign for several reasons. One, the lock on my door is not an easy one to overcome; second, I always lock the door when I leave and third, if someone is inside, it was not Lydia. She left early to visit her ancient mother and it was not my assistant Arnie Macgregor who was on a short vacation. I drew the .38 I keep in the small of my back and crept to the door. A look through the crack between the door and the jam said, unlike a few hours ago, no one was waiting to reopen my head. I dropped into a low crouch and flung it open ready to shoot.

The office was occupied, all right, but not in a threatening way. On Lydia's desk, centered for easy discovery, was my high-tech camera and recorder from Bill Sanchez. The killer not only knew who I was, but where I worked and was thoughtful enough to return both emptied of what I had recorded in the Plaza hotel's Palm Court.

Phillip "*Sleep and Slim*" Santori never showed up.

CHAPTER 3

Paul Santori handed his heavy coat to the flight attendant and pushed his carry-on bag into the bin above his Business Class seat. He was on a mission that would begin with a breakfast meeting at the Savoy Hotel in London with an Englishman named Alistair Baker.

Alistair did a one-hundred-million-pound business in high-end art in a country with about twenty-percent of America's population. Paul intended to make it known throughout England and Europe that he intended to replicate Alistair's business model in the U. S. To get the business started, he would broadcast that he was in the market to buy sculptures, paintings and other valuable artifacts from anyone who wanted to sell, tempting collectors to bring out that "priceless" artifact the family has treasured for decades. If it meets my criteria, Paul Santori would promise, I'm ready to buy.

To shore up his company's worth, he had informed Dun and Bradstreet, a firm that provides financial information on companies to other companies or individuals for a fee, that Santori Enterprise's policy had changed. It was prepared to give D&B key facts about itself, facts it had previously withheld as confidential. He deliberately inflated the company's numbers to increase his credibility with art sellers.

He gazed down at the cold, February Atlantic as the Boeing 767 whined its way to 39,000 feet. At about 20,000 a still-attractive flight attendant set a glass of straight-up scotch and a cup of mixed nuts on the console between Paul and the seat next to him. He breathed in the whiskey's strong smell with a massive inhale and took a hearty sip. Its hot, biting taste burned a channel down the center of his chest. He pushed one of the many buttons on the side of his seat and lowered himself into a more relaxed position. His thoughts returned to Manhattan. How were events playing out back there, he wondered?

He would make a call when he reached Heathrow Airport.

"Aye, 'ank. Give me twenty minutes."

Arnie Macgregor, my associate and ex-NYPD sergeant, was foregoing his two days off at my request.

"Arnie, I wouldn't ask this if a very good hit guy hadn't dropped me…"

"Aye, ye needn't go into it, 'ank. I'm on my way."

Arnie Macgregor stood six-foot-six, sported a mass of red, Scottish hair and weighed at least two-hundred-and-fifty pounds. Quickly told, his story turns on a black teenager who had just robbed a convenience store at night and was facing Arnie defiantly with a knife in one hand and a gun in the other. He started to raise the gun toward Arnie and Arnie shot and killed him. The gun turned out to be a piece of black pipe.

Arnie was retired early sans pension. With a wife and two daughters to support, he took a job bartending at the Thirsty Tongue, a restaurant and bar across the street from my office. I hang out there and we got to know each other. Thanks to a generous loan from the Mayor of New York's private company in return for work done for the city that couldn't be revealed, I was able to hire Arnie at a much better salary than he earned pouring booze and cleaning glasses. The loan also allowed me to hire Lydia away from two insurance agents next door to my office.

Lydia's story is much simpler. She is single, sixty-three, commutes by car from New Rochelle, New York, a place not known for thrills. Lydia was bored and jumped at the job. That changed quickly. Not far into her new job a killer broke into my office, put a gun to her head and dragged her down the stairs, threatening to kill her if anyone pursued him. Outside, he released her terrified, but unharmed, and fled. She must have thought long and hard about it, but she stayed with me.

The three of us comprise the dynamic firm of Hank Tower and Associates, LLC. We even advertise on Carol's web site, solve-it-ny.com.

As promised, Arnie made it to the office in twenty minutes.

I brought him up to date and waited. He said,

"We need a check on Phillip. I'll call the Seventeenth."

The Seventeenth Precinct where Captain Tom Holden was in command. I could pump Tom, but it seems a universal truth that sergeants know things before officers do. A friend of mine claimed that when he served in the Navy as a junior officer he would ask his chief petty officer for important information, not a senior officer.

"I'll check on 'is company as well."

I said, "Our client's twin, Paul, is in the phone book on Fifth Avenue, but there is nothing about him on Google or Yahoo! Strange. Phillip's description of the company the two of them ran made it large enough to warrant coverage. He claimed it made over two-hundred-thousand a week in profit on Sleep and Slim. That seems large enough for a mention."

Arnie asked, "What about the Better Business Bureau?"

"I went to its web site. All I saw was they received complaints about refunds and late shipments. Santori Enterprises is not a BBB member."

"It looks like Phillip and Paul like a low profile. I wonder why."

"Work your contacts in the Seventeenth and we'll compare notes later – after I talk to Holden. I want to give him more time to hunt and gather. Let's talk at eight."

I paused, swung my chair around to the window behind me and mused in a low voice,

"I need a drink to treat the whacked head. Then…then…" I trailed off. Arnie knew.

"Aye, 'ank. The 'ouse was never pleasant when I came 'ome with a bump or worse. The wife went into 'erself, busied 'erself with whatever was close at 'and – dishes, clothes, a newspaper or magazine. Things she would usually let pile up unnoticed suddenly had to be tended to. The girls would see a bandage and ask what happened. I would make up something like 'I caught me head on another door, lassie. Ye 'ave to keep telling me how 'igh yer daddy's goes up.' It passed; it always passed, but the air would get 'eavy before it went normal."

I spun my chair back to him. "Thanks, Arnie."

He smiled. "There's much to be said for a good drink."

"I'm off to the doctor." I put on my coat and walked across the street to the Thirsty Tongue, leaving Arnie to work the phone.

I slow-sipped a Remy XO for almost an hour, hoping the cognac's fire would burn off the throb and worry in my battered brain. It worked on the former; the latter withstood the cure. Carol probably wouldn't turn to stacking dishes or reading a magazine, but her coolness would be no less telling.

I got in a cab for our apartment in Greenwich Village and went through a gamut of moods. At Forty-second Street and Second Avenue, I was relenting. Maybe a child wouldn't affect my game, maybe it would increase my caution, even keep me alive longer; maybe it would bring more joy into my life than worry. Look at Arnie. He had two young daughters. He loved them and they loved him. He was a happy man despite nearly getting killed a couple of times while working for me. I never asked how many times he came close to the Reaper while on the force. Maybe I should just say "Carol, let's make love without the pill. Let's let Nature decide."

I mellowed on this solution; then somewhere around Fifth Avenue and Twenty-third Street I got pissed off. Why should I even have to deal with this problem? Why am I so occupied with some damned thing I want no part of? Why am I even thinking about it? A child will clearly screw up my work – my life. It would change everything. I am happy with the way things are. I have my job, my work, my fun. Why would I want to change that? Why is she pushing this child thing? No way. I'm not going to give up what I have, what I worked hard for, almost got killed for. That's that. Forget it, Carol. The cab stopped in front of our apartment. I paid him with less of a tip than usual and went inside. Carol was not home yet.

I shed my coats and the five-shot .38 I keep holstered in the small of my back. The gun was my father's only legacy to me. The man drank too much, yelled too much, and died as too many ex-cops do – broke; but I carried his gun despite others in the trade telling me to get something more powerful. Three years after he died his ailing wife, my mother, went into an Alzheimer's home, where she is today, where I dread to go and rarely do. And Carol wanted a child in this world? A slightly chilled glass of pinot noir helped brighten my mood.

I was pouring a second glass when Carol bounded in the front door and shut it with a bang. It was not her usual entrance. I turned to keep the bandage on the back of my head out of sight.

While removing her coat she bellowed,

"I can't handle the new IT person anymore. He's incompetent. I'm doing his job and mine, too. How did he get hired, for Christ sake? Who hired him? All the people looking for work and I wind up with someone who can't even change copy on the site!"

I heard a thud as her purse ended a five-foot toss to a wooden chair in our foyer.

"Tomorrow's the day. If I get in trouble for saying he has to go, so be it. I can't do his job and do mine well at the same time."

She tossed a shoe to the floor, paused, and carefully removed the other, as if her better self had said "Wait a minute. These are expensive."

Shoeless, she stared at me and said,

"I would like a drink." It wasn't a sweet, feminine tone. It was more how an angry Captain Kidd might ask for more rum. I said nothing and poured some pinot for her. She took the glass and flopped down on the living room couch. After a stage pause, she raised it to me.

"Here's to mutiny."

I remained quiet, smiling inside at the departure from her normal evenness.

My hospital smell had followed me into the living room – a trigger – but neither of us said anything. Finally, she sighed as if giving in to a great load, or getting ready to launch one, downed part of her wine and set the glass on the coffee table. Calmly,

"Hank, I'm sorry about the outburst." I waited. Something was off key. Mutiny at the office was giving way to a larger cause. She said,

"I've been thinking. I know you don't want a child and I understand why. So one way to keep you from going off your game and getting killed and making me feel guilty and miserable is for us to raise someone else's child. That way I have a child and you have something that's not you. You'll feel less responsible. We'd be together, but I would do all the parenting. I would get a nanny to fill in when I have to be at work. I think it's a wonderful idea. It keeps you emotionally distant from the arrangement. Your prowess would not be affected. You would be safe."

"You mean adopt a child?" I was sure I didn't want to do that.

"No, that's expensive and can take a long time; and you never know about the genes. Besides, it wouldn't be mine."

"Carol, I'm not sure how…"

She looked at me in a devilish way. "There's a guy at the office who is very good looking and extremely intelligent. I could speak to him…"

"Whoa! What are you suggesting, that you sleep with him?"

"Well, not all night, just long enough and often enough…"

"I can't believe this! Are you serious?" She appeared unmoved by my hysterics.

"Carol, honey, I love you. I can't let you…the mere fact that you would think of such a thing …" I fell into the chair across from her. "Have you spoken to this…this guy?"

"No, it's a recent thought. I have heard of others doing it…" She crossed her magnificent legs. "I'm sure he would…"

"Good Lord! Of course he would! Every bloody man in your office – in the city! – would…"

With a teasing smile that I didn't get right away, "But he's the best looking and very bright…"

"I don't care if he's Einstein and Gregory Peck! Holy God Almighty!…if you want a child that badly, then it damned well will be mine…" The teasing smile had changed into a very pleasant one.

I felt like a fool, a relieved fool, but nonetheless a fool.

She walked over and curled up in my lap.

She grinned like someone who had made a point. I said, "Sometimes it takes a two-by-four to get an ass's attention."

"I won't hold you to what you said, Hank."

She wound her left arm around my neck just below the smelly bandage. "Was it treated by a doctor?"

"Yes." Our eyes were only inches apart. Maybe that's what all lovers should do when one of them goes bonkers. Look into each other's eyes at close range, put your arms around each other and pull your bodies in close. Carol had teased her way into my gut with the odious thought of another man touching her intimately.

I said with a smile, "Please don't swing any more two-by-fours at me." She promised she wouldn't. I paused. "And…and…"

She drew her face back a bit. "And?"

I swallowed. "…and stop taking the birth control pills."

She dropped her head on my shoulder, her lovely hair dropping over her chin, and put the warm palm of her right hand on my cheek. The feeling between us curled up in that chair was as intimate as making love.

An hour later, at 8:00, I called Arnie at the office.

"'ank, Santori Enterprises, Inc., is ten-years old. Paul Santori is President and Treasurer. D&B doesn't list Phillip Santori. Paul's wife, Eleanor Santori, is shown as Vice President and Secretary, only seven employees. Everything is contracted out. The business is infomercials. Sales average thirty-to-forty million a year. Last year they jumped to sixty million. Accounts Payable are current and paid within sixty days. No long-term debt. Sounds pretty good, aye?"

I was doing some notepad arithmetic while Arnie talked, using Phillip's "…at six to one the money rolls in" comment as a benchmark. I dropped it to what I thought would be a more typical ratio, factoring out the wild success of *Sleep and Slim*, added in a standard figure for overhead, cost of goods and got a ballpark number that suggested the two Santoris made about a million a year each. If the jump to sixty million was from the Sleep and Slim product, their million-a-year would have jumped proportionately, while it lasted. The numbers provided adequate money for murder. Add in a gorgeous and playful wife and…

"Paul Santori is not at 'ome. The police are looking for 'im," continued Arnie. "Our client, Phillip Santori, isn't listed in New York City, but Google has one in Jupiter, Florida. No occupation or phone number. I got the dead guy's name."

"Good work, Arnie. From the Seventeenth?"

"No, from a fellow lodge member who works in the morgue. Giuseppe Bufono – Joe Bufono, in English. Italian passport. Arrived here a few months ago. The dead woman is definitely Paul's wife, Eleanor Santori. Both died instantly."

"Anything on Joe Bufono?"

"No police record here or with Interpol. No known wife or family. Sounds like a gigolo who caught up with Eleanor somehow for some reason."

"Two reasons. Looks and money. Good work, Arnie. Stay with Giuseppe – Joe. My gut says he's important. And hunt down Paul Santori. I need to see his neck. I'll be in the office about nine tomorrow."

I felt Arnie do a double take on the "I need to see his neck," but he let it pass. He had another concern.

"'ow do we get paid, 'ank, if our client has gone to earth?"

I gave him a bland not-to-worry answer. My mind was elsewhere.

Why wasn't break-his-legs Phillip Santori in the D&B report?

CHAPTER 4

Night was falling fast outside the big jetliner as it flew away from the setting sun. It would be 1:00 a.m. when it landed at Heathrow, and close to 3:00 a.m. when Paul finally retired to bed in the Savoy hotel. "Going flat" in his business-class seat would help his alertness at his breakfast meeting with the art dealer, Alistair Baker.

He maneuvered the small buttons on the console at his side and the chair lowered his upper half and raised a foot rest for his legs. The airline blanket covered his length, but not quite his width. He tugged it left and right and finally decided his bulk would keep him warm. Most of the other passengers had finished their dinners and were preparing to doze. But for the dull hum of the jet engines it was quiet in the dimly lit cabin.

Paul raised his head, swallowed the last of his scotch, put on the airline's eye blinders and released a powerful exhale. The hypnotic whishing of the engines drifted his thoughts into why he was going to London. Money was number one; Giuseppe Bufono was number two and three.

They had met several months ago at an exhibition of the works of Degas, Renoir and other Impressionists at the Metropolitan Museum of Art across from Paul's apartment on Fifth Avenue. Eleanor insisted he attend with her. What the hell, he thought; the place is a short walk. None of the humanities interested Paul. He liked numbers, long numbers with dollar signs in front of them. He understood numbers; numbers were definitive. He could talk comfortably about them. Paintings of fruit bowls and people drinking in cafés? Why not just take their pictures with an iPhone?

He had always excelled at math. He could out-compute his

grade school class by multiplying and dividing in his head. The gift grew as he aged – three advanced Sudoku puzzles lay completed at his side. Sometimes he would feel a deep respect for the beauty and logic of numbers and the unarguable statements they made. Numbers were one creation of Man that he couldn't twist and say, "Oh, it doesn't mean that, it means…" They could be deflated or inflated by liars, as he had done with his company's finances with D&B; but numbers themselves were unbendable.

Words were putty. A speaker or writer could shape them to his or her purpose or ideology. A glass half-full of water could be half-empty, if that supported an embedded view. But a glass with four ounces of water in it could not have three or five ounces, whether viewed by a devil or a saint. Four ounces is four ounces; and two plus two is four, and can't be interpreted differently. It was Giuseppe's willingness to listen to Paul expound on this and some of his other favorite subjects that let Paul tolerate him; for he knew why he was on the scene. He had seen the game of eyes between Giuseppe and Eleanor, but Paul had seen the game before and permitted it.

…as long as she didn't go too far.

Giuseppe and Paul had an occasional drink. Paul's reason was money. He smelled it. If Giuseppe really was as connected as his stories suggested, Paul could use him. Giuseppe's reason for the relationship was Eleanor.

Santori Enterprises had had a good run over the last ten years, especially with the recent success of *Sleep and Slim*. But things change quickly in the direct response TV business. The company had received a registered letter from the Federal Trade Commission requesting an array of documents. They wanted to see proof that refunds had been given and products had been shipped within the time limit required by law. Paul could handle that. The killer demand was the request for substantiation of the claims the infomercial made for *Sleep and Slim*.

Paul had seen other direct response TV companies go down shortly after receiving this kind of letter and he sensed doom for Santori Enterprises. He knew support for some of the claims made in the infomercial was shaky at best, and some refunds were probably not made on a timely basis or at all. The fines for late shipments and late refunds and false claims were devastating – up to ten thousand dollars an occurrence. Santori Enterprises had sold several hundred thousand *Sleep and Slim* belts. It took Paul a nanosecond to compute the math. The FTC could wipe out the company with a fine a fraction of the size it could legally impose.

In their conversations Paul sensed some truth in Giuseppe's tales of traveling the better rooms of Europe; his looks and suavity made the stories reasonably possible. Paul was certain Giuseppe had no money; but if he were to continue seeing him, and if he were to continue watching him and Eleanor ogle each other, he wanted proof of Giuseppe's tales. A few phone calls to contacts in Europe confirmed that Giuseppe indeed did socialize with many of the names he freely dropped; and more than likely, he learned, given his easy manner, many of their secrets. The calls gave Giuseppe credibility. Paul started listening to him more closely.

It was in the King Cole bar in the St. Regis hotel in Manhattan where Giuseppe launched into a story that grabbed Paul's arithmetic soul. It was another tale about rich Europeans, but in telling this one he was no longer the lighthearted, regaling "Can you believe these people?" chronicler of Europe's wealthy. This time Giuseppe Bufono was uncharacteristically serious.

His story included a *nouveau riche* Austrian billionaire named Carl von Tresser he had met skiing; a museum curator named Carlton Bouchard with millions of euros at his disposal; an English dealer in million-dollar *objets d'art* named Alistair Baker whom Giuseppe had met; and finally the *piece de resistance*: a cloistered nunnery somewhere in Venice that Giuseppe said was the key to a fortune.

At the center of his drama was a nine-hundred-year-old artifact of incalculable value that had been coveted by the richest collectors in Europe for centuries. The story was why Paul was flying to London to meet the dealer in expensive *objets d'art*, Alistair Baker.

Lydia and Arnie were already at their desks in the outer office when I arrived at 9:00.

Arnie came into mine and flopped his mass on my couch.

"'ank, I checked the Phillip Santori I found in Jupiter, Florida. Not much help. 'e's dead. Even alive 'e would be ninety. We 'ave a phantom client."

I said, "Let me check something." I called my bank and asked for a picture of the thirty-five-hundred-dollar check I deposited.

"If you deposited it yesterday afternoon, it won't be available on your account's web page until late this afternoon." I thanked the sweet, young voice and hung up.

"We won't know for a while if it bounces or goes through. Even if it bounces, it's a lead on his bank."

Arnie answered with a reasonable question, but one I embarrassingly could not answer. I was too busy justifying the catch-the-lover seediness of the assignment and never asked.

"Where is the company located?"

"I don't know."

Pause. "Aye. I'll track it down, 'ank."

"Ask Lydia to help, and have her call her computer-whiz nephew, if it will speed it up."

"Aye." He unfolded his long frame and went into the outer office. I called Carol at the *New York Post*.

"It's your gullible, but otherwise smart and loving mate. He needs a favor and hopes the guilt you feel for exciting his stomach acid will force you to provide it."

"What is it, smart and loving?"

"I need data on a company called Santori Enterprises, Inc. It's in the infomercial business, but probably uses print too – maybe the *Post*."

"I'll see what our salesmen know."

"Is that Einstein-Gregory Peck guy one of them?"

"Hank, my love, he doesn't exist. You're right. I do feel guilty, but not very. I don't plan to stop the pill for a while. Last night has to sink in. Call it a grace period before your policy expires."

I smiled. "Okay. Will you tell me when you stop?"

"No. you have to tell me not to stop. Otherwise, poof goes the grace period."

"How long is it?"

"Only the Shadow knows."

Damn. That's why I love her.

She said, "I'll have something for you before the end of the day." We hung up.

I Googled Santori Enterprises and found it located in Queens on Vernon Street just north of the Queensboro Bridge. I called and got a recorded "Please leave your name, number and the nature of your call..." I stepped into the outer office and while putting on my coat barked,

"Arnie, Lydia, the boss is off to Santori Enterprises in Queens. Here's the address and phone number. Give it half-hour calls. If a real person answers, say you're looking for Phillip Santori. You have a TV buy he will love. If you see an infomercial for *Sleep and Slim*, order it. Only two easy payments of $19.95."

I went down to Fifty-sixth and got a cab for Vernon Street, We crossed the Queensboro Bridge at Fifty-ninth Street and exited almost immediately on the Queens side. The address was near Vernon and Forty-first Avenue across the street from Queensboro Park. I told the cabbie to wait. It's easy getting to Queens by cab, but hellish getting one to leave it.

It was a plain, two-story building that housed several small service businesses. The ID board in the small, clean lobby said Santori Enterprises, Inc. was on the second floor. It was a modest headquarters for a company doing millions in sales.

The opaque glass door said Santori Enterprises, Inc., but was locked. No bell and no answer after several knocks. Was this some kind of front? Was I taken in by Phillip Santori? A flush of inferiority seized me. Fooled by Carol, now Santori?

There was an open door a couple of offices down the hall – Burns and Burns Insurance. Notary. Inside was an overweight woman eyeing her computer monitor in a kind of Zen state.

"Miss, I am looking for someone at Santori Enterprises. Do you know if..." A white cat leaped off a bookshelf and did a four-point landing on her desk with no effect on her Zen.

Still looking at the monitor she reached over and ran her hand down the cat's hunched back and dropped a tidbit in front of it. The cat grabbed it and started jerking its head back and forth chewing hard.

"Nobody there anymore. The landlord says they're moving out."

"Have you seen anyone there today?"

She finally looked at me. "All I know is what I said." I handed her my card.

"Please call me if you see someone go in the office." She studied the card, then me, then the card.

"You're a private dick. Like in the movies. There's been a murder, hasn't there?"

"No. Phillip Santori and I were in the Army together. I wanted to catch up with him."

"Army? He's too fat for the Army," she said dead pan, returning her hand to the cat's back.

"He's put on weight since we served together. Please call me if you see him or one of his employees."

She nodded. "You carry a gun?"

"No."

I left Burns and Burns Insurance, Notary, for the cab. No Phillip, no Paul, no employees. I was getting paranoid. Was I set up to take a murder rap? Nonsense. I had no motive to kill Eleanor and Giuseppe and the police knew my reputation was spotless. Maybe the visit was no more than what it was, a request for pictures of a cheating wife, but cheating wife and lover got killed and my client has gone into hiding. Was Phillip capable of two perfectly placed shots to the head and a perfectly placed whack on mine? Would he have even fit behind the door to the hotel room? No. I was certain it was a hired gun.

An accident on the bridge had cars moving a foot at a time. It was 1:00 when I finally reached the Manhattan side – 1:30 when I reached my office and got the call.

"Tower, Santori."

"Where the hell are you?" The screen on my cell phone was blank.

"No need for you to know."

"No need? Phillip, there are two murders. The police are looking for you and Paul – who is also missing. I have a bandage on the back of my head that says I need to know."

"You would have to lie to the police. I'm not sure you would. Ergo, no need to know. Tell me where things are. I'm still your client."

"They're nowhere. I called on your office in Queens. Closed. A neighbor says you're moving out. You're a prime suspect, Phillip – Paul, too. You left my office at eleven and the murders were two hours later. That's plenty of time for you to…"

"Hold it! We have a client relationship. You can't reveal that."

"Answer me this. Why did you send me over there?"

"To get pictures."

"Well, I can cut some out of the dailies, if you still want some. Now, where the hell are you?"

"Top secret, Tower. But I won't let you get fingered for the murders…"

"That won't happen, Phillip. I hope that's not the real reason you sent me there."

"No. I just wanted pictures to get even with my prick brother."

"Why doesn't D&B list you as part of Santori Enterprises?"

"Because I didn't want to be."

"Why?"

"Neither Paul nor I like publicity of any kind. If he's listed, I suspect he did it for some other purpose."

"Why are you calling me?"

"Remember my check? You work for me. I want you to keep me informed as this murder thing plays out. You are my eyes and ears."

"I need a way to get in touch with you."

"No. I will call you. Don't try to trace me or Janet. She's with me."

"Where do – did – you live? We can't find a Phillip Santori anywhere."

"Hank, my friend, that is not an accident. Now, remember those dollar facts I gave you about *Sleep and Slim*? They're true, but they're based on claims that I knew from Day 1 would not stand up. Now, what I knew would happen has happened. The FTC is after Santori Enterprises. In a month or less the business will be gone. I have taken my share – my fair share – out and flown the coop with Janet. My last hurrah is sticking it to my cheating brother, but it seems someone has outdone me on that. Think of me as a ghost who will call you occasionally for worldly information."

He hung up. I tried to retrieve the incoming number, but there was no record. The ghost was gone.

CHAPTER 5

Paul rose at 7:30, showered, shaved, put on a dark, pinstripe "British" suit and tie and took the elevator to the lobby of the Savoy, the very beautiful Savoy, thanks to a 150-million-pound renovation. He strolled slowly – his bulk gave him little choice – alongside a magnificent gazebo framed under a glass-domed cupola into the River Restaurant. The maître'd ushered him to a table next to a window opening to the Thames. It had expensively appointed plates, silverware, crystal glasses and a bouquet of fresh flowers. The table cloth was crisp and spotless. He requested coffee instead of tea. The maître'd told him Mr. Alistair Baker was detained for a short while, but would arrive shortly.

Paul searched for a comfortable position in the table's small arm chair and settled for perching his bulk on the front edge of it. The sky, the street below his window that paralleled the river, the misty air were all shades of winter gray. Even the Thames itself, at muddy low tide, was cheerless. Pedestrians had their collars up and heads down into the wind as they made their way to nearby office buildings and the underground station. February in England is not a walk on the beach.

He had looked forward to an English breakfast and with a touch of anger at Baker's absence ordered without him. Eggs and bacon and scones and jellies and butter and honey and a rack of toast had just arrived when the well-known dealer in expensive objets d'art showed up.

"My dear Mr. Santori, I must apologize for my lateness. I hope Henry advised you."

Alistair Baker was also dressed in a dark, pinstriped British suit and tie. However, his attire agreed with him. He had thinning dark hair, delicate hands, a large emerald ring on his left hand, perfect teeth beneath a thin, barbered mustache. He stood five-six and carried less than half of Paul's weight. A man Paul's size could crush him with one blow.

"I see you have started. Excellent. I would not want to be responsible for any more discomfort than my tardiness may have already caused you." He pulled back the other small chair and sat comfortably in it.

"Please proceed with your meal. I am having tea only. I'm afraid my delay required my dining ahead of you." He signaled Henry and studied the large American sitting uncomfortably across from him. His tea arrived instantly.

He held up the cup. "Now, I am fully here. Without tea I find I am subject to distractions." He sipped and said,

"I understand that you are in the market for the kinds of objects which I am acquainted with. I also understand that you would like to establish yourself in a capacity similar to mine in America. If I can assist you in that regard, it would be my pleasure to do so. There is no conflict – my dealings are strictly England and the Continent. It's possible your success would be beneficial to both of us."

He paused and sipped again while Paul ate and studied Alistair in between bites. Alistair continued,

"I would like you to come to my apartment after we have finished talking here. My car is at the entrance. What items I cannot show you in the flesh, so to speak, I can show you with pictures." He stopped the tea cup near his mouth, waiting for Paul to say something. Paul was moving his eyes back and forth from his plate to Alistair's face.

"The apartment has a magnificent view of the Thames," said Alistair with pride.

The numbers man set down his fork and said,

"I have sufficient funds of my own and access to considerably more to purchase what interests me." Alistair smiled. The American was typically direct.

"Then we should not waste time. Please let me take the check."

Paul wiped his mouth with a stiff, white napkin and said,

"Mr. Baker, I am sure you have an inventory that every art collector of means would love to negotiate away from you, but…"

Alistair was taken back. "But…?"

"I am interested in only one artifact and I doubt you have it. My hope is that you can help me find it."

"My sources are impeccable, Mr. Santori. If what you seek exists, I can find it and negotiate a price for you."

Paul remained silent and held his napkin open in front of him. His question to Alistair would tell him if Giuseppe's stories, the follow-up calls he made to validate them and this trip to London were going to pay out. Alistair's reaction was critical. "Wait until you think you have waited long enough, then count three seconds more," advised his acting coach many years ago, explaining the stage pause. The three-second wait was up.

"I want to buy the Temujin."

Alistair froze for a moment, then leaned back in his chair, almost tipping it.

"My dear, sir, please accept my compliments. Few people in my business even know about that precious prize. Every collector on the Continent would want to buy it – if it exists."

Paul relaxed. The most influential dealer in collectibles in Europe had confirmed that he and others in his trade knew about something that came to him through a story told by a gigolo over a drink in the King Cole bar in Manhattan. With the firmness of a man who knows the power of sounding right, even when he may not be, Paul said,

"It exists."

Alistair had a half smile, but his eyes were hard on Paul.

"If it does, Mr. Santori, it would take a billionaire to buy it."

"I am aware of that."

Alistair held his stare on Paul, then signaled for more tea and coffee.

"Then you must know one."

The pinstriped art promoter with the delicate hands had done what Paul knew he would do. He had checked D&B and probably other sources to get a fix on Paul's net worth, and had learned that he was rich, but not billionaire-rich. But billionaires, even American billionaires, rarely reveal their true worth to anyone, so he couldn't be sure his sources were accurate. Alistair was playing Paul's game. His "Then you must know one" was a probe. Paul dodged it. Let him think I'm a billionaire, he thought.

Both men were silent while the waiter delivered another tea and coffee. Paul wasn't about to break the silence. Finally, Alistair said,

"I would like to continue this conversation, Mr. Santori. May I show you my apartment on the chance that the Temujin is either impossible to find or does not exist? It would be a shame, if you didn't return to New York with a work of lasting value. Do you agree?"

Paul agreed. Alistair's awareness of the Temujin was sufficient for Paul to stay in the game. This perfectly tailored little man could have information or know angles that would make Paul's hunt for the Temujin an easier chore; and besides, why not enjoy a view of the Thames?

"Splendid," said Alistair. "I am fairly aware of the Temujin's history, but my associate Jerome is an expert."

"Hank, the murdered man's name is Giuseppe Bufono. Italian passport…" I let Captain Tom Holden go on. Saying I already had the info would jeopardize Arnie's sources. Sergeants may know things ahead of their superiors, but that edge is best not flaunted to said superiors.

"We have located Paul Santori, the victim's husband. He's in London. We're having him brought home as a person of interest."

"It was a pro, Tom. Maybe he hired him, but he didn't do it. When did he leave for London?"

"Time of death was one-fifteen. His plane left JFK at one-thirty."

"Say no more."

A bit testily, "We need to talk to him."

"Thanks, Tom." I did not reveal to Tom when we were at the crime scene that my client was Paul's twin, Phillip Santori, and that he was holed up somewhere with a phone that blocked its number and whereabouts. I decided I would wait to hear what Carol and Arnie had learned about Giuseppe before opening up to Captain Holden. My cell started beeping with another call which allowed a diversion from Tom.

"Mr. Tower, this is Joyce at the bank. We have a picture of the check you deposited yesterday. Do you want me to e-mail it to you?"

"Yes. What bank is it drawn on?"

"Chase."

"Please send it right away."

Ten minutes later I got a JPEG picture of the check. It was signed "P. Santori," but had no address on it. So far it hadn't bounced. I looked at it reprovingly. A lousy thirty-five-hundred dollars – and my head still hurt! I was going to ask for five thousand more when the ghost called again. Our detective/client relationship needed a stronger bond.

An hour later Carol called.

"Dear smart and loving, my sources say that Santori Enterprises is run by Paul Santori. They have heard of Phillip, but he must be back-office. No one has met him. The company spends millions on advertising, almost entirely on TV. They have never advertised in the Post. The guys here who have been in the direct response TV business say Santori Enterprises goes to the edge with its product claims. The copy they use would never pass network scrutiny, but there are hundreds of smaller stations which are less rigid when presented with a hundred-thousand dollar buy."

"Are they still on the air?" She yelled to someone and I heard a muffled answer. "They are no longer on the stations my friend checked. See you tonight."

"Carol, thanks." I wanted to ask more about the birth-control grace period, but let it pass. I would find out soon enough.

Now, the case entered the dreaded out-of-my-hands period where all you can do is wait and keep from drinking too much while you're waiting. I yelled into the outer room.

"Arnie, Paul Santori is being brought back to New York from London as a person of interest. Tap into your contacts in the Seventeenth. What they learn is about all we will have to work with until something breaks."

"Aye, 'ank. I 'ave some information from them on Eleanor Santori."

He came into my office and we talked, but what he had added nothing to what I already knew from my truant client. It was wait-for-twin-brother-Paul time.

I learned during the early months of being on my own that any length of dead time over which you have no control is a time that can be either dangerous – the Thirsty Tongue is a short putt from my office door – or productive. But to accomplish the latter one must prevail over the human tendency to "veg-out" and do nothing, or watch someone else do something. TV accommodates the latter temptation superbly. One can weather time by watching the stock market tape parade by monotonously while listening to dull wisdom from dull sources, or by clicking on a professional or college – even high school – baseball, basketball, soccer or football game. I keep a TV in my office, but I keep it off and have situated it where you have to stand to watch it.

So having hardened myself against these distractions, I decided to learn about identical twins before meeting Paul Santori. To do that, I did not have to suffer through large books. I could simply call Dr. Edna Housman. Together, we had solved a complicated case a while back. I was the Sherlock sniffing out the clues and eventually killing the killer; she was the Freud who psyched out the best trail to follow. Edna was between patients when I called, a rarity.

"Edna, it's Hank Tower. I hope you are free for a moment."

"Mr. Tower, it is a pleasure to hear from you. Yes, I am free. I hope this isn't the kind of call it usually is. I don't hear alarm in your voice."

I refrained from going into the murders, for now. "I am unalarmed, but if that changes, I will call."

"You may always call me, of course. Sometimes an outsider sees things those closely engaged do not."

"I am in the market for knowledge on identical twins. Just how close are they?"

"You refer to the murders at the Plaza hotel." I jumped.

"Don't look for clairvoyance, Mr. Tower. Since our collaboration on the Army general's murder, I have become fond of New York's tabloids. There is much to muse over in them. I would recommend their material as training for psychoanalysts. You have a client who is an identical twin of the murdered woman's husband."

"How do…"

"The tabloid said the widower was a twin so I reasoned that he would hardly be the one seeking additional scrutiny. He would be a prime suspect. So it must have been his twin that came to you. I could go on, but it would be too speculative. We need more facts."

We.

"Now, Edna, I don't want you getting involved in this…"

"Oh, please don't worry, Mr. Tower. I won't interfere."

"Interfere" allowed for a lot of room. I sensed my seventy-or-so, one-hundred-pound, five-foot-one, gracious and polite friend with a twelve-cylinder brain had been bitten by the detective bug.

"Can you give me a sketch of identical twins? My client says the two of them are the same in every aspect, including handwriting."

"Yes. They are a never-ending subject in the sciences. Identical twins come from the same egg and the same sperm. The egg splits in two. Therefore, the DNA is one-hundred percent the same for both. Regular siblings may have only a fifty-percent match. As a result, they not only look and speak identically, their mannerisms are the same. This seems to hold true even if they are separated at birth.

"One study of identical twins examined a pair that were separated at birth and thrown into environments that could not have been more different. One was taken to Germany where he was reared as a Catholic and a Nazi. The other was reared in the Caribbean as a Jew and lived for a while in a kibbutz in Israel. When they were brought together many years later as adults both were wearing wire-rimmed glasses and mustaches and two-pocket shirts with epaulets; both liked spicy foods, both flushed the toilet before using it, both read magazines from back to front and dipped their buttered toast in their coffee. Their personalities and mannerisms, not just their looks, were identical despite the vast difference in rearing."

"Good Lord, Edna. How could someone tell which one you were talking to?"

"Sometimes they are mirror images of each other. One might be left-handed and the other right-handed; one might enjoy the arts, the other mathematics. Otherwise, it would be most difficult, especially if one represented him or herself as the other. Have I helped, Mr. Tower?"

"Yes. It's important I know this. I'll figure out some way to differentiate them, but I haven't met the widower-twin yet."

"May I suggest something?"

"Of course."

"Plant an obscure fact in the head of one and work it into later conversations. The one who knows the answer is Twin A; the one who doesn't is Twin B."

"Any ideas for obscure facts?"

"I just read a kind of tidbit that sticks in one's mind. You might use it."

"I'm listening."

"Try dropping zettabyte into a conversation. It's a one with twenty-one zeros after it. You may think of another tidbit."

"Zettabyte, twenty-one zeros. Edna, you're wonderful."

"Perhaps you could call me occasionally as your case develops. I certainly won't interfere. I am quite busy."

CHAPTER 6

Paul and Alistair left the River Restaurant and walked back alongside the magnificent gazebo to the Savoy's tea room and to the entrance where Alistair's car was waiting. The two would have been a tempting metaphor to a cynical observer who knew their origins. Alistair was short and thin and perfectly tailored, an *uber* civilized Englishman; Paul was a large and powerful, uncomfortably tailored, less civilized American. If the observer were more astute than cynical and was close enough to see their eyes, he would have seen a more meaningful difference. Alistair's had the beam of a man sensing a profitable sale; Paul's had the focus of a predator eyeing a strike.

The car moved slowly away from the hotel's entrance down the fifty-yard half-street in front of the Savoy, the only one in London that allows driving on the right, and turned onto the Strand. A short while later the two men were in Alistair's penthouse standing at its large window, viewing the Thames, its bridges, the London Eye – a magnificent Ferris Wheel – and Big Ben atop Briton's Parliament. Paul listened while Alistair expounded on the sights, but his real interest was Jerome, Alistair's associate and the expert on the Temujin.

"My history is wanting, Mr. Santori, when it concerns anything I don't have for sale, and unfortunately I can't sell you what you want. I will hopefully overcome that when I regale you with the history of some of the artifacts I do have for sale." He caught the let's-get-on-with-it look in Paul's eye.

Turning to the other man in the room,

"Jerome, I am turning Mr. Santori over to you. I will get some tea from the pantry. I'm afraid we have no coffee, Mr. Santori."

Then with a hopeless, but tolerant intonation, he said to Jerome,

"He wants to buy the Temujin."

With that, Alistair disappeared into another room.

Jerome rose from his passive, on-call state as a starving man might respond to a dinner bell. He was thin, like Alistair, but taller and handsomer and dressed more casually. He wore a navy-blue jacket with an open-collar white shirt, sharply creased gray trousers and expensive loafers with tassels. His facial skin was flawless and his check bones were unusually high, as was his forehead, giving him a haughty look. He had no mustache and sported perfectly combed dark hair. He, too, had an emerald ring on his left hand. Paul put him at thirty-five to forty, ten or fifteen years younger than Alistair. Were they a pair? He didn't care.

Paul turned to Jerome. Neither offered his hand.

"Jerome, I have an understanding of the Temujin, but it came from a gigolo whose primary interest was my wife. My inquiries into his story, however, gave me enough confidence in the Temujin's existence to come here. Alistair says you're an authority on it."

Jerome was still grinning at the "…gigolo whose primary interest was my wife."

"I would be glad to enlighten you, Mr. Santori. The Temujin is the Holy Grail of collecting." It was said in a deep baritone worthy of the stage. Paul imagined Alistair holding a bouquet of flowers outside a West End theater's stage door, waiting for Jerome.

Jerome took a chair and waved for Paul to take the one across from him.

"First, I feel obliged to tell you that the Temujin is my consuming subject. If it seems I am getting rather professorial, I probably am;

but please bear with me." Paul nodded slightly and settled uncomfortably in the small chair. Jerome began.

"The Temujin has two values, Mr. Santori, an intrinsic one and a historical one. The manuscripts I have read tell me it is a miniature ship with oars extending from both sides. The references say it is two feet in length, made of solid gold and embellished with hundreds of precious jewels."

Alistair reentered the room with a tray holding cups of tea. "Does he have your attention yet, Mr. Santori?" Paul looked at him blankly and waved off the tea. Jerome continued.

"That alone makes it an extremely valuable find, but it's the historical value of the Temujin that puts it 'over the top,' as you might say, in the collecting business. It goes to the heart of the Mongol Empire and its advance on Europe.

"Genghis Khan and his successors built the largest contiguous empire in history. It was larger than Napoleon's, larger than Alexander the Great's. Only ours at its peak exceeded it in territory, if you combine all its pieces. The Mongol Empire stretched from the China coast to the Black Sea to within a week's advance of Vienna.

"Vienna at that time was a penny of its later value. It was the early twelve hundreds and the Hapsburgs had yet to establish their own empire; but Vienna is only three-hundred-and-sixty miles from Venice which was extremely valuable at that time. It had a sea-trading empire under a line of Doges that lasted a thousand years. It was perhaps the richest city-state in existence. It was the center of the developed world's maritime commerce. The Doges ran its riches smartly and with an iron discipline. Three-hundred-and-sixty miles is an easy distance for Mongol warriors. With his multiple horses, a Mongol fighter could travel a hundred miles a day."

Alistair had taken a chair next to Paul and was watching Jerome admiringly. The deep-voiced man went on, comfortable in his performance.

"Venice had something of an army, but the ruling Doge, Pietro Ziani, knew it was no match for the Khan's. A Mongol horde on the march was a terrestrial tsunami. Nothing could stop it. It lived off the land, drank blood from its horses if there was no water, ate its own, if there was no food. It slaughtered all the men and boys and enslaved all the women and girls in the cities and villages it conquered. It was a terrifying force and unstoppable."

He paused to evaluate Paul's interest. Only a fixed stare. He rose from the chair and walked to where Alistair sat. Make the audience move their eyes, thought Paul, reminiscing.

"The Mongol campaigns killed about eleven percent of the word's population and the part they killed was almost entirely male. As a result, genetic research has shown that one in every two-hundred males living in what would be the Mongol Empire today has Genghis Khan's and his descendents' genes. That's a half-percent of all the men on earth today.

"I say all this to describe what must have been in the Doge's mind as the reports of the Mongol's advance came to him. Think of the fear. Think of the extraordinary steps Pietro Ziani would have to consider to prevent the horde from destroying Venice and all its men, including Pietro himself."

Jerome was pacing slowly as he spoke. He paused to read Paul who was still blank-faced.

"Fighting it was pointless, so the Doge thought of bribery, not monetary bribery. The Great Khan needed nothing. The bribery of power. Genghis Khan was undefeatable on the land, but he was powerless on the sea. He had no ships and if he did, his army would not know how to manipulate them. Through the Venetian banks the Doges controlled a thousand ships. If Doge Ziani and the Khan joined forces, they could control the entire world, sea and land.

"The hundreds of jewels I mentioned lined the miniature ship's hull and masts, even its oars. Under a throne on its prow was a message in the Khan's language from the Doge Pietro Ziani. Remember, the Khan had no familiarity with ships or the sea. He was stopped in the East by the only force that could stop him, the China Sea. His military consisted of wagons and horses and archers. Ships and oceans were beyond his ken."

Jerome expected something, a leaning forward, a widening of the eyes, but the American remained still.

"The message under the throne of gold is reputed to read, 'A Universal Ruler must reign over sea and land.'"

"Genghis Khan means Universal Ruler. The Doge's gift implied that without the sea he could never be a true universal ruler, and without the ships of Venice and the men who knew how to man them on his side, he would never rule the sea. The Doge was no fool. He knew the Khan would never share power. His game was to delay the Mongol advance long enough for the rest of Europe to mobilize its forces and block the menace before it destroyed Vienna and Venice and their men and boys. Ruler of the land and the sea was meant to tease his ego, tempt him to send an emissary to Pietro for negotiations, another delay."

Jerome leaned back in his chair, confused by such an unresponsive listener. The American seemed totally uninterested in these facts, facts he had painstakingly accumulated from books and archives in Venice and Vienna and took pride in disbursing to an audience. Didn't the man realize that but for Pietro Ziani's ingenious gift the two of them might not be conversing in English, that this was what gave the Temujin its priceless value? He leaned back in his chair and with a tone of exasperation said,

"The Doge chose the largest of the jewels to fashion the name of the jeweled ship on one of its sides. He named it Temujin, the Great Khan's real name."

Jerome watched for a reaction from Paul, but the moment was interrupted by Alistair leaving to answer a phone in the other room. Finally, the American spoke, but it wasn't the question Jerome expected.

"Did it work?"

"Yes. It delayed the invasion long enough for Europe's opposing forces to gather at Vienna and for the Turks to mass in the south at Constantinople; but more important, during the time it took for the Khan to consider the promise of the gift, a political row among his generals required him to leave the western front. His absence left the horde leaderless and it slowly retreated. My research and the weight of the golden ship suggest the Kahn did not take the Temujin with him."

Alistair reentered the room shaken and pale.

"Mr. Santori, I have just received a call from Scotland Yard telling me that you are required in New York. Your…your wife and a friend have been…have been killed. A…a representative from the Yard will be here momentarily to assist you."

Paul rose, started to say something, paused, stared at Jerome with shock and collapsed in the chair. Jerome caught something disingenuous in Paul's reaction.

He had also perceived something wrong in the question he asked. Paul had asked if the Doge's ploy worked. His disinterest in the story of the Temujin didn't seem to square with such an inquiry. The large American was clearly a direct man. Why didn't he "go for it " and ask a question in keeping with why he was here, thought Jerome? Why didn't he ask, "Where is the Temujin now?"

Jerome had a breathtaking thought. The American was here to learn its true value. He already knew where it was.

Paul and the detective from the Yard paused at Alistair's door. Paul said,

"Mr. Baker, Jerome, I will be back. I cannot say if it will be in a week or a month, but once the police have questioned me and I have made arrangements for my wife, I will call you." He turned to leave, then hesitated and turned back to them.

"If you sense callousness in my reaction to this tragedy, please don't be mislead. As Jerome must have taken from my remarks, my wife and I were not close. My heart is not broken. Only my pride."

The two left.

Jerome turned to Alistair. "I must say, that was perhaps our most eventful ending to a presentation."

"Yes. We can now boast Scotland Yard's interest in our goods. Mr. Santori is a gruff person, but do you think he could murder?"

"I have no idea. His eyes were like steel when I was telling the story of the Temujin. I felt I was talking to a computer that was assigning a pound figure to each of my sentences. But there was something else…"

Alistair settled into a chair and straightened his tie and jacket. "I agree. How would you describe it?"

"I have two observations. One, I think he is a dangerous man. That's pure perception, of course. I have no evidence except Scotland Yard's interest in him. I feel on firmer ground saying he is an actor, or was an actor. I felt he already knew his wife was dead. It was only your surprise announcement that rattled him, but even that was for only an instant. He recovered quickly and went into what I believe was an act."

"Well, you would recognize that. What is your number two?"

"I think he knows where the Temujin is."

"Good Lord, man! Is that true? How…what…?" Alistair was alive.

"We…we…have to…it could be worth a hundred million…how can we…?"

Jerome was calm. He walked to the window and looked at Alistair. "I don't know yet, but I will, with some help."

Alistair cooled. "Jerome, I don't want to…"

"He will be retained by the police for at least a few days, but he'll be back. I'll make…"

"I'm uneasy about this, Jerome."

"In your own words, Alistair, one-hundred million."

"I know, but…" His protest faded into an incoherent mumble.

The detective took Paul from Alistair's penthouse to the Savoy, then direct to Heathrow and to the airplane's gate. At JKF in New York a police lieutenant met him when he deplaned and the two of them went in a patrol car to the Seventeenth where Captain Tom Holden was waiting.

Paul's plane was landing at JFK when Phillip called Hank Tower.

"Your ghost needs an update, Tower."

The screen in Hank's phone was blank. "And I need to know where you are."

"No deal. Where I am will stay a secret until this murder is solved, and Paul signs off with the FTC."

"There is news, Phillip. Your brother is on a plane returning from London. The police will be waiting for him."

"London?" He paused. "What the hell is he up to? Well, I don't give a damn. Not anymore, not after he screwed me. He's all yours. Do you think he killed Eleanor?"

"And her lover, don't forget. No, it was a hired killer."

"Do the police think that?"

"Reluctantly. It makes their job harder."

He went silent for a moment. "Ask Paul if he knows about Eleanor's other affairs. If he says no, he's lying. He had every motive jealousy can provide to kill her, or have her killed; but I doubt he knew a professional killer or how to find one."

"Do you know how, Phillip?"

"Now why would I want Eleanor dead?"

"I don't know. Did you?"

"No. She was a whore, a beautiful whore, but a whore nonetheless, but there are lots of whores who marry for money. I have no idea who the guy was with her."

"Okay, if it's not you or Paul, who would want her dead?"

"Some guy she tossed for the dead one, or the one before him, or the one before him. It's a long queue. Chaucer was good bait." He paused.

"So you're going to meet Paul. Just remember I'm your client, even though he's a dead ringer for me. That's all for today, Tower, I'm signing off."

Shortly after that call and before Hank called Holden at the Seventeenth Precinct, Tower received another call. The voice sounded French.

"Mr. Tower, please hold."

A few moments later a strong, Germanic voice took the phone.

"Mr. Tower, I have one of your New York newspapers in front of me. In a lurid fashion it reveals two murders in your Plaza hotel. It also has your name as being the one who discovered the bodies. I had a relationship with one of the victims that I do not wish to walk away from. Nor do I want to involve the police in my affairs. You seem the perfect person for me to have as my representative. I want to hire you. What is your fee?"

Hank stated he had a client concerning the murders and that it would be unethical for him to take another client interested in the same case.

"I will triple his fee." was the answer. Hank thought and asked,

"Are you interested in Eleanor Santori?"

"Are you interested in my business?"

"It depends on your answer."

"No. I am interested in Giuseppe Bufono."

"Then I can take your business. Three times my fee is nine-thousand dollars for three days, plus expenses."

"Have someone give me your bank numbers and I will have the money wired today."

"I'll take your word for that. Now, I need your name and whereabouts."

"Carl von Tresser. I live in Vienna, Austria."

CHAPTER 7

"What is your interest in Giuseppe Bufono?"

Rather than answer, Carl von Tresser said,

"I'm an upfront person, Mr. Tower. Seeing your name in this rag of a newspaper someone gave to me was not enough to trust you with an answer to that inevitable question. Before I called you I spoke to an acquaintance of mine, a Mr. Edgar Corton, to inquire about you. He provided a sterling recommendation."

Edgar Corton was on the Mayor's private payroll as a special assistant. He was probably His Honor's most influential advisor. His job was to know, bring to and keep private money in New York. He is a powerful force in the City. We worked together on a few cases and developed a mutual respect.

"I know Edgar."

"So I will tell you my interest in Mr. Bufono, knowing you respect the confidentiality of your client's information.

"Giuseppe Bufono is – was – a handsome, charming, sophisticated lady's man, gigolo is perhaps a better word, who could persuade wealthy and footloose women to buy him whatever he wanted, from first-class air tickets to squire them to exotic places to expensive clothes to keep him dressed perfectly to racing cars he drove expertly. He had no money, but then he didn't need any. He was a poor sultan with a rich harem.

"Now, I believe the world's most useful secrets are revealed in bed. If I'm right, and I believe I am, then Giuseppe had a seraglio of secrets he pried out of his partners. One of those secrets he shared with me before I had a wily professional lure him away from my wife. Now the bastard's dead and he took the most important part of the secret with him. I need someone in New York who was close to his death to track down that part."

"The current theory, Mr. von Tresser, among those close to the murder investigation is that it was a jealousy killing."

Silence. "Perhaps. Sometimes Giuseppe barely made it out the bedroom window before getting shot. But there's another possibility."

"I'm listening."

Another pause, the kind that precedes a person deliberating whether he should answer or not.

"I am a collector, Mr. Tower. I own some of the most expensive art and sculptures in Europe. I invite you to ask Mr. Corton about me. I am a very wealthy person who became so by not wanting to lose in business, women or collecting. It is the collecting game that is in play at the moment.

"Giuseppe told me about an object that's the crown jewel of collecting, especially to a Viennese and a Venetian. I believed his story because I believe in the power of the bed when it comes to secrets and Giuseppe's power in that venue. The item in question is called the Temujin, Genghis Khan's real name. It comes up in collecting circles every five years or so one way or another, but always fades away as non-existent. Giuseppe convinced me it exists and I want it."

The "I want it" was said like someone with a gun.

"You mentioned a Venetian…"

"A French Venetian named Carlton Bouchard. He's the curator of the Doge's Palace Depository in Venice and has access to collector money across Europe – as well as millions in the Depository's bank account. Giuseppe could have spoken to him as well as me, searching for the best deal."

"You said 'perhaps' when I said Bufono's murder was jealousy. Why?"

"Because I believe Giuseppe had confirmation from a reliable source that the Temujin exists and was told where it's located. I believe he was also told that it could be bought for a price far below what a collector like me would pay for it. Before revealing its whereabouts, Giuseppe would have demanded a piece of the ultimate sale price to a collector like me. Now, if Giuseppe revealed the Temujin's location to the one who planned to buy the Temujin and resell it, that person might not have wanted to share the profit with Giuseppe."

"But the woman…"

"Collateral damage. She's a witness to Giuseppe's murder."

"How much is this Temujin worth?"

"Impossible to say."

"What would you pay for it?"

"Fifty-million euros without a blink."

"Does this Bouchard have that kind of money or access to it?"

"That and more."

"How many other collectors are as hell-bent as you are on getting the Temujin?"

"I'd say at least six."

"Send me a list. We have a complicating factor, Mr. Tresser. Bufono and his bedmate were taken out by a professional killer who could have been hired by the dead woman's husband or this Carlton Bouchard or any of your six collectors…"

"…or any of the women Bufono scorned for another."

"…or you."

"Not likely. If Bufono had given me the location of the Temujin, I would not be hiring you to find it. Saving a couple million or so in a finder's fee to Bufono would not be worth killing him. I was told you are very good. How hard is it to find a professional killer?"

"In today's world it's not impossible. But you have done another client of mine a large favor, one I will share only with the police and without revealing your name."

"Yes?"

"You have widened the motive pool for the double murder considerably."

"Your assignment is to find the location of the Temujin. Call me everyday. I get irritated when I'm not informed."

Arnie lumbered into my office and flopped down on my expensive couch. He's going to go through the seats one of these days.

I said, "We have an international client, a Mr. Carl von Tresser in Vienna. He's wiring in nine-thousand dollars today and is on board for three-thousand a day, plus expenses." Arnie's eyebrows went up. I briefed him on the conversation, then asked,

"Any ideas on how to track down this killer?"

"It's 'ard, 'ank. They can come from anywhere in the world and go back when the job's done. It's easier to dig out who might want to 'ire one."

"That will be hard, too. I'm getting a list of six collectors our new client said would lust for the Temujin, and maybe hire a killer to get it. I wonder if Paul or Phillip Santori knew about it. Phillip said his infomercial company was about to be closed by the FTC. If so, both twins would need lots of money to keep up their standard. Phillip said he took his fair share before he disappeared with his wife, Janet, but maybe that's a lie, maybe there wasn't any money left to take. If he knows about the Temujin, he would see it as a comfortable IRA.

"I think Paul's a better bet. Say despite his wife's proclivities, he got along with Giuseppe and Giuseppe told him about the Temujin. Then Paul has a jealousy motive to have his wife killed and a money motive to have Bufono killed. The killing of Eleanor wasn't collateral damage, as Tresser suggests, it was a deliberate double murder."

I paused. "Any ideas?"

"I'll talk to my sergeant friends. There may be word on the street about a professional killer. It's also possible..." He hesitated.

"Yeah?"

"Well, cops can go bad. It's a way for the really bad ones to pick up extra money."

"Can you run that one down?"

"Aye."

"I'll put Lydia to work on the collector list when we get it. We can at least try to find out where they all were when the murders were committed. It might suggest something. She should open up a Giuseppe file as well, but if Interpol has nothing, it's unlikely she can uncover anything. Then there are his many women friends, one of whom had a piece of explosive knowledge and whispered it to Giuseppe under the covers." I swung my chair around and looked out the window.

"I have a feeling there is a large amount of money in this mess for us, if we can find the Temujin. Tresser's ready to lay out at least fifty-million euros for it." Then I swung back and faced Arnie.

"What has the world come to when someone in Singapore or Tunisia or Cape Town or Vienna or Venice can hire a faceless killer to do his or her work thousands of miles away and then evaporate? Doesn't the world realize how hard that makes it for the good guys to catch the bad guys?"

With a grin, "Aye, 'ank, it clogs up the pipes. I 'ave a call into the Seventeenth to get what was on the security cameras in the Plaza."

"They'll have some good pictures of me, but the killer will have his head down and collar up."

"Aye," said my large, red-haired associate.

Paul Santori landed at JFK and was escorted directly to Tom Holden's quizzing room in the Seventeenth. He kindly invited me. Paul entered and any doubt I had about differences in twins was blown away. Here was a Xerox copy of Phillip. Even his walk, the turns of the head, the movement of his eyes, arms and hands, his bulk and finally his speech were, as Phillip said, dead ringers for him. Was this Phillip? I thought back to Phillip's writing the check in my office, I was positive he used his right hand.

Paul squeezed himself into a chair with the same motions Phillip used when he jammed himself into the one in front of my desk. I stood to the side. Paul saw me but registered nothing. Tom said,

"Mr. Santori, we apologize for bringing you home so abruptly, but I am sure you would have returned immediately on your own once you learned of your wife's death." Paul nodded. There was no indication of nervousness. His fingers and feet were relaxed.

"It was a shock of course, but the long flight from London has helped soothe it. Please ask me what you need to."

"Your wife Eleanor. Were you on good terms?"

"No. She had lovers." It was said factually.

"I see. Mr. Giuseppe Bufono. Was he one of them?"

"Yes, the current one. Captain, you will learn from your inquiries what I have just told you. Eleanor was a beautiful, promiscuous flirt. I tolerated it for obvious reasons. Take a look at me. I am no George Clooney. It was painful, but having her with me was worth it."

"I see. We know you could not have committed the crime – you were getting on the plane when it happened – but there are other ways to murder. The man standing over there was the first on the scene and was knocked unconscious by the murderer, a professional killer. Your business does not suggest you had access to professional killers, but…"

"Captain, I wouldn't have a clue where to find one, even if I needed one."

"Jealousy can find ways."

"I was not jealous. I was lucky to have her as a wife. She was beautiful. I am not."

"Then there's money." Tom waited. Paul looked at him quizzically.

62

"She didn't have any money."

"No, but Bufono might have."

"Bufono? He was penniless. All he had was looks."

"Yes, but he knew where millions could be found." Paul's eyes narrowed. There was a breath of stiffening in his body.

"I'm not sure what you are…"

"I am talking about an artifact of great value called the Temujin." Paul's eyes and body went from caution to full alert.

I had given Tom the details of my call from Vienna, but not my client's name.

"Giuseppe might have known about it and told you. Your trip to London seems to suggest that. You breakfasted with a famous art dealer, then went to his apartment. Perhaps it was Bufono you wanted dead, not your wife, and the killer you hired killed her because she saw him."

"Wait! This has gone far enough. No more. You're suggesting something I won't tolerate. Yes, Bufono told me about this so-called Temujin and that it was worth millions, but the art dealer you mention doesn't think it exists, that the thing is a rumor built over the ages. You're suggesting I killed someone, or had someone killed, on the basis of a fairy tale? Captain, please. This has gone far enough. If you're going to charge me with something, I will call a lawyer. Otherwise I am walking out of here."

"You are free to go, but keep us informed of your whereabouts."

"Why? Why should I do that?" He leaned back against the chair and said,

"Captain, I have lost a woman I cared for. I need to make

arrangements."

He stood. Tom remained seated and waved at the door. Paul left. He did not look at me.

The room stayed quiet for a moment. Tom turned to the sergeant standing across from me who offered nothing, then looked at me.

"Well?"

I was still enthralled with the resemblance. Paul's rant against Tom was delivered with the same up and down volume, the same intonations, the same rhythms, the same verbal punctuations as Phillip's *Sleep and Slim* rant against Paul in my office. But for Edna's telling of the hundred-percent genetic sameness between identical twins, I would have sworn it was Phillip sitting in front of me. My fascination had a cost. I neglected to determine if he was right or left-handed. There was no opening for Edna's one with twenty-one zeros after it. I said,

"Tom, at first I thought it was an act, but he gained credence as he progressed. If it was an act, the only slip in it was when you mentioned the Temujin. That surprised him."

Tom emitted a humming sound which generally meant, "Is that all?" He said,

"If it was the Temujin that sparked him, then the motive is money and the hit was Bufono. What are you holding out on me?"

"Only that which I cannot reveal, like the name of my client."

There was more in my von Tresser call, but I would keep it to myself for a while. If the damned thing existed, I want to be the one who finds it – not the New York Police Department or some Venetian curator.

"Tom, I suspect he will return to London after the funeral. That perk up tells me he believes the fairy tale is real. Maybe he has to believe it. His company is going kaput…the Temujin could be his only shot. Bufono probably told him something, maybe the location of the Temujin, and Paul believed him. It's a risk worth taking. The money is enormous, if the thing is real. It's enough for someone to kill several times over."

Tom smiled and said, "Genghis Khan rides again." Then he added regretfully,

"Unfortunately, we can't hold him. But I get the feeling you are going to keep him in your radar." He looked at me quizzically.

"I'm right, aren't I?" He grinned sardonically. "Well, I'll be damned. The hard-assed Hank Tower believes in fairy tales."

Then he went thoughtful.

"If you are going to tail him, I want to know where he is, just in case this fairy tale is real. *Entendes*?"

"*Si, senor capitan.*"

And with a parting salute I took a cab back to my office to arrange a tail on Paul Santori. That fifty-million Tresser said he would pay in a snap for the Temujin had found a home in my mind.

Across the street from Tower's office at the bar in the Thirsty Tongue, a non-descript man was holding a glass of scotch a bit awkwardly to his lips, as if he were using the wrong hand. His other hand was hidden inside the right-hand pocket of his jacket.

CHAPTER 8

"Another thought," I said to Arnie.

"If our client in Vienna is correct that Giuseppe's talents under the sheets provided him knowledge of the Temujin's whereabouts, how does one track down European women who like to pass million-dollar secrets under the sheets to handsome gigolos?"

Perhaps it was an unanswerable question. I say "perhaps" because although Arnie is not one to tackle the social consequences of income equality or the crime consequences of high-food prices in low-income areas, or to ruminate about the broken-window theory of lawlessness – on those subjects he would demure – but if you asked him a question like the one I had just asked, one which left me clueless, his innate common sense comes through as dependably as the morning sun. He said,

"Seems to me, 'ank, that the best way would be to 'ave the lassies come to us."

I stared at him. "How…"

"We could run ads in the proper newspapers as Giuseppe's estate attorney and say we 'ave some letters 'e wanted to go to the press after 'is death unless they were claimed…"

"…that would scare the hell out of some of them…"

"Aye. Or we could say we 'ad a personal something 'e wanted to give to an unknown woman he said would recognize what it was."

"That would attract women who actually fell for him."

I called in Lydia.

"Lydia, answer this question without thinking. Which of two women would more likely give a gigolo a high-powered secret, a woman who was simply having fun or a woman who actually loved him?"

"The woman who loved him, of course. Why would the others waste it on him?"

Arnie nodded. We were down to the women who actually fell for Giuseppe.

"I would concentrate on Vienna and Venice, 'ank. If the lass knew about the Temujin, she would likely live in one of the two towns."

"Okay. Lydia, do your Internet thing and find the top paper in both cities. I'll draft an ad. And see what you can find on a Mr. Carlton Bouchard. He's the curator of the Doge's Palace Depository in Venice. Arnie, get a tail on Paul Santori. He lives on Fifth Avenue across from the Met."

"Aye, 'ank."

"Arnie."

"Aye?'

"Ask Lydia for two-hundred from Petty Cash and take your family to dinner somewhere nice."

He smiled appreciatively and went to his desk to round up police buddies for the tailing job.

I started to fiddle with some words to reel in a woman naive enough to believe Bufono had a post-mortem gift for her. Remembering his looks and charms in the Palm Court, there was no reason it was impossible. Giuseppe might flip a lesbian.

I had penned "Law firm for the estate of Giuseppe Bufono seeks…" when my cell phone rang, announcing Phillip Santori.

"Tower, did you see my brother?"

"Yes, at police headquarters. He just returned from London."

"I don't get the London thing. We have the FTC about to chain the doors, backorders on the *Sleep and Slim*, and he's in London. Only my wife would do something like that. Why was he there?"

"Well…"

"You work for me, Tower. Speak up. Why was he there?"

"Phillip, I am sure you have experienced price increases on items that suddenly become more valuable. Airline tickets come to mind. On Monday you get a good price, then when you call back Wednesday to buy the ticket you find that the price has gone up. Now maybe the first price was too low…"

"How much?"

"I think another five thousand would get you the ticket you want."

"I'll have Chase cut a bank check for you. This is not kosher, Tower. We had a deal…"

"Wait a minute. You wanted pictures of Paul's wife and lover and you got them. Just because I didn't take them…"

"All right. You can pick up the check at the Chase branch closest to your office."

"Besides, there is a lot more at play than the *Sleep and Slim*.

Things have multiplied; there are more angles, more complications. Keeping you on the inside is technically a new assignment."

"What's in play?"

"An *objet d'art*."

"What the hell is that?"

"In this case an extremely valuable artifact that I believe Paul is chasing."

"How valuable?"

"Do you know what a zettabyte is?"

"If I don't know what an *objet d'art* is, how in hell would I know what a zettabyte is?"

"Imagine a one with twenty-one zeros after it and a dollar sign in front of it."

"Tower, cut to it. What did Paul say? What's he up to? You'll get your five grand. I need facts."

I did not want to reveal we were putting a tail on Paul. "He said he has to make arrangements for Eleanor's burial, but went no further than that. I suspect he will return to London afterwards. The police can't hold him. He has his passport."

"How long does it take to bury a murdered person?"

"A week, maybe less. The cause of death is clear."

"I might go to London as well. That's confidential, Tower."

"Of course it is. I'll let you know when your brother goes. Where are you?"

"No chance, Tower. I'm incognito until this blows over."

"Do you think Paul could have had Eleanor killed, could he be that jealous?"

"No. He knew she was what she was. His concern was himself, of being exposed as a cuckold. That's why I wanted those pictures spread wide and far. They would have been my best shot at payback for his stealing from me."

"What would you do in London?"

"Now, is that hard to figure out? I don't care what a zeta-meta is, but twenty-one zeros interest me. My brother might be a thief, but he has a bloodhound's nose for money. And Janet is driving me nuts. I need a break."

With that he rang off.

Arnie. "I 'ave three men lined up for the Santori tail. I e-mailed one of the media pictures to each of 'em."

"Good. Tell Lydia to bill it to Carl von Tresser's account. I'm going home. You, too, Arnie. Call your lass before she prepares a dinner."

"I did. There's a Japanese restaurant near the 'ouse that flames up what they cook in front of you. The girls have 'eard about it, so we're going with two of their friends tonight."

"Lydia, if you want to do that research from home, go to it."

"Can't leave yet, Hank. I'll stay a little longer to get behind the traffic."

"'til tomorrow."

I left for the subway to Greenwich Village. It was about 6:00.

Carol Tomkin's best friend in New York is Didi Harrington. The two became friends at the University of Missouri. Carol was attending its School of Journalism; Didi was pursuing a degree in a sports program Carol never completely understood and Didi never explained cogently. Both were at the top of every male student's wish list. After graduation, Carol took a job as a crime reporter for the St. Louis *Post Dispatch* – then moved to the *New York Post*. Didi went to New York immediately after graduation. Both were now thirty-two years old.

Upon arrival in Manhattan, Didi committed her savings and credit cards to a fine wardrobe and an apartment in a good building in a good neighborhood and had parties, inviting only the better off, then the better off of the better off. Eventually, a wealthy hedge-fund male entered her life and they were married, followed a few years later by a marriage to another hedge-fund male of equal wealth. Both men had mistaken her blue-eyed, Midwest freshness as easy-on-the-eye and low maintenance – she came from a farm in Kansas – and assumed she would be awed by the sophisticated ways of the East.

Didi's divorce lawyer corrected that assumption. He insisted that a two-bedroom condo overlooking Central Park from the thirty-third floor of the Essex House on Central Park South would be in more caring hands, if it were tended to by her; and convinced her second husband that his three-bedroom cottage on the beach in East Hampton, New York, would be a happier place, if he deeded it to his beautiful and wounded client. These homes, plus sizable monetary settlements, helped Didi conclude that men were too fickle to marry. She would stay single.

Dressed in a form-fitting, dark green *Escada* dress that bared most of her arms and ended a few inches above her knees – she waited at a table in the Union Square Café on Sixteenth Street for Carol to arrive for lunch. Her blonde hair was bunched in the back of her head. Two young men a few tables away were observing her as hawks might study a mouse. Carol, dressed in a conservative, black dress with her radiant, brunette hair falling over her shoulders, arrived before the hawks could decide to swoop or not to swoop.

"I'm sorry Didi. We just got a new murder reported and I wanted to get the details on the web site before we run the next go-to ad."

"You made it just in time. The two over your right shoulder were discussing who would buy me a drink. Speaking of that, let me buy you one. Chardonnay?"

"Yes, but the house wine is fine. Nothing fancy." With the effectiveness of a person who has done it many times, Didi waved a hand and a waiter appeared.

Carol settled into her chair. "Didi, I need to vent. Do you mind?"

"Mind? Vent away. We're not here to discuss world affairs. What good is lunch without heart gossip?" She paused. "What has the lout done?"

Carol smiled. Her street-wise friend's style differed from hers, but their friendship was deep and sincere. Together, they had navigated some rough waters at Mizzou – male and female. The four years had created a special bond.

"It comes down to family. I want one; he doesn't."

"Why not?"

"He thinks a child will affect his prowess, put him off his game, as he puts it, maybe get him killed. But I'm not sure that's…"

"Horses. I don't believe that. We'd have eunuchs for police, if that were true." Didi waited a moment, then as was her habit, went to the core of it.

"Does he love you?"

"Yes."

"For sure?"

"For sure."

With a serious look, "Then tell him to get off his butt and unzip his pants."

Carol laughed, then recalling her miscarriage said, "Missing those birth control pills was probably on purpose."

"But they said you can still have a child. Get pregnant again and tell him this is it. Get aboard. You're going the distance."

The drinks arrived. Carol sipped hers thoughtfully and spoke quietly into the air, "I'm thirty-two. I make a good salary and have a good resume. I can support myself. If he leaves…"

Didi swallowed a healthy sip and stared at her friend, "He won't leave."

Her answer was what Carol felt instinctively, but she wanted someone she cared for and who cared for her to confirm it. Carol took a another sip, set down the glass and asked,

"Now, tell me about this guy at Goldman Sachs. Is he a partner?"

Didi gave her a look of surprise. "Of course, he's a partner."

The two explored that affair and a variety of other subjects while enjoying two more glasses of wine. The two hawks were looking at them more intensely now, waiting for them to pay the check. Perhaps it was the wine and the college reminiscing and the fecklessness of the male gender they had just reaffirmed that made them mischievous. They paid the bill and with teasing smiles walked up to the two gawkers and looked down at them. Didi said with a fake drawl,

"Hello. I'm April. This is my friend June." The two hopefuls couldn't believe their luck. One of them took the bait and said with an off-color grin,

"I want to be May."

Carol gave a small pout and said in mock disappointment. "Too bad it's only February."

They took each other's hand, grinned at the dejected pair and with a bit of a wobble, sauntered out of the restaurant. In the cab back to her office, Carol decided to tell Hank the grace period was over. She was going off the pill.

Paul had gone directly to his co-op on Fifth Avenue from Captain Tom Holden's quizzing room in Midtown. A man of a more sensitive nature might have had misgivings about returning to his apartment house after the murder of his wife. There are written and unwritten codes of behavior within "co-op" ethos which are meant to protect the upper-class reputation of the building and its occupants. "Hollywood" parties or raggedly dressed visitors, for instance, would trigger a letter from the Board of Directors. More important, in addition to proper in-house behavior, residents were expected to behave ethically and honorably in their social and business affairs, or more advanced measures would be taken. Paul had concluded that suspicion of murdering one's wife might fall in the latter category.

Selling the apartment was already in his plans. He didn't need the space and certainly not the luxury now that Eleanor was gone. He was sure that a ten-million price would bring a quick sale and after allowing for a small mortgage and taxes would provide enough money to finance a comfortable but unexciting post-Eleanor life. It could also finance his hunt for the Temujin and the more exciting life it would bring.

The doorman opened the cab door and presented a silent half-nod. The ostracism had begun. He toyed with hanging around the building for a while just to spite the snobs. He took the elevator to his apartment.

He stood at the entrance and scanned the expensive furnishings, all selected by Eleanor. The double-paned windows blocked the traffic noise from Fifth Avenue, leaving the apartment soundless but for the swish of his shoes as he shuffled across the sixty-thousand dollar Oriental carpet she had insisted on. "It was on sale! The company was going out of business." The company had been going out of business for three years and to reinforce the charade recently posted a court-issued bankruptcy notice in its window. Paul was certain it was a fake, but he admired the ruse, even smiled in respect. He glanced around at other appointments Eleanor had purchased. What a waste. He wanted all of it out of his life, the apartment, the building's snooty residents, the extravagant furnishings, the whole damn thing. It was time to move on. A six-million-dollar-bank account after all the payouts would do the job nicely. He decided to cut the selling commission to three percent.

His first call was to his lawyer to arrange for a service for Eleanor and her burial. A small service would be fine, he told him; her mother was dead, "…inform her father and her sister, both are in Atlanta, here are the phone numbers." Then he had an idea. Set up the formalities in Atlanta, that's where she was from and where her remaining family and friends live, tell them I am being detained by the police…tell them the pre-nup gives her estate a million dollars and all the furnishings in the co-op, including the art. That will stir the family pot, he said. "Send me a power of attorney to sign and follow up on what's left of the company. What? I don't know and I don't care. Just do it."

He walked through the rooms to the master suite where he opened a small wall-safe hidden in his closet behind some clothes and withdrew a stack of hundred-dollar bills.

His second call was to American Airlines to reserve a first-class ticket back to London and another visit with the two emerald-ringed art dealers. He had read Jerome carefully. Jerome and he could deal.

CHAPTER 9

Across the Atlantic, Jerome Manchester was thinking about Paul Santori. He was as certain as his English caution allowed that the big American knew where the Holy Grail of his life was hidden. Anyone who could listen to the history and value of the Temujin described as he had described it and not ask at the end of the account "Where is it?" either knew where it was or was not interested in the item or its tale. Paul's trip to London proved he had a high degree of interest. How Paul knew its location was not important. His knowing was the answer to an obsession Jerome had had since he learned about the Temujin in his late teens.

It was while touring the Natural Museum of History in Vienna with his classmates from Cambridge when the fixation took root. It came from a guide, a man in his thirties, who took a "special interest" in Jerome. The man's attraction to him enabled Jerome to get historical information that would have gone unmentioned otherwise.

While the young men strolled about the rooftop observatory of the museum, viewing the spectacular panoramas of Vienna, the guide whispered Jerome aside and told him that all the bones and skulls and dinosaurs they had seen and learned about were nothing compared to the greatest relic of them all, the relic without which there would be no Viennese art or music or beauty. The city that stretched out for miles and miles before them would not exist. The relic saved Europe, he said; for without it, the Mongol hordes of the thirteenth century would have destroyed every church and castle and murdered every male from Vienna to the English Channel.

While the two of them looked across the sunlit gardens and historic buildings of the city, he regaled Jerome with descriptions of the miniature ship's gold and jewels and the meaning of its shape. He praised the ingenuity of the Venetian Doge who was responsible for the ploy and how his stopping the Mongol advance had allowed the Hapsburg Empire and the rest of Europe to root and flourish.

Jerome was enthralled. A sorcerer could not have lighted a more beguiling candle in his curious mind; or have launched a lifelong quest more effectively.

Now Santori's appearance had set that candle ablaze. The prize of a lifetime was within his reach. He didn't want to sell the Temujin; he wanted to possess it, to control it, to view it, to treasure it. He wanted ownership of that fabulous relic as intensely as Paul wanted to sell it.

As soon as Paul and the detective from Scotland Yard were out of Alistair's penthouse door, Jerome had told Alistair he wanted Paul followed when he returned to London. Alistair was uneasy with these tactics, but knew there was no stopping Jerome when his Temujin fire was blazing. He simply nodded his head and Jerome made a phone call.

Carl von Tresser. It was the name Giuseppe had confided to Paul in the King Cole bar of the St. Regis hotel weeks ago. Fifty million is a finger-snap for Tresser once he sees you have the Temujin, Giuseppe had told Paul. Giuseppe's price was only ten million for revealing where the prize was. Only ten million! What a bastard. He's doing my wife and he wants ten million from me, thought Paul at the time.

You are right, Paul, Giuseppe had admitted. I have no money to retrieve it from where it's hidden, and von Tresser would never trust me with an advance of any size; but then without my knowledge of its whereabouts neither of us has anything. You're getting a good deal, said Giuseppe with a cocky smile Paul remembered angrily. I could ask for half of the price you get from Tresser.

Yes, you could, Paul had thought; so why aren't you? Perhaps you have another way of getting half, even all of the sale price.

Jerome had similar concerns. He wasn't afraid that the big and gruff Santori would withhold the location of the Temujin. He would get that information from him in return for the promise of the buyers he and Alistair could provide. After that came the hard part. Alistair Baker and Paul Santori would want to sell the Temujin to the highest bidder they could find as quickly as they could settle on a price. Both would laugh at keeping it. Once it was sold, it would be out of his reach forever. It was a problem Jerome was starting to work through, as Paul had started working through his problem with Giuseppe after their meeting in the King Cole bar.

Paul waited impatiently at the fax machine in his apartment. Finally, the documents crept onto the machine's tray. He signed the power of attorney giving his lawyer all the authority necessary "… to conduct in my name all transactions in connection with the termination of Santori Enterprises, Inc., a Delaware corporation doing business in New York, and all affairs attendant to the final affairs and burial of my wife, Eleanor Santori, including disbursing the amount due her under a Prenuptial Agreement signed and dated __ and all fixtures and furnishings, etc., etc.; and to act on my behalf at the closing of the sale of my co-op apartment at __ Fifth Avenue, New York, NY, and to deposit the proceeds of said sale into my account, etc., etc." and faxed it back to his lawyer.

He also signed a real estate agreement with a top Manhattan agency at a commission of three-percent and faxed it back to an ecstatic agent who already had a customer straining to buy the co-op at the ten-million-dollar price Paul had set. It was an instant three-hundred-thousand-dollar commission for her. With his apartment, business and wife now out of his life and a large wad of hundred-dollar bills in his pocket, he packed a carry-on bag and took a cab to JFK for his flight to London. He did not want to see New York again.

He was followed to the airport by an agent of Arnie's who watched him until he went through the security line, and remained watching for two hours to be sure he hadn't faked a departure.

Carol and I live in half of a vertically split building with two apartment doors inside an outer door. A four-step stoop with an iron railing leads up to the entrance. The building is worth millions. Greenwich Village is one of Manhattan's most expensive neighborhoods. Before I gave up my own (damn nice) apartment on the Upper East Side and moved in with Carol, she was getting help on the rent from her Uncle Jack Tomkin in St. Louis. Jack is her deceased father's brother and his paternal stand in. He's devoted to her. Jack retired from the stock brokerage firm he founded and now at seventy takes life easy, except when he's in New York. After drinking close to a full bottle of Kettle One vodka during cocktails and dinner with Carol and me, he would stride out the door to examine the city's possibilities. He always made it back to his hotel, if the absence of police calls is sufficient evidence.

I wondered if Jack had given Carol a "not getting any younger" talk. Probably not. He's not one to preach, but if he dropped a subtlety here and there, she would get the message. I had a strong sense that my friend and informal father-in-law Jack Tomkin was meddling in the background in re the matter of a child.

I poured myself a glass of a slightly chilled pinot noir, shed my gun and jacket and wondered how one contacts the Shadow to learn when birth-control grace periods end. My gut said it was ending soon.

From the foyer, "I'm home. Grab the big bag fast. The bottom's coming out." It was.

"Milk, orange juice and bread, the basic stuff of life. Can you store them? I need an aspirin. Didi and I had three, I think, glasses of wine at lunch. My head aches." She tossed off her shoes and started for the bedroom.

"How is the Princess of Profit?"

From down the hall, "She's fine. Looks spectacular."

"She had advice, of course."

"Yes."

I didn't need details. Didi and I get along, but underneath she thinks Carol would be happier with someone "normal."

"I have a feeling the grace period is ending."

From the bedroom, "What grace period?"

"My god, it's over."

"Yep, it's over. You can no longer unzip your pants with impunity."

I swallowed the rest of the pinot.

Desperately, "How long does it take for the pill to wear off?"

She sauntered into the room, sat across from me on the couch, crossed her wonderful legs, now bare to the hip under an open robe, and gave me a rebellious look. She was waiting for a reaction, which I was not prepared to give. We stared for a three-second eternity and, gratefully, my cell phone rang. Arnie.

"'e's on a plane to London. I 'ave someone picking up the tail when 'e's off the plane."

I mumbled something like "Good work."

Holding the phone on my knee, I said,

"I have to go to London. Let's go together – tomorrow."

She stared at me for a second and then, looking down, started moving her head slowly from left to right. She uttered a hopeless chuckle.

She pulled the robe over her legs. "I can't do that, Hank, not on such short notice."

Fortunately, she didn't say you know that.

"You could join me in a few days. We could…" I stopped. There was a forlorn look of helplessness in her face, but what shut me up was the tear forming in her eye.

Something powerful seized my insides and took me to her side. We looked into each others eyes; mine dry, hers moist. She was silent. I said,

"Carol…I love you very much."

It helped loosen whatever it was still trying to rip out my stomach.

The following morning Lydia announced she had selected the newspapers *Il Gazzinttino* in Venice and *Der Standard* in Vienna.

"But we need them in German and Italian. I *speak-a* only *der* English, *Herr* Tower."

"Call New York University's language department and ask for an advanced student in both languages. E-mail them the English. A hundred dollars for each translation. Bill it to von Tresser."

"I need the English."

"Right. Give me a few minutes. Make a reservation for me to

London on a flight that gets me there tomorrow morning. Also, a hotel reservation at the...at the what...the Ritz. It's on Piccadilly. Make it a deluxe room and put it on von Tresser's account. Did the nine-thousand hit the bank?"

"Yes, yesterday."

"Make it a junior suite. Now I need quiet for my creative juices to flow."

Arnie came in. "'e's checked in the Savoy hotel on the Strand."

"Fine. The Ritz is a walk from there. Now, I need quiet for my creative juices..."

"Aye."

After a few re-dos I handed the following to Lydia.

Important Message from the Attorneys Representing the Late
Mr. Giuseppe Bufono.

Mr. Bufono's last will and testament has instructed our firm to locate a woman he was exceptionally fond of. He wishes her to have an item from his estate that he believes will remind her of the closeness that he and she shared during his life. His instructions further state that she will know who she is and what the item is. The person can claim the object by calling Mr. Hank Tower collect at (cell phone number).

Lydia studied it.

"What do you think?"

"I can't think of anything to add. The question is does she exist and will she see it?"

"Let's not be pessimistic. Run it for three days in both papers. Make sure his name is printed in large type."

"Will do."

My cell rang. In crisp Germanic English, "Tower, von Tresser. Update."

"Carl, we are running ads in Vienna and Venice to lure in whoever may have told Bufono the location of the Temujin. I'll give you the insertion dates. It will be in the *Der Standard*. I also have tails on Paul Santori who's back in London for reasons we will find out and I will pass on."

"A liberal paper."

"I didn't know that, but it could help. If our lady exists, she's probably a softie."

"Hmm. E-mail me the advert."

"I'll be in London tomorrow night at the Ritz. Can you fly over?"

"The Ritz? Not the penthouse, I hope."

"No, a junior suite."

"Hmm. Yes, I'll fly over. We need to talk about Carlton Bouchard. Keep ten tomorrow night open. We'll drink."

I sensed the next morning might require medication.

"Lydia, what do you have on Carlton Bouchard?"

"Hold on. I'm getting my notes."

She slid easily into the black chair that Phillip Santori nearly took with him when he stood up.

"Carlton Bouchard comes from a wealthy French family that settled in Tuscany, Italy, right after the First World War. They bought thousands of hectares – a hectare is about two and a half acres – and grew Chianti Classico grapes primarily. They used the profits to buy more vineyards and to open wine stores, first in the small towns of Tuscany, then in the more populated Northeast around Verona and Venice.

"The Bouchard family now owns chains of wine stores under different names across Italy that sells its wines and everyone else's. I might add that the figures I saw show Italy drinks more wine than the rest of the world drinks water.

"The best off in the family went into philanthropy and many of the small museums of Italy depend on their contributions. The head of the family is Carlton who runs the Doge's Depository in Venice."

"Where in the world did you get all that?"

She grinned. "Smart, aren't I, but unfortunately also truthful. The Bouchard wine company has a web site."

"Any idea how wealthy Carlton is?"

"No. The company is private and the family is more private. I asked my nephew to crack open some secrets, but even he was frustrated trying to hack into the Bouchard dynasty. There were dead ends everywhere. It's an excessively secretive family, he said, but that could be the wounded pride of a professional."

"It's also information. Real wealth keeps to itself. If Carlton knows that the whereabouts of the Temujin is in play, it's possible he could outbid our Austrian client and put it in the Doge's museum, where it probably belongs, but don't quote me on that."

"Anything else, Hank?"

"No, just place the ads. I'm meeting von Tresser tomorrow night in London at the Ritz. He'll have more data on Bouchard, but I want to impress him with this first." My cell rang.

"Tower, I'm at Heathrow. Where is my cheating twin Paul staying?"

It seemed all roads had been diverted from Rome to London.

"At the Savoy. What are you planning to do?"

"To do? I'm going to find out what his nose smells. He doesn't leap frog over the Atlantic without a strong smell of money in his nostrils. Janet, on the other hand, leaped about – on my money – like the earth was a frying pan. If she hadn't insisted on Moscow, my seven-hundred-and-fifty would…"

"Doubtful, Phillip. As you said, the FTC would have gotten it, if your brother hadn't."

"Hardly a comfort, Tower."

"Phillip, do me a favor. Hold off a confrontation until we can meet. I'll be in London tomorrow night. I'm staying at the Ritz…"

"Christ! I'm not paying for that!"

"No. I'll take care of it. Just cool it until we can talk."

"All right. I'll call you as soon as I find a place for these weary bones."

Phillip Santori, Paul Santori, Carl van Tresser, a rich curator named Carlton Bouchard and maybe a call from a grieving woman with a multi-million-dollar secret. My lovely Carol was going to miss the fun.

CHAPTER 10

"There's an eleven p.m. flight from JFK to Heathrow, American Airlines 106. It lands tomorrow at eleven a.m.; but, it's coach. No other seats available. If your meeting with von Tresser isn't until ten p.m., you have plenty of time to straighten out and take a nice nap." So said my office manager, Lydia Larson.

"Book it. Did you get an insertion date for the ads?"

"Yes, the three-day run starts in both cities the morning after you and Tresser meet."

"Good work. Care to bet, Lydia?"

"What, on getting a response?"

"Yeah."

"Even money?"

I smiled. "You should give me odds. It's a shot in the dark."

"No. I'll refrain. The last time I made a bet I got in trouble for it."

"What happened?"

She handed me a note with the airline details on it.

"It was in grade school. I had noticed one of the nuns kept repeating 'incidentally' when she was teaching and bet a friend – Mary Pat – that if she said it more than five times she had to give me her new silly socks and if she said it less than five times, I had to give her my curved, red comb."

"Did you win?"

"No, but neither did Mary Pat. Sister Mary Joseph found out somehow and made us write something a hundred times on the blackboard."

"And you haven't bet since."

"Never." She grinned, "Except when I go to Atlantic City."

"Okay. I'm off. Put details in my voice mail. We have a five-hour difference."

I told Arnie the same and went down to the street. A light snow was starting to fall in unusually still air. The delicate flakes were falling straight down, as if they were descending strings. Snow in New York usually swirls in the wind chaotically. I decided to take a cab instead of a subway to Greenwich Village so I could watch it fall, at least I thought that was the reason I took a cab. Around Forty-second Street I called her.

"Hello, this is Edna Hausman."

"Edna, Hank Tower."

"Mr. Tower, how nice to hear from you. My last patient just left. I have plenty of time to hear how the case is going. Have there been any more murders?"

"No, just the two."

"I have a premonition there is going to be another."

When Edna has a premonition I listen.

"Why do you say that?"

"It's mostly a woman's instinct. I have no facts; but one should never dismiss a woman's instinct – mine or any other woman's, if it's sincere. We call it unconscious reasoning. The mind is assessing information that hasn't reached consciousness yet. There's only a feeling, an intuition. The person can't base it on anything specific. Now, if you were to give me some facts, perhaps I could…"

"Edna, Carol wants a child. Why don't I?"

Silence. "Forgive me. I should have known there was another reason for your call."

"I love her; she loves me. I'm thirty-eight; she's thirty-two. She makes a good living; so do I. She has a college education; so do I. She loves to travel; so do I. I've met her parental stand-in. He likes me; I like him."

"The check list is impressive."

"I think the responsibility of a kid will put me off my game, make me worry about getting killed and then get me killed. She, well, she doesn't believe that's the reason."

Silence.

"And another thing. Why in hell am I willing to go after a guy with a gun pointing at my head or a nut with a knife at my throat – risk my damn life – and not be afraid, and then be afraid of having a child?"

"Are you afraid of having a child? That's different from thinking a child would endanger your life."

"Why?"

"What do you think?"

It just came out. "Because it would overwhelm me…it would sink me…"

"Why?"

"I wouldn't know how to act, how to care, what to do, it would screw me up...my life would change...the responsibility would replace things...I wouldn't have as much fun...I couldn't just... just do as I please..."

Silence.

"I sound like an immature boy."

"Do you think boys have less fear than men?"

"Well, they take chances grown men wouldn't."

"Physical chances."

"Yes."

"Like going after a guy with a knife at your throat."

"I get the point. But I have to do that sometimes as part of my job."

"I don't detect recklessness in your work."

"Hell no. I'd be dead."

The cab was turning onto our apartment's street.

"I must still be a little boy looking for a high bridge to walk over or a dangerous tree to climb or a car to drive fast..."

The cab had stopped in front of our apartment. "I have to go. The cabbie wants his money."

"Think about that dangerous tree, Mr. Tower."

I paid the cabbie and went up the steps to our door. Flakes of snow were landing and instantly disappearing on the steps. Inside, I thought, Edna didn't ask again about the case before we hung up; and I didn't bring it up. See, this damned distraction about a child is…well, I did get one opinion from her – another murder.

If so, who would it be? Paul, Phillip? Would one identical twin kill the other? It seemed unlikely, but maybe having the same DNA isn't enough to overcome jealousy, anger or greed. Tresser? No, he's the guy with the money. Ditto Bouchard. But, would Tresser knock off Bouchard, if it came to war between them over the Temujin? Would the reverse occur?

Giuseppe's dead because he learned where the Temujin is located, and because he most likely wanted too much money for that knowledge after he revealed it. Not very bright. Eleanor's dead either because she was there with Giuseppe or because she had gone too far for Paul or a spurned lover to tolerate. If that's the case, then Giuseppe is dead because he was there. One thing seems certain. Anyone who knows the location of the Temujin is in danger, and that means our mystery woman, if she appears, is target number one; and once I know it, I'm number two.

Carol came in slapping the wet snow off her coat.

"What time is your flight?" came echoing down the hall to the kitchen where I was pouring a pinot noir.

"Eleven. I'll have to leave here a little before nine."

"Jack is coming to New York. He should be here about eight-thirty, unless there's a traffic snarl with the snow. Anywhere else it wouldn't be noticed, but the city is so finely tuned the slightest thing fouls it up."

Jack Tomkin, Carol's uncle and parental stand-in and a fine guy. I hoped I wouldn't miss him.

I wandered into the bedroom to begin packing. She came in, let her hair fall and pressed herself sensuously against the wall.

"It's only seven and you might be gone for awhile…"

I pulled her into my arms and we fell on the bed. It's amazing how the brain can perform on different levels. Part of mine was heating my blood to the exclusion of any form of rational thinking; but another part was whispering like an offstage prompter "It may be the last time you know there will be no consequences. Go for it." I did and so did Carol.

An hour later we rose and dressed. I finished packing while she made a couple of sandwiches. At 8:30 the door bell rang. Jack Tomkin stepped inside, dropped his suitcase on the floor and hooked his coat on a twisted, birch wood hat tree Carol found in an antique shop in Pennsylvania. He was holding a paper bag…

"I brought my own Kettle One, but I'm willing to share a couple of ounces of it. Carol, honey, how are you?'

She wrapped her arms around him and put a firm kiss on his cheek.

Carol lost her parents in a private plane accident about seven years ago. She survived psychologically, partly by leaving St. Louis, but her younger sister by four years still receives counseling, thanks to a generous Uncle Jack.

He released Carol and extended his hand. "Hank, It's been a while. You were out of the country the last time I visited." He scanned me up and down and said,

"I don't see any scars or bullet holes. All must be well. Am I right?"

The question suggested more than a health query. Carol was his charge; but for her sister, Jack was her only living relation; and to a childless widower that meant Carol and her sister were Jack's children. His eyes were asking if the two of us were still in sync, which meant that he was aware of something that might have caused us to go out of sync, which meant that he was fiddling in the children market.

"You're right, Jack. All is well." Carol snuggled to my side as proof. The timing couldn't have been more opportune for the two of us to show we were happy.

"Then I need three glasses." He pulled the vodka out of its brown paper bag and poured about an ounce and a half into the small glasses Carol provided and handed them out.

"Here's to the two of you. You look wonderful – more, you're aglow."

"And here's to you, Jack." I lifted my glass to him and downed the vodka. It went down like a liquid razorblade.

"I wish I could join you two, but I have to leave in about twenty minutes for the airport. London."

Sincerely, "I'm sorry. It's the curse of the retired class. When we're ready to party, the working class has to go to work. Can you discuss any of it?"

"Part of it. It seems there's a multi-million-dollar relic that several people are wiling to kill to own. I hope to find it and return to New York with a chunk of its worth."

Concerned, "Be careful, Hank."

"I will. I'll give you the whole story when I return."

We chatted for a while. Jack said he would take Carol to dinner and watch over her while I was gone. Carol handed me a wrapped sandwich and we kissed at the door with Jack standing in the background. I was closing the door behind me when I heard him say again, "Be careful, Hank."

I found a cab easily and settled back for the trip to Kennedy. The snow was denser now, but still falling straight down in the windless air. Jack's surprise visit, surprise to me, brought up thoughts of Carol in St. Louis. It's a shock to lose a parent to an accident, but two at the same time? It must have devastated her. She would have been twenty-four, about three years out of the University of Missouri, settled in her reporting job at the *Post Dispatch*, on track for a career in journalism, maybe even a young man was in her life, someone she met at drinks after work, or someone she worked with. And then.

It was certainly a strong reason why she came to New York. New York is filled with young men and women escaping from something unpleasant back home. There is privacy in the city's teeming population. There is also loneliness. Carol's a private person, despite her fast-paced job at the *New York Post*. She speaks when appropriate, but doesn't start or encourage a chat. Sometimes I feel she is somewhere else, thinking about a subject far removed from the one last at hand. I hear that's what writers do, drift and assimilate. Perhaps that's what deeply hurt people also do.

Carol is well-formed, mature and comfortable in her skin, but the memory of the plane accident must occasionally invade her thoughts like a platoon of tanks. "Carol, it's your Uncle Jack. Something horrible has happened. Please, honey, sit down."

I haven't met her sister. All I know are tidbits Jack drops in conversation, which are minimal. He mentioned that she had some undemanding charity job in St. Louis. Carol has mentioned her only once that I can recall. It was during Jack's first visit to New York. He had to make arrangements for her – I'm not even sure of her name – therapy before he could leave St. Louis and he wanted Carol to know he had. I thought of Edna. How would she treat a person like Carol's sister?

The cab was emerging from the Midtown Tunnel into Queens.

Edna. She had me spotted; or, better said, she had me spot myself. I'm an immature adventurer who doesn't want to change or chance anything in his life that might cause a change. The dangerous tree. At ten or twelve it's not so dangerous, even though a fall could kill you. So what's different now? Only the proportion. Now, it's a gun or a knife instead of a tree that has to be challenged.

I shook my head to free myself of the thoughts. I needed all my pistons pumping on the job at hand.

The cab pulled up to the curb at the American Airlines terminal at 9:45. I had to check my luggage because of my .38 so I got through the security check a little faster than other passengers. Lydia finagled an aisle seat up front in coach for the 3,600 mile trip over Newfoundland in a 39,000-foot arc that would terminate at Heathrow Airport just west of London. We weren't 5,000 feet in the air before the guy in front of me pushed his chair back in my face. I pointed out what he had done as politely as a testy New York PI could and thought of the king-size bed in my junior suite in the Ritz.

Six rows behind Hank Tower a plain-looking, clean-shaven man with neatly combed hair was also settling in for the long trip. He was in a window seat where the prior occupant had left the shade half down, blocking a magnificent night view of the Wall Street end of Manhattan Island. To miss seeing those twinkling window lights sparsely scattered about in their high, shadowy homes would be an act of esthetic negligence. He glanced at the person dozing next to him and with an exceptionally long fifth finger on his right hand pushed the shade the rest of the way up.

CHAPTER 11

I had just cleared Immigration at Heathrow when my cell phone vibrated in my breast pocket.

"Tower, I'm in a poor man's hotel not far from your fancy Ritz. We need to talk. Where are you?"

I told him. "Phillip, give me a few hours. I was in coach squeezed in between a Sumo wrestler and a snorer. I need some rehabilitation before you descend on me. I also need your phone number."

"Eh...all right. No, the deal stands. No calling me – I'll call you. Meet me at six at the Mayflower pub in the East End. Any cabbie will know it. You need to visit with the common people, Tower. Six o'clock." He clicked off.

I picked up my baggage and .38 and decided to take a cab instead of the airport train to London. The train leaves you at Paddington Station where you have to continue your journey by some other means. It's cheaper, but not as relaxing as a taxi when your body is tired and bent. About a hundred dollars later I checked into the Ritz and was led to a very comfortable and quiet junior suite. It took five pounds to dismiss the footman who insisted on showing me every feature in my room, including how to regulate the hot and cold water, before I was able to slide under the sheets.

At 5:35, with straightened legs I was in another cab on my way to the Mayflower pub in the East End of the city. Unlike the crisp, snowy air in New York, the air here was filled with a thick dampness somewhere between fog and rain. The fading light didn't help. It made the city drearier. In an older, gas-lit, horse-clopping

London it would be easy to imagine that Jack-the-Ripper or Professor Moriarty or some similar fiend was stalking you in this mist with an open straight razor. In February, London's weather is worse than New York's, and only a wee better than Moscow's.

Rather than a fictitious fiend, I had only barrel-chested, break-his-legs Phillip Santori to cope with; but as the cab made its way east the changing neighborhoods suggested even he better be watched cautiously. Why so far away, if his hotel was near the Ritz? Adding to the eeriness, the Mayflower was on the Thames which at low tide reveals its worst picture – sloppy, gooey mud, lots of it, with a trickle of a river snaking down the middle of it on its way to the sea.

My imagination was only that. The Mayflower is charming, older than its namesake that sailed Pilgrims to our shore and the quintessential English pub. It's dimly lit and has a large, brick fireplace with a deer head over it. To the left of the fireplace is an upright seat backed to a booth and a regular chair with a small table between them. In the former sat Phillip Santori with his pepperoni face and a pint of dark ale. In different attire he could have been Falstaff.

"Phillip, why in the hell did you drag me all the way here when your hotel is near the Ritz? I should charge you for the taxi. In fact, I will."

"To see the city, Tower. This is an historic pub. People come from far and wide to sip its ale. You should appreciate my *savoir faire*."

Savoir faire didn't ring true from someone who when we spoke last didn't recognize *objet d'art*, or pretended he didn't. I filed it.

"Have the police contacted you?"

"No. You see the benefit of not being easy to find? But I am now contacting you. What is my brother up to?" He raised the pint to his lips and peered over it. I wrestled for a moment with how much to reveal about my better-paying client. I ordered a half pint of Speckled Hen ale and decided.

"He's after an artifact called the Temujin. It's worth at least fifty million, maybe double that. Art is in the eye of the beholder with the most money."

He looked at me respectfully. "How did you learn that?"

"Phillip, I can't reveal my source. He's a client…"

"Wait a minute! You work for me!"

"Yes, I did and I do. You needed evidence to discredit your brother. I have provided it well beyond your expectations. Regarding your second assignment, Paul was interviewed by the police and will probably be tossed out of his co-op because of the murders." He smiled at that.

"I remind you I almost got killed in your employ."

"Yeah, but I'm in for another five grand that's supposed to help me find what my brother smells."

"I just told you. I could call the case closed."

He studied me. "Okay, don't tell me how you learned it. Where is the thing?"

"If I knew that I could retire from the almost-getting-killed business,"

"You're after it, too?"

"No. I'm after a huge fee from the guy who can afford to buy it, if I can find it for him."

"The guy paying for the Ritz."

"A junior suite."

He hummed into a morose silence, then asked, "Who else is after it?"

"A London art dealer with access to a lot of money. I don't know if Paul is aware of that."

"What art dealer?"

"I don't know."

"Tower, I'm outgunned. I need your help, but I can't afford anymore five grands. This whole thing started because the idiot stole seven-hundred-and-fifty from me. Now, we're talking a hundred million. Jesus, that's not my league. How can I get my seven-fifty back with something for my mental anguish on top?"

"I don't know, but for god's sake, Phillip, stay inside the law. Let this play out. I have a feeling if the Temujin is found there will be money for all. If you do something foolish with your brother, you and I and my client will lose the keys to the kingdom." I paused and said,

"I think he knows where the Temujin is."

"Jesus. Then all I have to do is…"

"Confront him and you're lost. Leave him alone and he'll come home. Got it?"

He nodded and we ordered mushroom soup and free-range chicken. All was quiet while we ate but for the occasional "No" to "Is it all right 'ere, mateys? Do ya need somethin'?" from the waitress, and the mumble of background conversations. But neither sound was strong enough to keep the workings of Phillip Santori's brain from my invisible ear. I imagined hearing electrons zapping from synapses to synapses, so deep was his concentration. He could have been solving a difficult Sudoku puzzle in his head.

Billionaire Carl von Tresser was supposed to be in his late forties; if so, he should start spending rather than making. Maybe he was sick, I thought, but his "We'll drink" seemed to rule that out. He saw the question in my eyes as he approached the small table in the tea area, now a hard-stuff area, in the lobby of the Ritz. He stood for a second before taking a chair.

"You expected a hardier person at forty-eight. It's a disease that accelerates aging. There are medicines that slow it. Want·to guess how old I look?"

We were standing, facing each other. I had him by at least four inches, but he had the slim and taut body of a serious exerciser. Another way to stay young. He had a full head of brown hair laced with gray and was well-tailored in a typical London pinstripe suit. The aging problem showed in his face – it sagged. I wondered if he had lifts to keep it from sagging more. There's an old rule to follow when you are forced to guess a woman's age. Guess as low as you dare, then subtract five years. I applied it to von Tresser.

"Fifty-five."

"You're polite. I don't know if that's good."

We sat and I signaled for a waiter. Our table was removed from the others.

"I saw no harm in being polite to my boss."

"Ya. A good answer. I'll have a double martini, vodka." I ordered a Remy XO cognac.

"Now, I need to know what you know."

I said, "The best shot is the mystery woman. She would be a straight line to the Temujin. The second best shot is Paul Santori. Giuseppe may have told him where the Temujin is."

"Did he kill him?" The tone of the question was "Is it raining outside?"

"If Giuseppe demanded a big part of the sale to you, he might have."

"We need to meet this Paul Santori. If he knows where it is, I can wrap it up at a good price. Where is he?"

"At the Savoy. Hold on." I called the Savoy for Paul's room. No answer. I left a voice-mail message for him to call me, "Very important."

"Splendid. You're polite, but probably worth the money. Tomorrow early, maybe tonight, we call on Mr. Paul Santori. Now, we drink."

The martini and cognac arrived. Von Tresser downed his like an empty camel. Perhaps his aging disease is more common than he led me to believe. He ordered another.

I said, "Carl, a middle man might be a better approach to Paul."

"Do you think he knows I'll pay fifty-million euros?"

"Did Giuseppe know it?"

"Yes. A mistake, but fifty is a low price. It's worth far more."

"Then he used the money to get Paul in the act. Why didn't he go direct to you, get the money necessary for her and go to the mystery woman we hope exists?"

"Because he knew I wouldn't trust him a cent. He's a gigolo, even went for my wife, the ass. I could have had him killed. Does this Paul have money?"

"Yes, but not in your league. He has no interest in the Temujin, if you think he's gone to the mystery woman. His only interest is selling it, presumably to you."

"Presumably? Who else? Does he know about Bouchard?"

"I see you do. I don't know, but he came to London, not Vienna or Venice. Why would he do that?"

"To price it properly. Damnation!"

"How would he do that?"

"Art dealers. And that means Baker and Manchester."

"Who?"

"Alistair Baker and Jerome Manchester, two dandies that rule the art world here in London. Damn it! I'm late, Tower, maybe fifty-million late. If he's met with them, he knows the value. Jeromee-boy is fixated on the Temujin and probably lorded over Santori with its jewels and history. The bastard will want maximum value. Crap! Order more drinks."

I did and my better-paying client went into some kind of deep private world, only instead of solving a Sudoku puzzle, he seemed to be writing a script. His face said it wasn't a comedy.

I tried Paul's room. No answer. I shook my head and Tresser drained the remains of his current drink. A refill arrived, but he was lost in his mental scriptwriting. We sat and sat. He finally surfaced and swallowed the martini.

"I'm going out for a while, Tower. Call me if you reach Santori."

"It's lousy outside."

"I can take care of myself."

I set the alarm on my phone to call Paul Santori at 3:00 a.m., walked through the beautifully restored lobby and went to bed.

Alistair Baker waited for Jerome to leave on an errand and dialed.

"Please tell Mr. Bouchard that Alistair Baker is calling from London." A soft Italian voice said she would. A moment later...

"Alistair! What a surprise. We haven't spoken for far too long. How is your health? How is Jerome? Ah, don't answer. I sense you have a prize for me, no? It doesn't matter. I am always pleased to hear from you or Jerome."

"Are you free to talk, Carlton?"

"Si, always to talk, to eat, to drink. How can I help you?"

"I'll go straight to it."

"Please. You English are too circuitous. It's an old saying, but true. The more you say the less they hear. Is it right, Alistair?"

"Perhaps. Circumstances suggest I may have a lead on the Temujin's whereabouts."

"*Mamma di dio*! I want it. You know that. I must be the first person you call once you are certain. How certain are you?"

"Jerome is certain a client of ours knows, but is playing it coyly."

"Jerome. He's fanatic on it. You have to keep him out of anything we do. It has to be between you and me, only you and me. I insist."

"I will do my best, Carlton, but we are partners."

"You're the senior partner. If he gets possession of it, he'll sleep with it. That's terrible competition, Alistair."

Alistair laughed. "You are right. I will do my best…"

That wasn't good enough for Bouchard. "I highly recommend it, Alistair. I'm coming to London. I want to be in the middle of this. That piece belongs to Venice. No one else should have it, including Jerome."

"I understand."

"Keep him out of it. I don't care how, or I…"

"I understand, Carlton. Where would you like to stay? I'll make a reservation for you."

"The Savoy. I'll be there tonight."

After an evening flight from Venice, a large and determined Carlton Bouchard blustered into the Savoy's lobby just after midnight, minutes after a remarkably sober Carl von Tresser stepped into the London night from the Ritz.

Hank Tower woke at 3:00 a.m. and called Paul Santori's room at the Savoy. No answer. He left another message.

Von Tresser returned to the Ritz at 4:00 a.m., about an hour before the *Il Gazzattino* and the *Der Standard* newspapers appeared on newsstands in Venice and Vienna.

CHAPTER 12

"Meet me in the restaurant," said my better-paying client in as soft a tone as his guttural English allowed. It was 7:00 a.m.

The restaurant at the Ritz is old-world and extraordinarily beautiful. There are high-ceiling, golden draperies adorning large windows that reach to the ceiling, crystal chandeliers and sconces, a lot of them, elegant magenta-cushioned chairs with arms that Phillip Santori might not fit between, topped by a large mural of Roman pillars with laurels curled around them with nymphs at their bottoms cuddled playfully. Today, we'd call them lesbians. Tresser was already at a table in the far corner to the right of the mural. Orange juice had been poured. I pulled up a chair.

"Tower, a middleman is a good idea. I want you to represent me."

"Okay…Santori never answered my voice mail."

"Then go to the Savoy and collar him. Wait, it should be more subtle. How can you ease up to him?"

"I'll figure a way. He knows it's worth more than fifty million."

"I damn well know he knows!" A diner at a near table looked our way. Tresser saw it and pulled in his neck like a turtle.

"So how far can I go?"

In a lower voice. "I don't know." He paused. "As far as we know Bouchard is my only competitor…"

"Maybe he hasn't been contacted."

"Sure he has. Baker would have called him the minute he knew the Temujin might be located, probably behind Jeromee-boy's back. Bouchard knows all right. He is probably in London now or on his way. Check that out." Eggs and toast arrived. We both had coffee.

I sipped and looked at Tresser. "How did you make your numerous millions?"

He narrowed his eyes. "Azerbaijan."

"Rough territory."

Silence.

"Where did you go at one a.m. last night?"

"Too many questions, Tower. Stay with finding the Temujin and I'll deliver your triple fee. Don't wander."

I returned his hard look. "I need a number."

He went quiet "Ya, ya." We ate eggs and toast. He clearly didn't want to declare yet.

"Let me get an appointment with Paul Santori. When I have it I'll call and get your instructions."

He finished his coffee. "Good. I'll get this check. I'm paying for it anyway."

We parted. He went I don't know where; I went to the Savoy to hunt up the *Sleep and Slim* widower, Paul Santori.

It's an easy walk from the Ritz to the Savoy which put me at the entrance to the hotel's splendid River Restaurant about 8:30. I asked the maître'd if Mr. Santori had arrived yet for our breakfast meeting. He said he hadn't seen him this morning. Then, on a long shot I asked,

"Has Mr. Bouchard arrived yet?"

"Yes, sir. He's at a window table. Would you like to join him?"

Another long shot. "No, Mr. Bouchard said we were expecting another guest, but I've forgotten his name. Can you bail me out of my embarrassment?"

"Certainly, sir. He's expecting a Mr. Baker, Mr. Alistair Baker. He's a regular here."

"Thank you. What's your name?"

"Henry, sir. Would you like me to take you to the table?"

"Thank you, no, I'll wait in the tea room for Mr. Baker."

I strolled out of sight of the diners and called my triple-fee client. Voice mail. I left a report on Bouchard and my opinion that fifty million was clearly no where near enough to bring home the goods.

Where was the commodore of that ship, the only one who knew where it was harbored? No answer to my voice mails, no answer at 3:00 a.m., no show at breakfast. I went to the registration desk.

"I have an appointment with Mr. Paul Santori. Could you ring him up for me?"

"Just a moment, please." She scanned the computer.

"Mr. Santori has checked out, sir."

"I see. What time did he leave?" She looked at the screen.

"At six this morning, sir."

I knew the answer, but asked anyway. "Did he leave a forwarding address?"

"No, sir, he didn't."

Jerome Manchester was in a fitful, semi-conscious dream. His anxiety over possessing the Temujin was too elevated for his eyes to remain closed. His boyhood discovery and manhood obsession had him locked in a preconscious state. He was neither asleep nor awake. He rolled this way, that way, slipped his hands into the coolness under the pillows, pulled the covers to his chin, put his right leg on top of his left, then his left on top of his right. It was no use. Like corks in water, his eyelids would not stay down.

He was beset by a battalion of possibilities that would never let him rest again until they were resolved. Was he really certain he could get the hiding place from Paul Santori in return for delivering a high-price buyer like Bouchard? Did Santori already know about Carlton Bouchard? Once they had the Temujin, how could he keep his partner Alistair from arranging a sale to Bouchard, or an even higher bidder? Did Paul Santori have his own buyer, one Alistair and he were unaware of? Was he only using the two of them to determine the best price he might get from that buyer? Would someone give Santori a price no man could refuse, except me? How could he wrest the Temujin from the money, how could he steal it, which he intended to do, somehow?

He slipped out of bed, put on a robe and started for the kitchen. Alistair was asleep in the adjoining bedroom. He pulled its door shut. The refrigerator offered weak help. He went to the wet bar in the living room and poured two ounces of cognac into a snifter and swirled it. Its pleasant smell and burning taste dispatched part of the half-sleep. Jerome was an average size and well-muscled from sedulous exercise. Two ounces were not enough for his conditioned body to relax. He poured two more and hung the robe's waist tie around his neck, letting the robe hang open. His mind was alive now and back into his obsession. He was a true collector, one of those few who collect only to collect, the kind that must have total control over their treasures, whatever they may be. For these true collectors, selling a prize possession is a repulsive idea. To Jerome, selling the Temujin was unthinkable. Only possession mattered.

Jerome stepped beyond the collector's normal neurosis that day on the roof of the museum in Vienna when the male guide put a caressing hand on his bare forearm. Jerome had listened to his story in a trance, too fascinated by it to catch the true meaning of the man's gesture. Here was a prize he would someday, somehow, have for himself. Now, nearly twenty years later, that prize was at the door of his dream. He would steal it; somehow, he would steal it.

A click. Alistair's door? He placed the cognac's snifter on the bar and looked down the hall. Perhaps his friend wanted him in bed. No, the door to his bedroom was still closed. He looked down the longer, wider hallway to the flat's foyer. The front door looked ajar a few inches. He hesitated. A shiver started to form up his back. He went slowly to the door and reached to close it, and froze. The robe's tie was quickly doubled around his neck and cinched. He grabbed at it, tried to turn to see the person behind him, but couldn't move his head or breathe or utter a sound. Deeper and deeper the cotton tie dug into his flesh. He struggled to get his fingers under it, to turn his body to fight the source, but a sharp knee was in his lower back, bending him into a bow and leveraging the noose even tighter around his throat. His brain was blasting into space, then it exploded like a flare and he went into eternal blackness. He was lowered quietly to the floor. Moments later the flat's door clicked shut.

"My god, Alistair! What…how…he's…?" Carlton Bouchard had leaned back from his breakfast table and was staring out the window to the Thames.

"What time this morning…you found him naked…his robe was

removed…the police are, what…? *Mamma di dio*…can I help, can I come to your flat? Okay. No, there's no need to meet me. Do what you must do. I'll be here at the Savoy. Are you sure there is nothing I can do? All right. I'll wait to hear from you, come when you can. Yes, it would be better to meet here."

Carlton pocketed his phone and waved for more coffee. What a development! Jerome strangled, naked. Who would want to…? Was it a sex crime? He doubted that. Jerome and Alistair seemed to get on. Why would Jerome branch out? If not a sex crime, then… then it's the Temujin. Someone wanted Jerome off the stage. Was the person afraid if Jerome got near it, he would steal it? It was a valid concern. The relic exerted a power over him a mistress would envy. Poor Alistair, well, maybe not poor. Alistair was no softy. He couldn't be at the top of the world he had chosen, if he were. The competition in high-end art could be cunning and vicious. A weakling would be eaten.

Jerome's murder suggested caution, if the Temujin was behind it; and Bouchard was almost certain that it was. Someone wanted the relic badly and wasn't going to take a chance on some fanatic art dealer whisking it off for himself. Bouchard returned to his breakfast and searched his mind for someone who would want the Temujin badly enough to kill.

Von Tresser heard the news on an early morning news report and immediately called Tower.

"Tower, you heard?"

"Yeah. I recognized the guy's name, but never met him. The second half of Baker and Manchester."

"He was a fanatic…meet me in the middle of the Waterloo Bridge at twelve-thirty. We need privacy."

When I heard Jerome had been murdered I thought about having Arnie join me. If this case turned on art dealer number one killing art dealer number two or vice versa, I wanted his help and protection for New York PI dealer number One. It may be just a piece of art, but apparently art people turned into fire ants when one-hundred-million dollars was in play. It was only 7:00 in New York. I'd wait a while before calling him. I would need Tresser's approval of the expense as well. A last-minute flight to London would run in the thousands.

At 12:15 I turned onto the footpath of Waterloo Bridge and walked slowly to its middle. The tide had graciously returned the Thames to its deeper depth and good-size ships were plying their way up and down its water. The Thames has one of the more vicious tides in the river world. It can rise twenty-four feet or so before it turns. The current created can render a swimmer or small boat helpless in its speed. Now, looking down at it, the river seemed docile. It was probably at flood tide. I was leaning over for a better look at the activity below when Tresser leaned over next to me.

"We have to find Paul Santori fast. I suspect Alistair will plead ignorant of knowing any reason why Jerome was killed, but he will know. If the police get the Temujin story out of him, every collector in Europe will come out of their cage, sending the price to Pluto. I do not want that to happen, Tower. You are on triple fee to prevent that. Now, where is the bastard?"

I hesitated. I wanted to ask where he was from 1:00 a.m. when he left me until he returned to the Ritz this morning.

You can't make a billion in Azerbaijan without sharp instincts.

"It wasn't me, Tower, for the reason I just explained."

I looked at him. Maybe not, but if killing were necessary to win something, he would. I wanted Arnie, which meant it was time to talk about my other client.

"Carl, when you called me I said I couldn't take you on because of another client. That client is Paul Santori's twin, Phillip Santori."

"Twin?"

"Identical twin. Same size, mannerisms, speech, everything. Their DNA is one-hundred-percent the same. Now, Phillip was ticked at Paul because Paul stole from him and Phillip wanted to expose Paul's wife as a cheater to get even. Enter me. I go to the Plaza hotel to get proof of the cheating and find Paul's wife and Giuseppe shot dead naked in bed."

"Go on."

"Here's my point. It was a professional killer and he's still free-ranging about the world. He could have killed me, but for some reason knocked me out instead. He could be on this bridge watching us or cooking a goat in the mountains of Azerbaijan. I have no idea. I have escaped death once in this case and I don't like the odds on escaping it twice. I want my assistant here with me – on your bill."

He looked at me dead pan. "Is he good?"

"Damned good. He's an ex-cop, bigger than both of us and has more common sense."

"Have you met Paul?"

"Only as a bystander in a police interrogation room after his wife was murdered. He saw me on his way out."

"Okay. Get him. I might need him, too. Jeromee-boy was taken out to prevent him from stealing the Temujin or from messing everything up some other way. I didn't give the order. That means someone else wants it as badly as I do. The only person I know of that wants it that badly is Bouchard. Does he have the balls to order a kill? I don't know." He looked down at the river and said reflectively,

"Collecting can be as wild as a fight to the death. It possesses the brain. God knows, it's possessed mine."

I took out my cell and called my office. Lydia's voice mail answered.

"Lydia, tell Arnie to get a ticket to London as fast as he can. Get a cab at the airport and go to the Ritz hotel (I saw Tresser flinch). I'll make a reservation for him. Tell him to bring his gun and check it. Keep looking for something on Phillip and call me if you find anything."

"Checking on your other client?"

"He's in London, a ghost. I can't call him, he calls me. We meet, he disappears. I'll hear from him as soon as he learns about Jerome."

"Is he after the Temujin?"

"He's says no, only the money his brother stole – about seven-hundred-and-fifty-thousand. Would he take a piece of it if he could, yes."

"Can he kill?"

"I'm not even sure he exists…"

"Really?"

"I'll worry about that when I have to. Right now I want to find the Temujin for you and the supremely generous fee you will give me when I do. The ad ran in Vienna and Venice this morning with no response. It's running again tomorrow. Cross your fingers. If we find the lady who whispered to Giuseppe where the Temujin is, we win."

He gave me a look Bismarck might have used to warn an enemy.

"I always win, Tower, one way or another."

"Let's see what tomorrow's papers bring."

CHAPTER 13

Paul Santori had a problem. From his meeting with Jerome and Alistair he had determined what he would demand for the Temujin –one-hundred-million - and from Giuseppe he had Carl von Tresser's name and city of residence. He had two parts of a three-part bonanza. The missing part, of course, was the product. All he garnered from Giuseppe on the product part of his enterprise was Giuseppe's strong hint that the Temujin resided in a cloistered nunnery in Venice. Did that mean the Temujin was hidden behind dark, sliding windows guarded by a platoon of armed nuns? Did cloistered nunneries still exist? If so, what the hell would a bunch of sequestered nuns want with the Temujin? Would they sell it? Do they need or even care about money? Not caring about money he considered impossible.

Nor could he contact his customer, von Tresser, without knowing exactly where the prize was. Maybe that knowledge alone would be worth a few million to Tresser. Take a much lower amount and let him figure out how to penetrate the dark chambers of a cloistered convent; but Paul Santori was a man of determination. Doubt was not in his blood. All he had done so far would not be wasted on a few million. Definitely not. It was the big number or nothing.

He was sitting in the lobby of a modest hotel off Piccadilly waiting for his room to be readied. It was nearing noon. A clerk placed some of London's infamous tabloids on a table near his chair and he picked up the Sun, perhaps the most accomplished in the world of sensationalism. In a quarter-page insert on the front page of probably the largest circulation newspaper in the world was a picture of Alistair Blake of Blake and Manchester surrounded by a gang of police, trying to get a large hat between the cameras and himself. The headline read…

Murder in the art world!
Victim's partner sobs "I loved him."

Paul read the short article inside the paper and read it twice more. There was no speculation regarding a motive for why anyone would strangle the handsome, deep-voiced storyteller Paul had listened to patiently in his penthouse. The police were in the wrong ballpark, if they thought Alistair was involved. Even if he wanted to, he was too slight a man to overcome the muscular Jerome. But they would question him aggressively and if he caved, the Temujin would become public knowledge.

Was that bad? Yes, thought Paul. The more customers the better, usually, but in this case the repercussions would most likely be detrimental. First, it would introduce the unpredictable – always a threat. Second, maybe the nuns in Venice would get the news and retreat deeper into their cave, if they truly wanted to protect the relic; or worse, fall prey to the Devil and push the price heavenward "for the benefit of the good sisters." Until he had his fists wrapped around his prize, it was best its existence remain a secret.

Cutting Alistair in on the sale might be a prudent way to accomplish that, he thought. It would insure his silence and if Tresser wasn't the Temujin-craved billionaire Giuseppe claimed he was, Alistair could access other customers. The key was keeping the convent a secret. Now that Giuseppe was no longer among the quick, it was a secret only he knew. How many cloistered convents can there be in Venice?

"Your room is ready, sir."

He pulled his roller-bag behind him and got off the elevator at the third floor. The room was smaller, a bit musty, but its location was unknown to all but him. He wanted anonymity and quiet to plan, which was even more critical now that he wanted Alistair in the mix. He thought of Henry the maître'd at the River Restaurant in the Savoy. He would ask him to give Alistair a message on his behalf.

Paul undressed to his shorts and rolled his hulk onto the bed. Beautiful Eleanor floated into his mind, then the *Sleep and Slim* belts stored in the warehouse of a Connecticut fulfillment firm, then the small office in Queens, then the apartment on Fifth Avenue, then Eleanor again, Eleanor naked under one of his tent-size shirts, promising him pleasure, if he takes her shopping in Paris for a week, then the son-of-a-bitch Giuseppe whom he tolerated, but hated. "If your nun story is false, Giuseppe..." but you're already dead. He dozed off thinking of a message to give Henry and when to call it in. Not too soon. He had to keep himself safe from Alistair's new coterie, the London police.

I got three calls around 2:00 in the afternoon. One was from Lydia saying Arnie had a ticket and would land tonight about 11:00. Another was from Phillip Santori.

"Tower, I need information. Who is this guy in the paper who got knocked off? Is he the dealer you were talking about?"

"Yes, one of the two partners. Phillip, listen to me. Are you sure you want to mess around in this? First, there's Eleanor and her Italian lover, now there's an art dealer. Three murders. Maybe Paul is next, and you're a carbon copy of him. Accidental murders are common. I know of wrong throats being cut in New York because of mistaken identities. You're a dead ringer for Paul. I'd get out of London."

"Tell the s.o.b. to give me my seven-fifty and I will. In the meantime I'll take my chances. Do you think Paul could get axed because he knows where the Temujin is? Seems to me knowing that would protect him."

"Until he was persuaded to reveal it."

"Hmm, yes. If someone can strangle, I suppose he can pull fingernails. What the hell should I do?"

"Stay put wherever you are while this plays out. The police will also look for Paul. If he were one of the last people to see Jerome alive, they'll want his story. He checked out of the Savoy early this morning. Alistair can probably give very good descriptions of people. They could snatch you for him. Where are you?"

"No deal. I'll call you."

"Stay out of sight and read the papers."

He gave a throaty grumble and rung off.

The third call I got was the kind that often kills people in my business, but, forgive me Carol, I have to follow up on it. It went something like this.

"I saw the Sun this morning. I want to talk to you. I'll be in a cab at the entrance to your hotel at five this afternoon. I'll hold up my right hand for recognition."

He said it had an exceptionally long fifth finger.

I cursed myself for not calling Arnie sooner. This kind of summons was exactly why I wanted him here. "I saw the Sun this morning," he said. Okay. But I wasn't mentioned in the Sun's article. So how does he know me? Why call me?

The next question was easy to answer. He didn't want to talk to the police. The third question was the disturbing one. How did he find me?

I get my name in the paper in New York occasionally, but I'm unknown to London's press, so far. So the caller knows me from New York, and knows that I'm involved in a case he obviously knows something about. That would be the Plaza murders which were widely covered and included my name. Arnie, I don't like the feel of this. Carol would…I don't know what Carol would do, leave me? So I have an anonymous caller who knows something about the Plaza murders. Was he the…no, that's preposterous. A double murderer reveals himself to a private detective closely connected to the police? I dismissed it. Then I thought he might think I saw him before I lost consciousness. That would mean I'm next in line. But if that were his motive, he could take me out anywhere. It must be a witness to the Plaza murders unable to contact the police for some reason. That made sense. It was also more comforting.

Whoever he is, there was no way I was not going to be in front of the Ritz at 5:00.

At 4:45 I was on the front steps. At 5:00 a cab pulled up, the back window went down and a hand with a grotesque finger waved at me. I walked to the open door.

"Step in Mr. Tower. I have a proposition for you." I took the seat that folds down behind the driver so I could sit face to face with my host. My coat was open, if I needed the .38.

"Driver, we'll get out midway on London Bridge." He signaled silence to me and the driver stopped where he was told. It seemed bridges over the Thames were the preferred meeting places of my London acquaintances. We walked to the concrete railing.

The man was smaller than me and his hands were visible, purposely, I thought, for the wind was sharp and he probably would have preferred not to expose the hideous finger on his right hand. I was ready to take him, if he suddenly turned on me. He pulled his coat collar up against the February wind rising off the river and after a long pause spoke, looking straight ahead.

"Our business models are the same in two respects. We have clients; we get deposits. But I work alone." He paused again, still looking down the river.

"I have a habit. I watch events *after* I collect my fee. The incident in the Plaza hotel is a case in point. My research of your career said you weren't the kind of person to take pictures of naked arms and legs. So I sensed something bigger was in play. I spared your life because you were not a threat and I wasn't paid to take it.

"Now, here you are in London without your woman. Someone has been strangled. My instincts are aroused. I feel sparing your life entitles me to know what it is."

He stopped and turned his head slowly to me. His hands remained exposed on top of the concrete barrier. A blank face with cobra eyes. I was standing next to a professional killer who knew about Carol.

He turned his head back to the river. I turned my back to it and folded my arms. "Who hired you?"

He turned his head briefly to me, then back to his river stare. It was a foolish question, but it bought some thinking time for how to handle this development.

"I use a sliding scale. If the amount of money transferred from one party to another as a result of my efforts is less than five-hundred- thousand dollars, I insist on only ten-percent. Anything over that is fifteen. Cheating on the amount is not recommended. Those are my standard terms. If a circumstance has unusual twists, I am flexible.

"Now, I'm going to walk over into Southwark and disappear. Take a cab and go back to your hotel. I will call you periodically." He started walking, turned and said.

"The strangling wasn't me."

I could stop him with my .38 and hold him for the police, but on what basis? Not on what he just told me. Who would believe it? I would be the one put under the light bulb. And what would he do in retaliation? Murder Carol? Here was another reason to avoid a child, even avoid Carol, or any kind of close relationship. A loved one could be murdered by an enemy for something I did or didn't do. I watched my new acquaintance as he walked off the bridge toward the buildings and winding streets of the Southmark section of London.

I believed him about the strangling. If he was following me around New York and London, he had no way of knowing about Baker and Manchester until Jerome's murder appeared in the *Sun*. I never met either of them. I saw him stop to let a London bus cross in front of him. He skipped across the street before another one approached and was gone after it passed, not to be seen or heard until he contacted me.

The man was a psychopath, but he was logical, spoke in an educated manner and professed a code. That made his insanity doubly dangerous. The solution my little voice suggested when he said I was here without my woman was now confirmed. There was only one way out of a situation that endangered the one I loved. First, I would make a deal with him; then I would kill him.

Arnie cleared Immigration a little after 11:00 and dragged his roller bag to the taxi stand. A driver was leaning against his cab's front fender. He opened the back door for Arnie.

"Aye, ye could be of me clan. Yer a Scotsman, if my eyes ever saw one. Where are ye from?"

"America, but my elders came from Glasgow."

"I knew it. Me father, grandfather and all the greats before him hail from it. Where are ye 'eaded, mate?"

"The Ritz hotel?"

He slipped in behind the wheel, still talking.

"Aye. If only me own ancestors had gone to America maybe I'd be staying with ye. There was a back up on M-4, but it should be open now. Would ye like a paper?" He handed a copy of the Sun back over his shoulder through the window.

"Do ye see the fairy on the front page, trying to hide his face? 'e's the one that did it, if anyone wants me opinion. They 'ad a love quarrel and 'e choked 'im with his robe tie. I'm told fairies 'ave meaner arguments then we normal people. That's what I've read."

"But I 'eard 'e was smaller than the victim."

"Don't matter, mate. 'e sneaks up behind 'im, wraps the tie round 'is neck and pulls it tight as a piano string. Takes the fight out of 'im. When small fellas get their adrenalin going they get unnatural strong. Yea, 'e's the one. Quarreled over money, is my bet. Lots of it in that world."

Arnie read the article carefully. No mention of Hank. "Maybe they fought over an art piece."

"Ye mean who owned it? Aye, that could be. Lots of reasons for fairies to fight. Could 'ave been the lady one served the wrong tea." He laughed at his insight.

M-4 was clear and so was A-4. The cabbie spoke sporadically with "Are ye staying long?" and other occasional questions, but Arnie's perfunctory answers convinced him to let his fellow Scot rest after his long flight.

At 12:45 a.m. Arnie paid the most he had ever paid for a cab ride and entered the fanciest, most expensive hotel he had ever visited. He felt uncomfortable with the attention he immediately received.

At breakfast, he ate heartily while Hank briefed him on events, but Hank withheld the solution he had reached on the London Bridge regarding the Plaza hotel killer.

In Vienna and Venice the second insertion of Hank's ad was on the newsstands.

CHAPTER 14

Tresser approached Arnie and me at the corner table to the right of the snuggling nymphs in the mural that dominates the back wall of the Ritz hotel's main restaurant.

"Arnie, meet Carl von Tresser, our client and host." Arnie rose from his chair with an extended hand that smothered Tresser's.

"Arnie arrived late last night. Everything I know and should know can be trusted to him."

Tresser nodded and pulled up a chair. A waiter immediately arrived and took his order – a fruit plate and black coffee.

Matter-of-factly, "I see Jerome Manchester's murder is in the paper. As I said, he was a Temujin fanatic. If he ever got it, I doubt he would sell it. He won't be a problem now."

It was a frank observation from a man who is willing to pay many millions for the Temujin, who only yesterday asked in a "What time is it?" tone, if Phillip Santori could kill and followed up with "I always win, Tower, one way or another." I looked hard at him. If he sensed he had just admitted how much he benefited from the removal of the relic-mad Jerome, he gave no sign. He was merely pointing out a fact.

"Carl, we have a new development, a serious one." He stared at me and waited.

"I mentioned that Giuseppe and Paul Santori's wife Eleanor were shot by a professional killer – who spared me." I waited. He sipped his coffee and stared over the cup at me.

"The killer is in London and wants a piece of whatever is behind his killings. He doesn't know what it is, but he's convinced something big is involved. He says I owe him because he spared my life. This is true. He could have shot me as easily as he shot Giuseppe and Eleanor.

"He has a rate card for this kind of 'follow up,' as he calls it – fifteen percent of whatever changes hands when it's over a half million. I'm certain his follow-up knowledge goes no further than me and the person who hired him. He doesn't know you or Arnie." I waited and added,

"But if you see an otherwise normal looking male with a yardstick for a pinkie on his right hand…handle yourself with care."

Carl set down his coffee and asked,

"Do you think Alistair could have killed Jerome?"

"Jesus, Tresser. Let's deal with the problem at hand. This psycho will not spare me a second time, if he doesn't get an answer."

He stabbed three blueberries onto his fork and held them inches from his mouth.

"Tell him there's a Renoir involved worth five-million euros when it changes hands. That's a seven-hundred-and-fifty-thousand follow-up fee. Arrange a pick-up, then kill him." He pulled the three blueberries off the fork with his teeth.

Arnie was poker-faced. I was angry – with myself. For a lousy extra thirty-five-hundred dollars for an assignment I would normally never have taken I wind up in this world-class mess. What was wrong with spying? Why did I leave it? The kind I did successfully for fifteen years involved tracking and recovering money suspected of going to terrorists or drug lords. I tracked people and banks and companies. I came close to an early end a few times, but at least my departure would have had a whiff of nobility. But to go into blackness for taking pictures of naked lovers? No hero buttons there.

Oh, yes. I decided it wasn't a taking-pictures assignment. It was a recovering-stolen-money or something as equally self-serving. Now, I have a professional killer who wants a slice of something that may not exist and if it does exist, may never be found. And if it can't be found, Carol is in danger for her life. Then there's Phillip Santori, the client who started all this, a corpulent, late-night TV hawker of phony products who has decided to behave like a homeless ghost. Now add a second client who recommends paying the parking ticket and shooting the judge to get his money back. A screwy picture by even my own experience, but it took only a nanosecond to see one thing clearly. Tresser's shoot-the-judge-solution was different from mine only in motive. He wanted his fifteen percent "commission" back; I wanted to protect Carol from a psychopath. We were in harmony on how to solve the two problems. Kill Long-Finger.

Arnie said, "Hank, if ye are the only one 'e knows about, then I have to follow ye until the Temujin is sold to Mr. Tresser and the money is delivered to the psycho."

"An excellent idea," said Tresser, quickly absolving himself from any responsibility for my life, "but I have a better one. Incidentally, it's *von* Tresser, Mr. Macgregor. Von is the German equivalent of Sir in Britain."

"I'll remember that," said Arnie unmoved. Tresser said,

"I suspect Alistair will be free to take up bachelorhood by tomorrow. I doubt the police can hold him. Bouchard will certainly contact him as soon as he's free of the police." Then with Germanic sureness, he said,

"Currently, there are only two ways to the Temujin – Paul Santori or your newspaper adverts. Let's not count on the adverts. Let's find Paul. Ask for a meeting with his twin the next time he calls you and have Mr. Macgregor follow him. You should be safe from your follow-up menace for awhile. Twins are very close and could be working together, with one of them using you as their information collector. If I'm right, your client Phillip will lead Mr. Macgregor to Paul. Once I have Paul Santori's location, I will take charge and you can submit your bill and go back to New York."

"So we're stuck until Phillip calls."

"Can you think of a better idea?"

"No."

"Can you, Mr. Macgregor?"

"No. It seems a good way to go, but it leaves us sitting on our ends until 'e calls 'ank."

"Most of war is waiting," said Tresser, philosophically. "War" wouldn't normally be a strong comparison to searching for an artifact, but it seemed appropriate coming from Tresser.

"There's another opponent who needs attention," said Tresser. "Bouchard. He's staying at the Savoy and Alistair Baker certainly knows that. With Jerome gone, Bouchard is our last remaining enemy. He has the money to buy it at any price once he knows Paul Santori or Alistair have it. I don't want that to happen, Mr. Tower."

There was an iron tone in Tresser's voice. It reminded me of Long-Finger's tone during our chat on the bridge.

"Bouchard needs watching. He knows me. That leaves you, Tower." He waved to the waiter.

"I'll take care of the bill. Meeting over."

I felt like goose-stepping out of the restaurant, but decided it would attract unwanted attention.

Carlton Bouchard, Curator of the Doge's Palace Depository in Venice, ordered plain toast and butter and a mild tea for breakfast. He stared at the ceiling of his Savoy hotel room most of the night while his dyspepsia churned the contents of his stomach like a Mississippi stern-wheeler. "Mild, it has to be mild tea," he said with a suffering face to the waiter.

The Temujin. Was it really within his grasp? If it were, it had to be ensconced in *perpetuity* in the city it saved. That's where it was conceived and created and that's where it belonged. Every ounce of his curator blood decreed he would make that happen.

There were two engines powering the stern-wheeler in his belly. First, the possibility of losing the relic to a private collector was terrifying; it could be gone forever. Second, the amount of revenue it would bring to the Doge's Palace was colossal. He might not ever sleep again, if he lost the prize.

About twelve-million tourists a year visit the Queen of Cities and a great bulk of those tourists wouldn't possibly leave Venice without seeing the small, golden ship that saved the city, its inhabitants and perhaps the Western world itself from the Mongol horde.

He would have a short movie of the story produced. He visualized the assembled audience, the big screen, the advancing horde, the maps of their empire and their impending march on a helpless, barely defended Vienna, then Venice and the rest of Europe. There would be tense music, a deep-voiced narrator showing past brutalities of the Mongols and their grizzly methods of destruction and killing. It would show the terror in the eyes of the men, women and children of Venice, and then!…the genius of Doge Pietro Ziani's response, his challenge to the Universal Ruler's insatiable ambition by telling the Great Khan that to be a true Universal Ruler he had to preside over the sea as well as the land; and then, the brilliant use of his name on the golden ship to show respect while suggesting a partnership.

He would create a special Movie Hall and charge five euros per visitor to see the movie, then five more to see the Temujin encased in glass and surrounded by guards. The vision was what kept him awake last night. He estimated forty percent of the tourists would pay one or both fees. What was the cost to see England's Crown Jewels encased in glass? He would find out. He foresaw his plan recouping an investment of as much as 100 million euros for the Temujin in two or three years. After that the Temujin was a money-maker *extraordinaire*. Renovations delayed, purchases and cleanings postponed – everything that was on hold could go forward, *if he had the Temujin*. His fire equaled Jerome's. Only their purposes differed.

"May I offer you a palliative, sir?" asked the waiter.

"I'm that obvious, am I? No, but I will have some more toast and butter."

"Yes, sir."

And now Jerome was gone and Alistair was probably suspected. Was that even possible? Far-fetched, he thought, but he's seen many surprises when large amounts of money are involved. If Alistair had access to the Temujin, he would want to sell it; Jerome would have wanted to put it in his closet and hug it. He smiled at the strangeness of that psychology, but he knew it to be true. So intense is the desire to own in some collectors they will hide their most precious artwork from view and show it only to their most trusted friends. "Let me show you something I keep to myself…"

He was taking the last piece of toast and reading the *Financial Times* when Henry the maître'd leaned over his shoulder and said politely,

"Mr. Blake is on the phone, sir. Would you like to take the call here?"

"No, please tell him I will call him in three minutes from my cell phone. I have his number. If he's at a different number, let me know."

"Yes, sir."

Bouchard finished his buttered toast and calmed himself, then he walked into the Savoy's tea room and found a lounge chair in a private corner. He pushed a button on his phone and Alistair Baker answered.

"Carlton, I'm in my apartment after a ghastly experience with the police. My loss is immeasurable, then they have the impertinence to...they actually thought I strangled Jerome!"

"Alistair, where can we meet? I don't want to use the phone."

"My apartment. Come as soon as you can, my friend. I'm distraught. I need company. Jerome is everywhere. I'll probably sell... never mind. Just come."

Bouchard immediately took a taxi to Alistair Blake's penthouse. As it always happens in the minds of men on the edge of the biggest deal of their lifetime, adverse possibilities were creeping into Bouchard's thoughts. Sell? He meant the penthouse of course, but he cut off the sentence. Did he have the Temujin? Did he have another buyer? No, at the minimum he would give me a chance to bid. The penthouse. He could get several-million pounds for it. Would that influence his interest in the Temujin? Would he simply retire to the countryside? Alistair was Bouchard's only link to the relic. The traffic was slowing down; his dyspepsia was acting up.

The driver tried another street only to become ensnarled in a different jam. He maneuvered the cab onto another street and finally found a route that got the cab within a hundred yards of Alistair's building. Bouchard paid him and for a man more used to a desk than a running track made the trip to the building's elevator at admirable speed.

An ashen Alistair welcomed him at the door.

"Carlton, thank you for coming. The mess, this horrible mess has me as weak as a kitten. It happed right here where I'm standing. I found him...his eyes were...Please come in and sit."

"Would you like some tea?"

"Yes, I would, Alistair. Thank you." Alistair took his coat.

"This is a very sorry affair. I haven't known Jerome very long. Did he have a family?"

"An older sister who lives in Cornwall. He never mentioned his father or mother, only her. I called her just an hour ago, but she had seen the *Sun*. What a horrible way to learn your brother has been murdered."

"Yes." Bouchard was not good at condolences even to those he was close to. Thankfully, Alistair was out of earshot in the kitchen making tea. He strolled over to the large window and its panorama of the Thames, the London Eye and several of the many bridges that crossed the river. A magnificent view, easily worth five-million pounds. A man can live quite comfortably on that in the countryside, but he couldn't imagine Alistair in a small house with a garden, sitting in front of a warm fire, with a book, a dog or a cat. They didn't fit the man. Trepidation was creeping back into Bouchard's head.

"It's English Breakfast. It's the only tea I have at the moment." Bouchard took the beverage.

"Alistair, I am truly sorry..."

"It's all right, Carlton. I know you are. No need to say anymore. I will get over this..." He looked out the window. "We were together here for almost fifteen years." Fifteen years, thought Bouchard. The apartment has appreciated immensely.

He should have enough money from its sale to dispense with thoughts of the Temujin.

"Will you sell this place?"

"Yes, but not immediately, not while I'm in this state. Besides, the market is gaining strength."

That was a mixed relief to Bouchard. "I think that's wise, Alistair. There are few apartments like yours in London." He paused.

"Is it all right if we talk about the Temujin?"

"Of course. The police station experience has subsided. Can you imagine how they treated me…?"

"No, I can't, but they have to investigate all the possibilities. Are you sure you are all right, Alistair?"

"Yes. Give me a moment to collect my thoughts." He sipped his tea and said,

"The key to the Temujin is a very large American named Paul Santori. He sat in your chair while Jerome gave the history and value of the Temujin and said nothing. Jerome said he was a blank face during his entire presentation, a presentation Jerome does very well. Jerome's conclusion was that Mr. Santori knew where the Temujin was and was merely getting an appraisal of its value from us; that he had a buyer already in mind."

A rapier went through Bouchard.

"Where is this Mr. Santori?"

"I don't know."

"Do you think Jerome knew?"

"It's possible. His fanaticism might have put him on the American's trail, as it's said. My god, I wonder if that was the reason…"

"I doubt it," said Bouchard, but he didn't. He was certain that was the reason. Murder for a priceless artwork isn't uncommon. He looked hard at Alistair.

"Do you have any idea how I, we, could find Mr. Santori?"

"He was staying at the Savoy when I met him, but he's no longer there. If you know someone in the police maybe they…"

"No! If he is taken into custody, we no longer have a way to the Temujin. We have to find him, Alistair. We have to find him."

Arnie and Hank were suffering the pains of war waiting helplessly in the lounge of the Ritz hotel for a call from Phillip Santori. The fidgeting and the absence of relieving refreshment were starting to drive both men to desertion when Hank's phone started vibrating in his breast pocket. He answered,

"Tower."

A silence, the kind that precedes an uncertainty of what to say, then in a soft, melodious Italian voice…

"Mr. Tower, I…I am answering a notice in the newspaper that had your name in it…"

CHAPTER 15

I pointed to a newspaper lying on the table in front of us to signal Arnie the source of the call.

"Yes, Signorina, we were hoping someone would see the notice and call me. The firm was worried we could not fulfill Mr. Bufono's request. Are you calling from Venice?"

"Yes, I…"

"May I have your name, please?"

"My first name is Jolanda. I prefer to keep my full name confidential."

"We will need it before we can release the item Mr. Bufono requested us to."

"I understand."

"We will need some proof…"

"I think I can satisfy that by describing what I am sure Giuseppe intended for me. If I am correct, would that do?"

I tried to picture her: young, late twenties perhaps, soft voice with a musical lilt. A singer? Her volunteering to describe what to us was a fantasy item was fortuitous. I hit the speaker button and leaned the phone toward Arnie.

"Yes, that would certainly do, but it has to be very specific. We have had crank calls."

"Crank, what is crank?"

"False calls from people trying to take from Mr. Bufono's estate what is not rightfully theirs."

"I see. I am not a crank, Mr. Tower. Giuseppe and I were very close. We were together only a month or so before he was…" I heard a crack in her voice.

"Please describe the item he wished to leave you."

She cleared her throat. "It's a picture…"

"We need to know who is in the picture."

"Our three-year-old daughter. I took it of Giuseppe and her in the San Marco piazza. Giuseppe is on his knees dangling a puppet of a clown in front of her. There are pigeons surrounding them. The frame is gold."

"Just a moment, Jolanda." I covered the speaker with my hand and looked at Arnie.

"It's very specific, 'ank," he said, "that helps me believe. It's a good bet Giuseppe fathered a child. 'e was in enough beds. It's all we 'ave."

His last point was inarguable.

"Signorina, you are correct. There are two ways we can deliver the picture to you. We can use money from Giuseppe's estate and provide you with a round-trip air ticket to London, or I can send an emissary from our firm with the picture to Venice. We do not want to chance a delivery service losing it."

"No, no, please don't do that. I can't come to London. I have to work and Margherita must be picked up from…and…"

"Then we will send an emissary. I will need your address in Venice?"

"Si, of course, but I won't be at home. We can meet. There are two columns next to the Doge's Palace at the entrance to San Marco piazza. I will be holding a bouquet of violets at the foot of the one with the Winged Lion on its top. When can you come?"

"We will need air tickets. Where can I call you?"

"I will call you tomorrow at this time."

The line went silent and I thought I had lost her, then,

"Mr. Tower?"

"Yes?"

With her voice cracking, "Thank you."

I clicked off the phone. Arnie and I looked at each other for a few long seconds. He finally said,

"The business isn't all 'ero buttons."

"No, it isn't, but if she's legitimate, there's a way to get her co-operation on the Temujin. See about tickets for the two of us to Venice. And call the Danieli hotel for two rooms with a canal view. Von Tresser is going to take another hit on our expense account."

Arnie got out his phone; I called Lydia in New York and told her to call Captain Holden. It was possible, just possible…

"Lydia, ask him if there is a picture among Giuseppe Bufono's personal effects. If there is, sign for it and overnight it to me at the Danieli hotel in Venice with hold-for-arrival instructions." I described the picture and went to my room. Arnie wandered out onto Piccadilly for a short walk about.

Next step – wait for an answer from Lydia and wait for a call from Phillip Santori and hope we can tail him to his twin Paul. A big maybe. Waiting and being helpless to change it is the worst part of an otherwise rather eventful job.

Signorina Jolanda Marcelli was lightly tanned, soft-skinned, slim, shapely, dark-haired and strikingly beautiful – a perfection of Italian femininity worthy of Michelangelo. But her soft, dark eyes, deep-set above a classic Roman nose, suggested sadness and vulnerability. A summer day roughly four years ago an adventurous man detected the gullible innocence in those eyes, and sensed a sexual opportunity.

At the time, Jolanda and others had been dismissed from rehearsal at Venice's famous opera house *Teatro La Fenice* an hour earlier than they normally were. The permanent chorus, of which she had just become a member, played a minor role in the production they were working on. She had free time, so she took it to relax with a cup of coffee in San Marco piazza.

It was June, perhaps the finest month of the year in Venice, and puffy white clouds were parading under the noon sun. It was a near-perfect moment in what Napoleon called "the drawing room of Europe." She was signaling for an inattentive waiter to bring her a refill when one of the handsomest men she had ever seen arrived at her table with a neat, white napkin draped over his forearm and a tray with two large coffee cups on it.

"Signorina, the waiters here are blind to beauty. May I be of service to you? I assure you this is the finest coffee in Christendom. My elderly aunt says it comes from a grotto high in the Andes where miracles are common among the villagers. May I offer you a cup of it and my friendly company? My name is Giuseppe Bufono."

It was said with a smile that might have weakened Lucretia Borgia. To a twenty-one-year-old recently freed to the world, it was a melting introduction. She had dismissed previous overtures like this since leaving the convent eighteen months ago, but today? Today, she was enjoying the free time, the open air, the off-and-on cooling shadows the clouds played across the large piazza. A light breeze was flapping the overhanging tablecloths – they're white doves trying to fly, she thought. The violinist was smiling and playing Haydn and roaming from table to table. The moment was magical and made for company. He was handsome and charming and something new was fluttering inside her chest.

Now, she was sitting in the warmth of a tea room only yards away from that fateful table, thinking about the stories he told that day and remembering the laughter, the walk in the city's narrow streets, the ride in the gondola. She had her first cocktail in the elegant salon of a private palace on the Grand Canal owned by a friend of Giuseppe's who was in Verona. She remembered the lightheadedness that followed it. He took her arm and guided her up the sweeping staircase to see the view of the Grand Canal from the bedroom's balcony and watch the boats and gondolas plying their trade from the left and the right. There was the blue sky spotted with what she giggled and called floating marshmallows. There was the wonderful dizziness she felt when he put his arm around her waist and pulled her to his side and with soft fingers lifted her chin and put his lips on hers. She remembered her rubbery legs when he picked her up and…

…and months later the pain of delivery followed by an occasional check and worst of all, the excruciatingly long absences.

She stopped thinking and crossed her arms around her chest and squeezed tightly, as if to protect herself from the memories.

She had her cell phone in her hand and was about to call her aunt to check on Margherita, but decided against it. Let the two of them enjoy each other, she thought. She still had a half hour before starting her second job at a nearby retail store.

A violinist stopped next to her table and asked if he could play something for her. She smiled and shook her head and looked out the large window to the spot in the middle of the vast piazza where she had taken the picture of her daughter with her father, the only picture of them together, only a few weeks ago. She turned away and looked at the few outside tables where they met four years ago. It was occupied by another pair of lovers. She tried to smile at that, but couldn't. She left the tea room and stared up at the gray, winter sky. Tomorrow, after rehearsal, she would call Mr. Tower again.

I had run out of newspapers and travel magazines to read and was staring at the room's Honor Bar. Waiting for something to happen that might not happen can be tolerated for only so long. I tossed "Daring Travel Adventures" on the bed and started for a sample of the good stuff when my cell phone stopped me.

"Tower, it's a new day. Where are we? Have you located my brother?"

"Phillip, let's meet. I'm at the Ritz. Meet me in the lobby bar."

"Last time we talked you said stay put, that I could get recognized as Paul and arrested or better yet, kidnapped and tortured. You were rather convincing. Why the need to meet?"

"You'll be safe with me. The Ritz has security all over the place. I have questions and, frankly, I'm not comfortable talking on a phone that is blocked from recognition. I could come to you."

"No. What's the latest on this guy Alistair Baker?"

"The Ritz, Phillip."

"All right. Give me a half hour."

Arnie needed to ID him. He was out of the office when bear-size Phillip marched past Lydia into my inner sanctum. That seemed like a decade ago. I'd keep Phillip in the Ritz long enough for Arnie to get a few good looks at him before following him, although one look at Phillip would probably be enough.

Henry, the maître'd at the River Restaurant in the Savoy hotel raised the phone on the dais to his ear.

"Henry, this is Paul Santori. I checked out yesterday and have misplaced Mr. Alistair Baker's phone number. I know he dines in your restaurant. Do you expect him?"

"Yes, sir. He has a one-o'clock reservation."

"Please ask him to call me when he arrives? Here's my number." Henry wrote it down and said he would give it to Mr. Baker.

The number Paul gave Henry was from the phone on the bar in a pub on the Strand about a quarter mile from the Savoy. It was just after noon and the pub was starting to fill. He took a seat a few feet from the phone and ordered a dark ale. At three minutes after 1:00 Alistair called.

"Paul, where are you? Jerome is…"

"Yes, I saw it in the newspaper. Please accept my condolences."

"Thank you. It was ghastly. The police…" He stopped abruptly. "Do you know where the Temujin is?"

Paul smiled. Grief can be fleeting when a large amount of money is on the loose.

"Yes, but some interim steps are necessary. Jerome was certainly killed because of the Temujin. Someone knows about it besides me and is playing rough. Do you have any idea how Jerome fit in this?

Did he have a way to buy it?"

"He didn't have that kind of money, but he has always been obsessed with the piece. I believe if he became aware of its location he would steal it or steal it from whoever bought it. He was convinced you know where it is."

"I believe I do, but it's imperative this is between us. If too many people..."

Sensing an opening, "I agree, absolutely, but the police might discover the piece is involved in Jerome's murder and the papers..."

"I will include you in the sale I have in mind, if you keep everything you know about the Temujin quiet."

Cautiously, "What kind of arrangement did you have in mind, Mr. Santori?"

"Five percent of the sale price for pleading ignorance."

"I think that's appropriate. Now, how can I help you find the piece?"

"You can't. Your contribution is ridiculing its involvement in Jerome's murder as absurd. It's a legend, a fairytale, it probably doesn't exist, that kind of thing."

"Do you think it's a fairytale, Mr. Santori?"

"My gut says no and it rarely fails me. I think it exists and I believe I know where it is."

"Do you have a buyer?"

"Yes, but if he evaporates, you need to find one."

"That would increase my commission."

"Take it from your buyer, if I need one from you. Five percent, five million dollars, maybe more, for keeping your mouth shut."

"When will I hear from you again?"

"Within days this should be a done deal," said the man with a large, dependable gut.

Phillip Santori paid the taxi driver with his head down and topcoat collar up, like a spy in a movie, and entered the Ritz as furtively as one could from a street that is as busy as Piccadilly. I greeted him inside the entrance and quickly shuffled him into a dark corner in the lobby's lounge. Arnie was sitting a distance away with the *London Times* open in front of him.

"Phillip, how do you expect to get your seven-hundred-and-fifty-thousand dollars back from Paul? Would he part with that much money?" I waved away a cocktail waitress.

"Hell no, but I have ways."

"Pray tell your humble servant what those ways might be so he can avoid getting his head bashed again."

"I'm sorry about that, Tower. I had no way to know."

"Apology accepted; now, to my question."

"You aren't business partners for over ten years without knowing things, tax things, for instance."

"You have evidence he cheated?"

He nodded.

"You would use that on your own brother?"

"Tower, you forget over and over that the bastard stole seven-hundred-and-fifty big ones from me. Goddam right I would use it. Now to my question. Where is he? If you say I don't know, follow immediately with but I will know within…fill in the blank."

I let that go. "He checked out of the Savoy…"

"You told me."

"I'm betting he's holed up nearby in a lesser hotel, rearranging his plans. He wouldn't want to be too far from Jerome's partner, Alistair Baker. I have someone going hotel to hotel with a picture."

I looked hard at Phillip and said,

"He might be hiding because he's scared. Maybe he's next."

He blinked.

"And the murderer might find you."

"I just thought of that. Hold off for a couple of hours until I can get out of the area." He donned his massive coat and headed for the door. He turned and said, "I'll call you."

It was a bluff. My only 'someone' was sitting about forty feet away and hadn't had time to search for anyone. But the ploy had Phillip Santori on the move. If he and his brother were playing as a team, hopefully he would inform Paul in person about the search and the two of them would dig in somewhere together.

Phillip hustled down the front steps and hunched himself into a taxi. Arnie climbed in the one waiting behind it. The airline tickets he bought to Venice would have us at the Danieli hotel tomorrow afternoon. From there, it's a five-minute walk to the east column at the entrance to the San Marco piazza where Jolanda wanted to meet me. I reached for my phone to inform my Austrian client of the call from Venice and ordered a Remy XO cognac to quell my guilt about the lie I told the young mother about the picture of her daughter with her father.

It occurred to me that inside a one-hundred-million dollar transaction rests enough money for a three-year-old to attend some of Europe's finest schools.

CHAPTER 16

"A woman called me from Venice who says she had a child with Giuseppe."

Tresser barked back, "What's her name?"

"All I could get was Jolanda. I'm guessing twenty-something, a singer's voice."

"That's enough to find her. Next steps."

"We meet in Venice."

"Good. I want to be there. What about Paul Santori?"

"Arnie left the hotel a few moments ago in a cab tailing twin-Phillip. We're hoping he leads us to Paul."

"Next step."

"A return call from Jolanda to set up a time for our meeting in Venice and a report from Arnie on the tail of Phillip. We are booked on a flight to Venice that gets there early afternoon tomorrow. I'll call you around six in the evening. We'll be at the Danieli."

"Jesus, Tower, you're fast with my money. Sleep in a gondola."

"Can't. Arnie's too big and I get sea sick."

"All right. I'm going off the air. I'll call you."

"Where do you go on these excursions?"

"I'll call you."

And so ended the briefing of my billionaire client. I sipped the last of my Remy XO and was contemplating another when Arnie's call came in.

"I lost 'im, 'ank. 'is cabbie took an alley to get out of the traffic. A beer truck blocked us before we could follow 'im."

"Any idea where he was going?"

"Nay. The streets go out like spokes on a wagon wheel. 'e could have taken any of them."

"Did he think he was being followed?"

"Nay. Too many cars and taxis. 'e was escaping the jam."

"Come on back to the hotel. It was a long shot anyway. Tresser has gone incommunicado again. He'll call me."

"Any word from Lydia?"

"I'm going to call her now."

Murano glass is made on a small island of the same name just off the north edge of Venice. The trade's location goes back to the ninth century when Venetians, fearing fire from the glass ovens, required that it be made outside of the city. Murano jewelry, birds, vases, animals, decanters are prize takeaways for tourists who want to preserve a memory of Venice.

Young Jolanda Marcelli graced a small retail shop that sold Murano glassware. Her beauty, smile, voice and manner were most likely as responsible for the shop's success as the quality and design of its products. Her salary was adequate to pay for the clean and respectable apartment she, her daughter and aunt occupied, but the shop and to a lesser extent the opera, demanded a level of dress that managed to zero out her bank balance at the end of every month. She loved the interaction with the tourists in the store and adored the opera and the talent she worked with. But the two jobs kept her away from Margherita for long and worrisome periods.

She had just returned home from a rehearsal when her Aunt Gina told her quietly that she had observed a man, hatless in a long, winter coat standing outside their building since early morning. He would walk back and forth, pause and look up at their windows, as if he were waiting for someone. Did she know who it might be?

"I didn't see anyone when I came in, Gina. Is he there now?"

"No, but I'm sure he was there just before you came in. He didn't seem like a tourist. They're usually hurrying somewhere when they walk through here."

Jolanda let it go. "Where's Margherita?"

"In the bath tub, playing with the rubber fish you gave her. She can identify all six of them. Now, I'm having her spell their names."

Jolanda shed her navy blue coat and red beret and joined her daughter. It was 3:00.

"It's a snapper, mammina. It comes from the Ca..rib..er..."

"Caribbean Sea, smarty. Did it snap you?"

"No, Gina says they don't snap."

"What this long skinny one?"

"It's a wahoo."

"A what?"

"A wahoo. It's my favorite. Gina says it comes from the Ca..ribb…and just about everywhere."

"Well, it's my favorite, too. I have to go out again, honey, but I'll be back before dinner. No store work for mammina today."

"This one is an angel fish, but I…I don't know where it comes from."

"Ask Gina. She's an angel, isn't she?"

"Angels aren't people."

"Well, no, so Gina is not a real angel. She just acts like an angel. I'll be back in a couple of hours, honey, maybe sooner."

Jolanda gave her daughter a kiss on the forehead and some instructions to Gina for dinner. She picked up a small bouquet of violets and slipped quietly out the door and down one flight to the street. It was a ten-to-fifteen-minute walk to the columns at the entrance to San Marco piazza where she had told Tower earlier in the day she would be at 5:00.

She had just made the first of several turns through the byzantine streets of Venice when a man in a long, dark coat fell in behind her.

There is one other person who knows as much as I do about the Temujin – the Austrian Tresser, thought Paul Santori. Giuseppe told him about the relic and its whereabouts before he told me in the King Cole room in New York. If Giuseppe hadn't been an untrustworthy roué, Tresser would have sent him on the mission. Ironic, he thought. Giuseppe lives off the success of others and loses out on the score of a lifetime because of it.

Paul didn't become a millionaire in the infomercial business where less than one in twenty succeeds without strong people instincts; and those instincts were saying it was Tresser who killed Jerome; *had* him killed, that is. Why take a risk when one can pay someone else to take it for you? Paul hadn't thought about murder when he decided to go after the Temujin, but here he was at the center of a sticky web that included one, and the next one could be him. He was learning that the bigger the prize the more dangerous the game. He wanted a fast sale and out. Alistair is my exit...Alistair has buyers, he thought. He picked up the phone.

"Alistair Baker."

"Paul Santori, Alistair. Meet me in the American Bar in the Savoy at three o'clock. We need to talk."

"Gladly, Mr. Santori. I am here to help you however I can. Is there something I can do for you now?"

Paul grunted and hung up.

Alistair had lived a life of negotiating with artists and some of the shrewdest art buyers in London and on the Continent. Paul's urgency was clear, but Alistair's professional ear detected something behind Santori's voice that suggested he could broker a much better deal than five-percent on a sale of the Temujin to Bouchard. The dream of matching Santori and Bouchard and winning a huge commission was diminishing Alistair's painful loss of Jerome.

At 3:00 the two of them were seated in two high-arm chairs snug against a wall in the Savoy's American Bar. Pictures of the roaring 1920's lined the walls of the virtually empty after-office-hours watering hole. Alistair ordered a martini; Paul asked for a club soda.

"Alistair, on a scale of one to ten, how sure are you of a buyer?"

"Is ten the surest?"

"Of course, for Christ sake."

"Then my sureness merits a ten."

"How much can you get for it?"

"Well, that's hard to answer. As you said, I will have to add my commission to the price and that might raise it to a level that would discourage the person I have in mind."

The drinks arrived. Alistair knew he had Paul. Something had happened since they last talked. He lifted the martini cautiously to his lips and stared over it at the corpulent, pepperoni-faced American.

Bastard, thought Paul, but this was no time for temper. Did this foppish art dealer know about Tresser's Temujin fever? Was Tresser known in the art market? Could he somehow end run me? Paul took a drag on his club soda and decided that in light of events selling half a loaf is better than being a dead baker, but his nature was to do better. He said,

"It's possible my buyer could fade away. I don't think he will, but things happen. People die, get hit by a truck, lose their money. Life is uncertain. I want a back up in case something goes wrong. If something does, then I am prepared to give you twenty-five percent of a sale to your customer."

Alistair was on solid ground. "Fifty percent and we are partners."

"That's too much. Sixty-forty."

"Very well, I feel comfortable with that. Now, Mr. Santori, I assure you that I have a buyer; but do you have the Temujin?"

"I will give you that answer in less than a week. Your job is to hype your customer into a fever. Make him drool. Tomorrow, I am going to a place I doubt any man has ever been. I will call you."

Arnie and I were at Heathrow waiting to leave for Venice in time for my 5:00 meeting with Jolanda Marcelli when Lydia called me back. Her report stoked a suspicion in me that had always been in Arnie's mind. She said,

"Hank, our client Phillip Santori is either in a witness-protection program or is one of those creatures that pop up helter-skelter, like cicadas, or whatever they're called. I have had my nephew on the case…"

"Lydia, the headline."

"The headline is we aren't sure he exists. I went to Santori Enterprises headquarters in Queens and found two people filling boxes with files. I had a picture of Phillip with me and asked questions. 'That could be Paul or Phillip,' they said. I asked if they had any idea which. They said no. I asked if they had ever seen the two of them together. They looked at each other and shook their heads. I asked then how do you know which one is Paul and which one is Phillip? They said they could tell by the way they acted. Paul was serious; Phillip always told jokes, mostly on Paul."

"Good, very good. I'll ask the boss if he'll give you a raise. What else?"

"Well, I asked my nephew to use all his cyber powers to track down Paul or Phillip. He found a Paul Santori at City College about thirty-five years ago. Guess what he majored in?"

"Lydia…"

"Acting."

"Acting?"

"Acting and finance."

"He was ahead of his time. Any other information?"

"Dun and Bradstreet had some, but nothing we didn't know. He found his marriage to the late Eleanor and his name on the City's real estate tax roles. He searched some show biz background – SAG, ASCAP and other organizations and found a play he starred in as a senior at City College. Guess what it was?"

"Lydia…"

"The Importance of Being Ernest. Oscar Wilde."

"I know it. The protagonist is a rich country squire who has a playboy side and uses a fake brother in London he calls Ernest as his excuse for whoopee."

"Paul played the lead. When will you talk to the boss, boss?"

"Soon. Good work, Lydia. Take five-hundred from petty cash for your nephew. I'm glad that wizard is on our side."

"One more thing, Captain Holden had someone go through Giuseppe's effects."

"And…?"

"There was no picture of any kind. You'd think he would have a picture of someone, his parents, a friend, a wife."

"He wasn't married and his parents might not have been his choice."

"That's sad. Carol called. She said everything was okay, but she hadn't heard from you." Then a polite, but firm add on,

"It's okay to let your loved one know you're alive."

"I'll call her. Also, put together a bill for all expenses and fees to date on the Tresser case and fax it to the Danieli to hold for me. Billionaire or not, I don't want him getting too far ahead of us."

We hung up and Arnie, who had heard the conversation, and I stepped aside from the crowd waiting at the airport gate.

"It's been on me mind for a while, 'ank. Think of this. There is no Phillip Santori listed in New York, 'e isn't on 'is company's D & B, the call ye got from Phillip might have been Paul calling from 'is plane. Ye can use yer cell phone as soon as it lands. Then Phillip calls from London *after* Paul arrives, Phillip calls *after* Paul has left police 'eadquarters, Phillip won't let ye call 'im in London or go to where 'e is...."

"Got it. And there's another incident, one you couldn't know because you weren't there. When Phillip and I first met in my office he described his brother's wife Eleanor sizing up men in front of Paul's apartment on Fifth Avenue. He said she used her bulldog Chaucer as bait. He said 'I saw it many times from the apartment window.' Phillip might have accidentally defaulted to Paul."

"I think Paul set up the killing of 'is wife."

"Maybe, but why would he involve me? I could have burst into the hotel room at the wrong time and fouled everything up."

"I think ye would 'ave been killed, if ye 'ad."

"Why involve me at all?"

"A frame."

"Not if he had background on me. He said he got my name from someone in the media. That could mean he read it in a newspaper. If so, his information was superficial. But I had no motive to kill either of them."

"There were only the two of ye in yer office. 'e could say anything about how ye talked. 'e could say 'e wanted ye to 'elp 'im get the Temujin and gave ye all the facts and ye went out on yer own. 'e could say ye decided to take out Giuseppe as a competitor and ye had to kill Eleanor 'cause she saw ye."

"It's possible, if he thought I was a do-anything gold digger."

"If I am right, 'ank. We 'ave to worry about Paul killing ye, not just Long Finger. If yer dead, 'e can say what 'e pleases about ye."

"Arnie…" I was about to say that living in a cloistered nunnery might not be a bad idea, but refrained. British Airways was calling for our flight to Venice to board and people were bunching at Gate 44.

As their plane was lifting off the runway, von Tresser arrived at the terminal for a flight later the same day. Moments behind Tresser's arrival another cab pulled up and discharged Paul Santori.

Already in the British Airways terminal having a scotch neat at a pub near Gate 44, was a medium-size man with his disfigured right hand in the side pocket of his winter coat, waiting to board the same flight to Venice von Tresser and Paul Santori were on.

The night before, Jolanda had gone to bed hoping Mr. Tower would have at their meeting tomorrow at 5:00 the only picture ever taken of Margherita and her father.

CHAPTER 17

Our plane landed at 1:30 at Venice's Marco Polo airport. There are several ways to get from this distant point to the place you want to go. In ascending order of euros and speed they are: land bus, land taxi, water bus and private boat. We hired a private boat to take us directly to the Danieli hotel. After roughly a half hour of open water and a biting, mid-forties wind, we landed "dockside" at the Danieli. We were instantly assisted and after an effortless check-in were shown to our two rooms overlooking the Grand Canal. My fifteen years as a money spy required staying at many upscale hotels around the world, but somehow I missed the Danieli. Too bad, it's unequivocally in the world's top tier. It would have been a cardinal sin to let the expense account of a billionaire client lie unused, especially when the billionaire client is as shadowy as von Tresser.

I let Arnie settle in and phoned him to meet me in the lobby. My meeting with Jolanda was only two hours away.

Arnie joined me in a private corner in the lobby near a large fireplace. "Did you see anyone on the plane?"

"Nay, but there's another one that lands at three-thirty. If Tresser's coming, 'e would be on that one."

"He's coming, and so is Paul Santori."

"And Long Finger."

"Yeah. Tresser and Paul know about Jolanda's pillow talk with Giuseppe. Long Finger doesn't. He's just watching the game, for now."

"Jolanda is the key," said Arnie. "No Jolanda, no game."

I nodded and looked at my watch. "If that plane's on time, anyone on it could make it here by five. Tresser would drop from a helicopter, if he knew I was meeting Jolanda then; but he doesn't. He will come as we did.

"Arnie, it's critical that I speak to her alone – no Tresser or Paul Santori to screw it up. I'm going to wander around out of sight until five. When he comes in let him see you and tell him…crap, tell him what…?"

"That yer buying a thing for Carol and will be back after 'e settles in," said my large and reliable assistant.

"Good. In fact, I will. Just keep him in the hotel until I return. I will need a lot of private time with her. It won't start out well."

"She could bolt when she knows there's no picture."

"I have a different kind of picture for her."

I left Arnie on watch for Tresser and found a jewelry store to buy a gift for Carol. Under the glass were beautiful diamond rings. Should I? I bought a diamond pendant instead and slipped the small, elegant package in my pocket.

Jolanda took the last of many street turns and walked slowly to the column with the Winged Lion on its top at the entrance to San Marco piazza near the Doge's Palace. She stood on the leeward side of the column to protect herself and her violets from the brisk wind off the Grand Canal only steps away.

She checked her watch. Five minutes to five. Would he come? She had gone through several pros and cons about showing Margherita the photograph. She wondered if she wanted it more for herself than for her daughter. The picture would bring up many possibilities. Would Margherita be hurt learning of her father's abandonment, even though she never met him? She couldn't imagine she wouldn't be. "Didn't he like me, mother?" Would the staging of the photograph help make a decent person of him? The picture showed Giuseppe's charm in full bloom, kneeling and smiling in front of his daughter, teasing smiles from her with the puppet clown. Would Margherita keep that memory of him in her mind? Would it soften future thoughts of him? She hoped so. But behind the fretting she knew why she was here. She wanted the picture for herself.

Men of various nationalities and sizes were passing her, some with covetous eyes – a beautiful, gentrified Eliza Doolittle standing alone with a bouquet of flowers. She hadn't thought of attracting the unwanted when she chose holding a bouquet of flowers for identification. Then a man, a handsome one with a sure gait, approached her with "Are you Jolanda?" With a smile of relief,

"Yes. Are you Mr. Tower?"

"Yes, I am. Let's take a table in that tea house so we can talk."

She fell in beside me and a few minutes later we were sitting inside the warmth of one of the many restaurants along the periphery of the vast San Marco piazza.

"Mr. Tower, I am grateful…"

"Jolanda, before you start thanking me please let me speak. I need to confess that I have misled you…" I paused; she stared at me. "…and before you walk away from me angry and disappointed, give me a little time to suggest something that may be as worthwhile to you as the picture you expected me to have."

This was unforeseen. She was off guard. A waiter arrived before she could respond and I immediately ordered a pot of tea.

She started to shift uncomfortably in her chair and was about to say something...

"Please let me continue, Jolanda." I had thought hard on what I said next.

"Jolanda, you are in danger for something that I am certain is far from your mind. Let me explain."

She was alert. Was this some sort of scam? Why would she be in danger?

"Giuseppe was murdered in a hotel in New York..."

"I know..."

"I am not going to dwell on that. I needed to be sure you knew. I am a Private Investigator in New York and I know the police captain in charge of the investigation into his murder. I asked him to go through Giuseppe's personal effects as thoroughly as possible to see if the picture you described to me was there. I am sorry to say it wasn't."

"Then why...?"

"Please let me go on." The waiter arrived with the tea and both of us remained silent while he filled our cups.

"I must get personal now, Jolanda, because there is no other way for me to explain why you are in danger. Please be patient. I have more then your safety in mind. You and Giuseppe were lovers..." She dropped her eyes. "Perhaps while you were intimate and he was telling you how beautiful you are you became embarrassed by his flattery and tried to change the subject from you to other beautiful things in the world, sunsets, music, art..." Her eyes were looking into near space as if she were searching for something in it.

"Perhaps you mentioned to him that you knew of a very beautiful piece of art, a secret thing no one knew about because it was kept in a secret place only you knew about…" Her eyes were wide and fixed on me, as if I were about to strike her.

"…and that beautiful thing was a golden ship that a thirteenth century Doge used to keep Genghis Khan out of Venice, that it had the Khan's real name on it…"

"Oh, Mother of God. Oh, Mother of God." She dropped her head into her hands and started to tremble. "Oh, forgive me, Lord, I didn't know…I didn't know he would…I didn't know he would tell people about it…now they want it. Oh, God forgive me."

I remained silent. She's a fast study. She raised her head and started to leave.

"No, no. Jolanda. Stay here."

"Mr. Tower, I have sinned far beyond my affair with Giuseppe… the nuns will…"

"You are luckier than they. You have a child."

She fell back into her chair and dropped her head into her hands.

"What can I do? Dear Mary, what can I do?"

"We'll come back to that. Drink some tea. I am on your side and I have resources. If you trust me, there's a silver lining to this."

"I can't imagine…"

I went on. "There are people, dangerous people, who want the Temujin and are willing to do terrible things to get it. They are also willing to pay a large sum for it. I am not one of them."

She lowered the tea cup with a shaky hand. "Mr. Tower, I…"

"Let me go on. First, do you know the Temujin is with the sisters?" She nodded her head.

"It was given to them hundreds of years ago to hide."

"Have they ever thought of selling it?"

"No, well, yes. It came up a few times when there was barely enough money for food, but the vote was always no."

"Do you think they could change their mind, if a sale gave them enough money not to worry about food or clothing or heat ever again?"

"I...I don't know, maybe. Money for food is always a problem, but they will fast and suffer. The big problem is the convent itself. It's sinking..."

"Sinking?"

"Yes. The whole city is sinking slowly, but the convent sits on pilings that are among the City's oldest. When there was a high tide, we went upstairs to dine."

"What if there was enough money to fix that, or move to a safe place?"

"They would most likely listen to that, but..."

"It will get worse, eventually they will have to move. Then what?"

"I don't know. There's no money to go somewhere else. I know they worry about it. We prayed it wouldn't happen."

"If they lose their home, it would affect their privacy, their sanctity, their mission."

"Yes."

Then I said something I never thought I would say in my lifetime.

"Then it's God's will that they sell the Temujin."

She looked at me with a fresh innocence. "Mr. Tower…"

"Don't speak, not yet. If you went to them and said if they sold it they could either move or fix the convent so it would last hundreds of years, would they listen to you?"

"Some of them would. Those that never liked the idea of selling it would weaken."

"Could you do it? Would they listen to…"

She knew what I meant. "I left on very good terms. We all prayed several days for guidance when I said I wasn't sure. Mother Sister told me that the sisters decided it was His will for me to depart, that He had chosen other ways for me to serve Him."

I had no idea of what it would cost to fix a sinking convent and to suggest getting an estimate seemed a bit off key. Two million should easily cover the job, I thought, and leave enough principal for the interest to buy food, heat and clothes.

"Now, Jolanda, there's your daughter." She perked up. The starry-eyed innocence disappeared. She went on high alert.

"What about her?"

"What if I could make up for my lie about the picture with a way to fund a superior education for her?"

She cocked her head. Lord, she was beautiful. Stay out of show business, Jolanda, I thought. Somewhere along your lifeline it will be offered. Don't listen. It will spoil you.

"How…what…"

"I may be able to divert part of the Temujin's price into a trust large enough to finance any of Europe's finest schools."

"Mr. Tower, that would be…she's very bright. I can see it in her eyes, so can Gina, my aunt. I make enough money in the store for us to get by, but I could never…she would excel, I would be so proud, I wouldn't have to worry…I can't believe that could happen…"

"It can happen, if you can convince your former sisters to sell the Temujin."

Her single-mother's soul had taken charge. "How much…"

"Two-million euros."

She sucked in her breath and crossed herself.

"Dear Lord Jesus, yes, they would sell it for that. That would save the convent and there would be food and medicine and books…Mr. Tower, are you an angel?"

I doubt getting an item for two million when a client said he's willing to pay fifty qualifies for a halo. A pitchfork seems more fitting.

"Jolanda, there would be a revolt of the Just in Heaven, if my name were put in nomination. Now, program my cell number into your phone and give me your number. Go home and prepare the best talk of your life for the sisters. Please do it right away. There are non-angels involved in this. As soon as I have your okay from the sisters, I will act."

I laid some euros on the table. We stood up. She stepped close enough for me to feel her body against mine and gave me a kiss on the cheek.

"Mr. Tower, I will ask the sisters to put your name in nomination."

Paul Santori took a *vaporetto* – a water bus – from the Marco Polo airport to his mid-level hotel near the Rialto bridge in Venice. Von Tresser took a private water taxi to the Danieli. Paul had prepared a list of convents in Venice, some of which he had learned doubled as small bed and breakfast inns. Ruling those out, left him with two possibilities: the Convent of St. Cecilia and the Convent of Mary Magdalene, both cloistered. He smiled at the latter. His memory of the Bible didn't jibe with Mary M. being locked up in a convent with other women.

It was 5:00 and not a good time to call on cloistered nuns. Tomorrow at 7:00 seemed more appropriate. Paul had created a pitch that highlighted how a half-million euros could benefit the sisters. There could be repairs that were needed and had been put off for years, a fund for proper medical care when a sister became ill, new prayer and hymn books and so forth. He couldn't imagine cloistered nuns bargaining for more money. They would either take it or be so enthralled with having the Temujin that no price would move them; or the worst of all possibilities, they didn't have it.

He got out a street map of Venice and spotted the two locations and drew a snaking line from his hotel to each of the convents. He had been told that tourists sometimes get lost in the city's maze of winding streets, sudden dead ends and dozens of foot bridges. With that done, he sat at the hotel room's desk and began writing his CTA, that part of an infomercial when the copy departs from the niceties and thunders home a Call To Action. Down deep, with the right words, he reasoned, a nun is just as susceptible to a good sell as anyone else.

Von Tresser and Arnie were seated in separate clusters of chairs off the main lobby when Tower returned. Tower pulled up next to Tresser and told him to delay any of his secret-excursion plans, whatever they were, for at least a day.

"If you don't screw things up, you might have the deal of your life," he said, referring to his meeting with Jolanda. Tresser nodded suspiciously and gave Tower his hardened "I never lose" stare, then went up to his room and made a call on his cell phone. It was taken by a man in a long, dark coat moments before he would have gagged Jolanda Marcelli and pulled her off the street on her way home from her conversation with Tower. He had been following her on Tresser's instructions since he located Jolanda through the opera's chorus and the Murano retail store where she worked. He dropped back thirty feet from her apartment door and waited in a doorway for new instructions, unaware that another man was following him.

CHAPTER 18

Alistair Baker was sitting in a comfortable leather chair with his feet on a matching ottoman, looking out his large window at London and counting his money. Enough of this city life, he thought, my next home is a chateau in the Loire Valley of France, one large enough to accommodate all my current and future art, with a massive dining table and a fireplace large enough to sit in. I want at least ten hectares of land with a stream winding through it and topiary and flower gardens and a butler and two or three maids and a three-star Michelin cook. He thought of a stable of horses, but knew his lifelong dislike of the animals wouldn't allow it. Forty-percent of one-hundred-million euros, plus the sale of his penthouse, would easily pay for all of it.

As it happens when mortals are within reach of their dream of dreams, his heart was racing. He was seeing it, walking it, living it. But as also happens when dreams overheat, he immediately feared losing it. The what-ifs attacked. Paul Santori. What if he couldn't get possession of the Temujin? What if he had possession and found another buyer? What if he found his buyer – Bouchard – and made a deal behind his back? He had nothing on paper, zip, *nada*, only a conversation in a bar in the Savoy. His worries intensified. He had gone too far, done too many things to let this life-changing deal fall through.

The conclusion was obvious. Go to Venice. That's where Santori is, that's where the Temujin most likely is, that's where Bouchard is. He picked up his cell phone and called British Airways for a ticket on the next plane. Then he called Carlton Bouchard who was back in Venice and arranged a meeting with him in his office in the Doge's Palace. It would be a long meeting, for Alistair was going to graft Bouchard to his side until this deal was completed. Then he called another friend in Venice and asked him to recommend a detective agency. He said he had a friend staying somewhere in Venice and needed to find him. A tragic personal matter had arisen and the person refused to carry a cell phone. He had to know where Paul Santori was staying.

God helps chateau hunters who help themselves, thought Alistair Baker, an atheist who right now would gladly accept help from Heaven or Hell, if Satan held a surer hand.

Jolanda shut the door and put on the chain lock. Tower's warning about her being in danger may have sensitized her, but she had a chill go through her about half way home from their meeting in the tea room. She sensed someone was following behind her in the shadows of February's early darkness.

"Gina, where is Margherita?"

"In my room. Dinner will be ready in twenty minutes. Vegetable lasagna."

"Wonderful."

She went into Gina's bedroom. "Hi, honey. Did you miss me?"

"I have a book of stars. Want to see it?"

"Let me see. Isn't that a beautiful picture? Look how small the earth is next to the sun. We're just a little ball."

"The sun is tiny, too. See this picture next to the big star."

"It's called Alpha Centauri, honey. It makes our big sun look like a pea, doesn't it?"

"We are almost invisible next to…Alba Century. Do you think God can see us?"

"Yes, He sees us. Do the stars fascinate you, Margherita? Would you like to know more about them?"

Turning the pages, "Yes, I see them in the book and then look up in the sky."

Dear God, thought Jolanda, I want this child to learn everything there is in the world. I want her to be…

"Dinner's ready."

"Okay, starry eyes. Let's eat. It's lasagna."

Holding the book, "Can we talk some more about the stars after dinner, mammina?"

"Yes, Little One, Mammina is going to make sure we can talk about lots of things."

Jolanda walked with her child to the kitchen table and whispered to Gina. "When we're though, I want to talk to you quietly."

Gina nodded and started ladling out the small family's supper.

Arnie and I freshened up and met at a window table in the Danieli's terrace restaurant, another benefit of having a billionaire client. The view was spectacular, a panorama of local boats, ocean-going ships and towers and cathedrals. If it were summer, the view from the open terrace outside our table's window would be unforgettable.

"Arnie, don't get used to this. Our next client could have us eating hero's at a Subway."

"Aye, 'ank. Me Scot blood would usually feel a wee guilty enjoying it, but with Tresser paying, it doesn't mind. I feel like sticking 'im."

"I know. There's something about him…You said you thought he could be behind Jerome's murder. Do you still think so?"

"Aye, and if ye can do one murder, ye can do another and another. It's a sand pit a fellow Scot got caught in a while back."

"Macbeth."

"Aye. 'e 'ad to keep protecting 'imself by killing."

"And he lost his head in the end."

"Aye, but Tresser's smarter than Macbeth. 'e uses faceless killers to do 'is work."

"We're working for a murderer?"

"Ay, 'ank. I think so. 'e says Jerome was a fanatic on the Temujin – 'e is, too. Ye can see it in the man's eyes and the tense muscles in 'is jaw. 'e's a stretched rubber band on the thing."

I had similar suspicions; now, I was nearly certain. Arnie had instincts honed by nearly twenty years with the NYPD. He was on the streets; he arrested punks and junkies and dealt with liars that must have strained the Deity to create. One acquires a feral warning system, working where life is cheap. One grows antennae.

"Thank God I didn't bring up Jolanda in the lobby. Tresser would have her kidnapped…"

I took out my phone and punched her speed dial number.

"Hello?"

"Jolanda, it's Hank Tower."

"Mr. Tower, I will speak to the nuns about our conversation tomorrow morning…"

"Jolanda, I don't want you leaving your apartment until I am with you. We will go to the convent together. Do you have strong locks?"

Not listening closely, "I think…it felt like…"

"What?"

"…someone was following me home after the tea room."

Christ!

"Locks, Jolanda, what kind of locks do you have?"

"A bolt and a chain."

"Lock both of them and the windows. What's the best time to call on nuns?"

"I was planning to see Sister Mother Michelle at eight-thirty."

"Give me directions from the Danieli to your apartment and stay inside. I'll be there at seven-thirty. I have an associate with me. Don't be alarmed if you see him standing outside your apartment, watching. He's six-foot-six and weighs about two-hundred-and-fifty pounds, red hair. His name is Arnie."

"Do you think…my daughter…"

"You'll both be fine. Just stay inside and wait for me to ring your bell."

She gave me street-by-street directions to her home. It took both sides of the hotel's note paper to record them.

"Arnie, you heard. Vulnerable time is eleven to dawn." I copied the directions on another piece of paper and handed it to him.

"Take some coffee. I wonder what an ethics professor would say about representing a murderer…"

"Lawyers do it," said Arnie.

"Yes, they do, but unlike a lawyer's murderer, ours is still at large. Let's order the most expensive meals on the menu, and be careful."

Paul Santori had located the Convent of St. Cecilia and the Convent of Mary Magdalene on a street map. He decided 7:00 tomorrow morning was most likely the best time to call on sisters. Breakfast and praying probably started at 5:00 or 5:30, he figured, which left an hour and a half to finish both. He had no way of knowing which convent Giuseppe meant when he told him the story of the Temujin in the King Cole bar of the St. Regis hotel in New York. It was a flip of the coin which to visit first. He liked the irony of Mary Magdalene dressed in black sequestered in a sunless room with other women dressed in black. The convent was also a shorter walk from his hotel, a feature his size favored.

He set the alarm on his phone, undressed and rolled himself into the middle of the queen-size bed. It was rehearsal time. Looking at the ceiling,

"My name is Paul Santori. May I please see the sister in charge? I have some very important news for her and the convent. I just need a few minutes to explain. What I have to say will help all the sisters and the convent for many, many years to come. I assure you my news is very real. She will be very pleased."

He spoke variations of the words and tested different deliveries. If he could get in front of the right person, he was confident his gentle segue to the Temujin wouldn't jar.

"It will be enshrined in a museum for the world to know it saved Christianity from the godless hordes." Then add that a half-million euros would easily pay for needed repairs and old bills, then close with…

"It would also free the sisters forever to converse with God without the weight of worldly matters weighing on their minds and souls." That was his clincher. He smiled, crossed his hands over his mountainous stomach and closed his eyes.

Downstairs at the reception desk, a small, self-effacing man was asking the clerk if a Paul Santori had checked into the hotel. There was an emergency at home in the United States and he was hired to inform him. Yes, he was, he said, but it's against hotel policy to reveal his room. I understand, said the man. "I'll use the house phone to contact him." Instead, he went outside, took out his cell phone and reported that he had located Paul Santori, as instructed. Alistair Baker thanked him and said he would have a check sent to his office.

It was 11:30 when Tresser's phone pinged.

"I have company," said a male voice.

"Where are you?"

"In a doorway about fifty feet from her apartment house. A big guy arrived about a half-hour ago. He's leaning against a wall directly across from her front door."

"Red hair?"

"It's dark, for Christ sake."

"About six-six?"

"Yeah."

"I know who it is. Lay off him…"

"Gladly."

"…but follow her to hell, if you have to."

"I've a feeling the big guy has the same idea."

"He does. Don't let him see you. I need to know right away where she goes. Got it?"

"Got it. I can't be sure, but…"

"But what?"

"I think I'm being followed."

"Jesus, Joseph! What do you mean think? I don't pay you to think – I pay you for facts. Are you or aren't you?"

"I can't be sure, just a feeling."

Calmly, "The big guy will be there all night. If someone is following you, take some time to find out who it is. Just don't disturb the big guy. He's the woman's guardian angel."

"How do I do that?"

"I don't care. If you're being followed, find out who it is and call me."

Tresser kicked the side of his bed violently. What the hell is Tower up to? He retrieved the phone he had thrown into the pillows and called Tower's room.

Long Finger was invisible inside a dark recess of one of the old, stone buildings along Jolanda's narrow street. He knew the big red-haired Scot was Tower's man, but the one he had been following was unknown to him. The young lady in the apartment was either a princess in hiding or she owned something sweet enough to attract Tower and citizens of London and Venice like bees. His nose said his follow up fee could be a large one.

He peered out of his crevice and saw the man he had been following was no longer in the doorway he was hiding in. Tower's man was still fixed in place. Where did the other guy go? He stepped out of the recess cautiously for a better view of the street. Nothing, but he felt something in the air. The one he followed was watching him from somewhere. The feeling would have raised the pulse of a normal man, but Long Finger's remained a steady sixty-four. *He wants to ID me, so there will be a close up.* The conclusion was as natural as "It's going to rain, close the windows." His fear was no more than worrying about a possible rain shower. He stepped a few feet out onto the street to assist the man's objective. On cue, he came up behind Long Finger pointing a stiletto at his back.

"Stand still and you'll live. Give me your wallet." Long Finger turned to face him.

"Relax, sir. I'll give it to you. Are you interested in my pockets, too?"

"Shut up. Give me your wallet and I'll let you go."

"All right." He reached around behind him and jerked the back of his pants.

"It's stuck sideways. I can't get it out of the pocket."

"Raise your hands and turn around."

Long Finger obeyed and waited for the man to raise the back of his jacket and touch his back. He started to feel across the top of his trousers for his wallet. Long Finger quickly dropped his arms, hunched low and pivoted to his left. The hard upper part of his fist came up low and rammed into the man's scrotum with the force of a hammer. He screamed and fell forward. The knife fell to the stone pavement. Long Finger rammed his knee under the man's chin. The man collapsed backward against the building's wall. Long Finger pulled him into the recess where he had been hiding and propped him into a sitting position in a corner. The street was quiet and dark.

"Why are you watching the apartment?"

Blood was running from the man's lower lip. The force of Long Finger's knee had driven the man's upper teeth through it.

"I don't know. I was told to…there's a woman in there…"

"Who told you to?"

"I can't say…"

Long Finger picked up the stiletto and touched its point to the man's throat.

"Do you want to live?"

"Yes, yes. His name is von Tresser. I don't know anything…"

"Where is he?"

"At the Danieli hotel. Please, man, I've a wife and kid. I was only doing what I was paid to do. I don't know why…I was just watching…"

In addition to being incapable of guilt, psychopaths are indifferent to feelings. To Long Finger, the man's plea was simply an annoyance to be silenced, like an errant car alarm. He slowly pushed the point of the stiletto into the man's neck. He gurgled up blood, then went limp inside his long coat. His wide eyes stared into the darkness. The killer wiped his fingerprints off the knife and left it protruding from the man's neck.

Long Finger had a name. Soon he would have answers.

CHAPTER 19

It was approaching midnight when Arnie thought a limited surveillance of Jolanda's street was in order. There were recessed doors in each of the side-by-side apartment houses where someone could move unseen toward him from one to the next. He took out his police revolver and went to the right of Jolanda's entrance inspecting each crevice until he could no longer see her door. The recesses were empty. He was about to turn back when he noticed a shoe extending from the shallow entranceway to a building just around a turn in the street. He gave the doorway a wide berth and with his revolver pointed bellowed, "Come out! I have a gun on you!" Nothing.

He edged closer and jumped in front of the entrance, gun ready. There it was, a corpse with a stiletto sticking out of its neck and blood still oozing from the wound. He was only minutes dead. He hurried back to his station across from Jolanda's door. All was quiet. Was the killing connected? Of course it was. He took out his phone to call Hank.

"How far away from her door is the body?"

"Fifty yards, I'd say."

"If Jolanda learns about it, she'll spook...do this. Call the police. If she comes out to see what all the commotion is about, ID yourself – she has your name – and tell her it's another matter, a...a..."

"'ow about a 'ome fight. 'e started after 'er and she banged 'im with a skillet and called 911..."

"Good. Add a butcher knife and flying dishes."

"The dead guy was Tresser's man, 'ank. I'm Scot-sure."

"I agree. I'm calling his room now."

"But who would kill 'im?"

"Your description of the method suggests my friend on the London bridge has followed us to Venice."

"But why would 'e kill 'im?"

"For information about what's in play, to get his follow-up fee, as he calls it."

"Do ye think the dead guy 'ad that kind of information?"

"No, but he knew who hired him."

"So Long Finger gets Tresser's name and kills the tail..."

"...so he can't identify him. Tresser will be delighted to know a psycho murdered his hire and has his name."

"Tresser's dangerous, too, 'ank. Be careful."

I nodded agreement and called Tresser's room.

"We have to talk. Something's happened..."

"Damn right we have to talk. What are you doing? What aren't you telling me? You put your red-haired Goliath on a street to watch..."

"Slow down, Tresser. You've not been honest with me. What I have learned I've told you. You put a tail on Arnie – your own employee – or you tracked down Jolanda and put a tail on her. Either way you could have screwed up what I'm doing to save you money, lots of money! So take a cold shower and shut up until we can talk. I'm on my way to your room."

I holstered the .38 in the small of my back and put on a suit coat, then thought, Christ, if I shoot the bastard, I'll have to pay the hotel bill. I could actually lose money on a seedy case I only took so Carol and I could go somewhere warm. The thought called for cooling down myself as well as Tresser.

Tresser opened the door and stepped back. He looked relaxed, but his cheek muscles were rippling. I said sternly,

"Let's sit down."

We walked together like two fighters approaching the ring. He sat in a chair with his back to the window; I took one facing him. I paused for about fifteen seconds and said,

"You're tail is slumped in a doorway with a stiletto in his throat. Arnie found him. The police are on their way."

Nothing. I kept my eyes fixed on him.

"I think I know who did it. He's searching for whatever it is that's going to change hands. If I'm right, he got your name from the tail before he killed him."

"The guy you met on the bridge in London, the one who wants fifteen-percent."

"Yep."

He went to the window and stared out into the chilly Venetian night.

"We have to kill him."

"Splendid idea, boss. It goes right to the nub of the problem. Speaking of killing, I believe you had Jerome Manchester killed. Did you?"

Without turning to me, "No."

"Why don't I believe you?"

He turned to me, still standing, "What motive would I have?"

"Should I laugh at that? Jerome had access to money...he knew the guy who knew where the Temujin is...if he got hold of it, he would hide it in some underground chapel for his personal adoration...you're obsessed in having it for yourself...you always win, always...need I go on?"

He walked slowly to his chair and sat. He said,

"A good argument for a jury."

I waited for more. Finally,

"Tower, I thought of it, but I didn't do it. The man I hired to stake out Jolanda was incapable of killing someone; still, I know men who are. If you must know the truth, someone beat me to it."

"You were prepared to kill Jerome, but someone beat you to it. That's either an honest confession or a smooth alibi. Which is it?"

"The former. Does it explain your instincts?"

"It makes you harder to know."

He smiled. Was it a reaction to winning our little game or admiration of my frank answer?

"The dead man had weak ties to Italy's unsavory class. The police will believe he made a misstep of some kind. Using a stiletto is very Mafia, so is leaving the body where it's easy to find. It sends a message."

I said, "I have to believe you didn't do it, if I'm to continue working for you. But in case you did, I would like to settle up on fees and expanses to date."

He smiled genuinely at that. "I will transfer thirty-thousand into your bank. That should cover your airfares and fees for another few days. Your hotel rooms and expenses are on my bill."

I did a quick calculation. Seven days since Arnie and I signed on, that's twenty-one-thousand, airfare five-thousand…not enough. Expecting forty, I said,

"Make it fifty-thousand."

"All right. Now, what's the next step?"

Fifty-thousand. If I can stay alive, maybe Carol and I *will* make it to the Caribbean.

"For me to accompany Jolanda tomorrow to a place I'm not going to reveal. And don't have me followed! Let me do this my way and you might get the Temujin for four of five million euros."

His billionaire eyes popped. "Do you really think…"

"It's possible, if you keep your goons in their cage."

"Tower, pull that off and your fee goes from fifty to two-hundred-thousand." I nodded and left his room.

Back in my room I called Carol. With the six-hour difference it was only 8:00 p.m. in New York. She was home, making a sandwich for herself. I joked that concerning my important parts I still had two of this and one of that, but it wasn't received with a chuckle. She said Jack returned to St. Louis two days ago after showing her and her gorgeous friend Didi Harrington some of the City's better bars and restaurants. She said Didi flirted with seventy-two year-old Uncle Jack and he flirted back. Jack is widowed and well off from selling his brokerage business, but Didi could probably buy him twice over with the proceeds from her two divorces. We laughed at the possibilities of an Aunt Didi, but ended the call in uneasiness. The question of having a child lurked underneath her words and mine. If I continued to resist, we both knew it was over.

I was walking out through the hotel lobby at 7:00 a.m. and met Arnie returning from police headquarters.

"How was it?"

"Routine. I said I was on my way back to the Danieli from an earlier walk-about and got lost looking for a shortcut. They checked my passport and 'otel and made me sit for 'ours while they waited for New York to verify my PI license. A lieutenant told 'em to let me leave."

"Get some sleep and keep your phone close. I'm off to take Jolanda to church."

He grinned at that.

I got out my notepaper and followed its street-by-endless-street instructions until I came to Jolanda's apartment house. Down the street fifty yards or so the murder scene was cordoned off with two policemen standing by looking bored. After a few knocks and pressing a doorbell button that produced no audible sound, a woman with a face older than Jolanda's opened the door with the chain attached.

"I'm Hank Tower. Jolanda is expecting me."

"Jolanda, Mr. Tower's here."

I heard a series of quick steps descending a flight of stairs. The chain came off and there she stood ready to go. She was dressed as plainly as possible for the meeting with her former boss, Mother Sister Michelle; but she couldn't hide what she was born with. Only a large bag could do that. I guessed Jolanda was twenty-five or six. She had soft skin with the color of a tan some women would die for. Her hair was a lustrous dark and fell to her shoulders. The gray dress dropped to her ankles and fit almost as loosely as my fictional bag might fit; but the experienced eye saw through the ruse. You needed to look no further than her face. It was finely structured, suggesting a figure desirably arranged beneath her attempt at disguise. Mother Sister must have seen it, too. Jolanda probably left the convent at least four or five years ago. I wondered when she entered it.

"I'm ready, Mr. Tower. Mother Sister asked if we could come a little later, about eight-thirty. The convent is only a twenty-minute walk from here." She threw a colorless coat over her shoulders and we turned to leave.

"Mammina, mammina!" came from the open door.

"It's all right Margherita. This man is a good friend of mammina's. He's going to help us know all the stars."

"When will you be back?"

"Gina knows. You stay with her until I return. Okay?"

"I have her, Jolanda. She knows this is your morning off. You go ahead," said Gina.

The two of us found a café to kill some time. She ordered hot tea; I ordered an espresso. I asked,

"Are you all right with this, Jolanda? I sensed when we

first met..."

"Si, si, I am very all right. The money will let the convent survive. I don't see how it can unless they fix the foundation and there's food for the sisters. The Temujin isn't part of their lives. I doubt anyone but Mother Sister knows it's there. It's in a steel case on the top floor out of sight. I know because Mother Sister asked me to help her carry it up there when Venice had a very bad storm a few years ago. It flooded the entire city."

"Do you and Mother Sister know its history? Have you seen it?"

"She let me see it as a reward for the climb. It's a small gold ship with jewels all over it. She said that it saved Venice from the Mongols back in the thirteenth century. A monastery in Verona had it hidden for at least six-hundred years, then somehow it came to the Convent of Mary Magdalene, maybe to escape Italy's unification wars."

With a soft honesty some men would fall on a sword for, she said,

"Mr. Tower, if I didn't think it would save the convent, I wouldn't...I wouldn't..."

"I understand. It will do more than save the Convent. I meant what I said about a fine education for your daughter. What about you? What do you do?"

"I sing in the chorus of the opera here, and sell Murano glassware in a shop just off San Marco."

"Would you like to pursue the opera?"

"Very much. Singing lets your soul free. I guess all music does. My father played the piano. He said when he was gloomy he played gloomy songs and it washed away the gloom. When he was happy, he played happy songs so he would be happier. It's the same with singing. It lessens sadness and increases happiness."

"If only the entire world sang or played an instrument." Then from nowhere…

"Are you seeing anyone, Jolanda?"

She lowered her chin. "No, Giuseppe was the only one. I still think of him…"

"You wanted the picture for yourself."

With a slight blush, "Yes, but for Margherita, too."

"I asked the captain in charge to have someone keep looking for it, but please don't count on it."

"I'm not." She paused.

"Mr. Tower…"

Our eyes locked. "Yes?"

She leaned back in her chair and hesitated. "Nothing, I was going to ask if…no, it's all right. Forgive me." She looked at her watch.

"It's time we left. Prayer resumes at ten. Mother Sister will have to attend."

She started to rise from the chair and her long dress snagged on a leg of it. I caught her around the waist before she lost her balance. The loose hanging garment gave under my grip and my hand felt the firm, shapely body underneath it. She smiled at me and blushed.

"Are you okay?"

"I lost my balance."

I smiled back and said to myself. "I hope you aren't losing yours, Tower."

At 8:30 Jolanda rang the ancient doorbell at the entrance to the Convent of Mary Magdalena. We waited for a response.

They have it! Paul was pumped. They have it and she'll sell it! He had just delivered a perfectly structured infomercial to the lady in black: thirty-minutes long, oiled with an enticing opening, filled with some arresting storytelling in between the three Calls To Action, then a soapy, happy wrap up and bang, a done deal!

But I had help, he admitted, fantastic help, help from the gods. Who would have known the creepy place was sinking into the sea? He was jubilant. There's no need for Alistair Baker and his absurd 40% commission. He's out. Forty-percent. Does he think I'm nuts? I have this guy Tresser in Vienna for a direct deal. How many von Tresser billionaires could there be in Vienna? One; and I'll find him as soon as I have my mitts on the Temujin.

But then the same invisible fiend that interrupted Alistair Baker's reverie, the same one that taunts all men near the deal of their life, descended on Paul Santori and whispered, "She might rethink it, she might want to keep it, she might look for a better deal, someone else might show up before you can pick it up?"

He countered, she's a nun, for God's sake. If you can't trust a nun who…Nonetheless he wasn't going to waste any time getting the goods. He planned to take a half-million from his own bank account for the purchase. Unlike Giuseppe, he wouldn't have to ask von Tresser for up-front money to buy it, or bargain with him over a finder's fee. Here's the Temujin you lust for Herr Tresser. It's yours for one-hundred million. My bank numbers are…

But the fiend wouldn't give up. "How are you going to protect yourself? Maybe you're earmarked for death as soon as you have the Temujin. Maybe Jerome's killer is following you now, waiting..."

A mix of jubilation and worry confused him on the walk back to his hotel. He turned onto one street, then another…their names meant nothing to him. He thought he recognized a building near his hotel and turned in its direction only to dead end in an empty piazza with a small church. The fiend had him imagining things. Was Venice entrapping him, purposely keeping him from his hotel, preventing him from calling his bank? Was it angry that he was selling the Temujin to an Austrian? Did it want it to stay where it was created, in the city that it saved?

He shook the absurdity out of his head, but he couldn't shake the labyrinth of streets that had him helplessly lost. The occasional walker would only frustrate him more with unknowable Italian directions and animation that embraced all points on the compass. Finally, he noticed the tip of the tower of San Marco piazza peeking over the five-story, narrow canyons surrounding him. Calming himself, he let it guide him to the Rialto bridge and the comfort of his hotel.

His wandering was long enough for Alistair Baker to find the same hotel and take a seat in a small tea room facing the registration desk. When Paul came in the door, Alistair held out his cup of tea as if to toast him and said,

"My dear Mr. Santori, please join me. I thought it would be helpful if I were at your side until our sixty-forty arrangement was completed. Tell me, do you have possession of the item? I have a highly qualified buyer eager to buy it."

CHAPTER 20

The door was opened cautiously by a short, elderly man with rounded shoulders wearing a tie and worn jacket that hadn't seen a dry cleaner since their debut. He recognized Jolanda, and like a drooping plant, straightened up as if she were sunlight.

"Sister Jolanda, it is you. Mother Sister said you were coming to visit. I must say you look wonderful. Please come in, both of you."

We stepped inside a dark, musty room. The floor consisted of loosely fit, water-stained planks that emanated the dank smell of rotting wood. There was one seat, a bench covered with faded, stringy velvet upholstery under a round, stained glass window, the only window in the room. The only art was a large, framed picture of Jesus in colorful robes with a large halo shining behind His head and a small red heart glowing from his chest. It hung on the wall across from the bench. The last item was a six-foot statue with a large, heavy base of, I guess, Mary Magdalene. It sat on a spot of the floor that looked like Mary might drop through the boards in a year or two. The entire room felt like the sea was only a few feet beneath it.

"Please wait. I'll tell Mother Sister you are here. What is your name, sir?"

"Tower, Hank Tower."

"Oh, yes, she mentioned it. Please wait a moment."

Jolanda moseyed around the small room while we waited. I made mental notes of its condition. If one ever needed proof the Convent of Mary Magdalene lacked money, one needed go no further. A high tide would certainly bring water through the cracks and cover your shoes; a storm surge might drown you. Clearly, everyone lived on higher floors. Jolanda whispered that his name was Gregory.

Gregory returned. "Please come this way."

I followed Jolanda up a flight of precarious stairs and – I can't help it – I focused on her ankles and calves each step of the way. Twenty steps later we were shown into a room slightly less dank and slightly brighter than the entrance. It had a modest metal desk, two chairs and a nun from central casting standing next to it, at least my vision of a nun from central casting. She was short, a bit hunched over, wore rimless glasses that were perched on the tip of her nose, had a wrinkled face and bony hands and, of course, was dressed in a black habit with a white chest. There was a stack of books on her desk and what looked like a ledger lying next to it. I noticed one book was *Sartre's On Being and Nothingness*, a massive tome that requires monumental concentration, and for a Catholic nun, monumental tolerance. Mother Sister studied her enemy.

"Jolanda, dear, I am so pleased to see you. I thought, sadly, that we had parted for good. The sisters will be happy to know you haven't forgotten them. Are you still living in Venice?"

"Yes, Mother Sister. I am singing in the chorus at the opera and working in a small shop. I am very happy." No mention of the child.

"And I am happy for you. We have followed God's will. I am sure He is pleased, too. Mr. Tower, please have a seat. You are American. I hope my English isn't offensive to your ears."

"Not at all, Mother Sister. You must have studied it for many years."

"Yes, I have a doctorate in language from the Sorbonne in Paris. If I may say with modesty, I speak five languages, if you allow me to include a struggling German. The Lord has been kind to me."

I looked around. *He doesn't look very kind.*

"Now, I think I know why Jolanda has brought you to us. It concerns the Temujin, I believe."

"Yes, Mother Sister. I believe it offers the convent a way to continue…"

"I agree. Mr. Tower, I would listen closely to whatever arrangement Jolanda was a part of. She's a good person, kind and giving, but…"

"But what, Mother Sister?"

"I have made a deal, as you might call it, that was, frankly, irresistible with a man who left here only an hour ago."

Tresser? Alistair? Santori? It had to be Santori. Christ! Jolanda looked at me.

"Mother Sister, was he a large man, shorter than me, but much heavier?"

"Yes, that describes him."

"May I ask what he said he would give you for the Temujin?"

"Yes, of course. He said five-hundred-thousand euros. I asked if it would be in a museum for people to see and to know its history. He promised that it would. That much money would solve the financial problems that are so pressing. I am sorry…"

How do you up-sell a nun? I was afraid a much higher offer would be unseemly, but without one, Santori had the relic and Tresser might kill him to get it and throw me in for sport. Jolanda was looking at me helplessly.

"Sister Mother, I know the man who made you the offer. He will not place the Temujin in a museum for the world to see. He will sell it to a private collector for much more money than what he offered you."

"I see."

"I believe Mr. Tower, Mother Sister," said Jolanda, looking at her, then at me.

"I see." There was more understanding in that "I see" than the matter at hand.

Then I took one of the biggest steps of my life, the kind that invariably boomerangs back where it hurts.

"Sister Mother, I am a private detective from New York. Jolanda and I met only yesterday. I have a client who will pay a fortune for the Temujin, but he will sequester it for himself. If the man you just saw – his name is Paul Santori – contacts my client, he will sell the Temujin to him."

She paused. "My, after all these years suddenly our treasure is popular. How did you meet Mr. Tower, Jolanda?"

She knew Jolanda was the only way the Temujin could be exposed. I started to answer with a fake explanation, but Jolanda interrupted.

She dropped her head. "I told someone about it, Mother Sister."

"You mean Mr. Tower."

"No Mother Sister, someone else. I…"

There was no need for this. I quickly said,

"The Temujin has been known by art collectors for decades,

Mother Sister. Jolanda's mention of it to one of them was largely dismissed as just another rumor. The man who just left apparently wanted to find out if it did exist."

"I see. Do you think I was naïve, Mr. Tower?"

"I don't think you knew its real value, Mother Sister. Mr. Santori took advantage of that."

"I see." She went quiet, looked at the stack of books and fiddled with what was definitely a green, hard-cover expense ledger.

Jolanda said, "Forgive me, Mother Sister. I…"

"It is forgiven, Jolanda. The will of God is in these doings. We must find it. Why would He bring this up now, centuries after its appearance? Some historians believe it saved Christianity from the pagan Hordes. If it did, then He would not want it hidden in a private collection or in our attic. Perhaps in today's world He sees a benefit from displaying it for all of His creation to see, Christian and pagan alike, for everyone to remember what it accomplished."

She paused and looked away from us. "And why has He given this precious relic to us, a poor convent, to hold and protect? Is He saying He wants us to continue to welcome young women who wish to escape a tempestuous world, women who want to devote their lives to sanctity and prayer, free of temptation?"

I listened mesmerized. To a cynical mind here was one of the top rationales of all time, far ahead of any I ever devised to justify what I wanted to do anyway. She was creating two reasons to stiff Santori – public display and saving the convent. Frankly, the only downside I could see to her decision was me getting killed by a hired gun of the man who always wins, always.

I could think of only one way to satisfy God, the convent, Tresser and my love of life – Bouchard, the curator of the Doge's Palace. Tresser had mentioned him as his most feared competitor and

Lydia had checked him out. He had lots of money. If I could get the two of them in a bidding war that Bouchard wins, God gets his display, the convent gets a new life and I should stay alive.

With a sly turn of her head, "Mr. Tower, how much money do you think it would take to repair the convent and provide a reliable sustenance for the sisters?"

"I believe two-million euros would accomplish the many repairs the convent needs and would generate enough interest to pay for the essentials of convent life."

"Oh, my."

Goodbye, Paul Santori.

"Do you think you could, well, get that much?"

Jolanda leaned forward, "I am sure Mr. Tower can, Mother Sister, he…"

Mother Sister smiled and Jolanda blushed.

"Yes, I think he can, Jolanda.

"Mr. Tower, you have my word that if you can provide the convent with that amount and guarantee the Temujin will be displayed in a public museum, it is yours."

"Thank you, Mother Sister. I will attend to it right away."

The three of us went to the door to say goodbye. Before closing her office door, she said,

"It is astonishing how God works his will among us mortals, how He mysteriously helps we who believe in Him to find our way."

As she closed the door,

"You have one week, Mr. Tower."

"Could we have another tea and coffee?" asked Jolanda. "I'm a bit shaky."

"Of course."

There was a concrete bench alongside the quay we had just entered. She sat on it.

"For just a moment. Going back there, seeing her…and having to admit…"

"It's the past. You have a wonderful new life."

"Yes, it's the past. Thank God it's the past." She got up and led me through a maze of stone-paved streets to a small tea room. A tiny gas fireplace was emanating a soft, intimate warmth. I sat her in front of it.

"How long were you in the convent, Jolanda?"

"From four to eighteen."

"I'm guessing you're twenty-five. So you've been out of it for seven years."

"Twenty-six. Yes, but from eighteen to twenty-one I was in Switzerland at a strict private school for girls. Mother Sister recommended it. She called it a transition place for me before facing the real world."

She shed the worn coat and opened three buttons of her colorless dress at her neck. The tea and espresso arrived.

"Mr. Tower…"

"Please call me Hank, Jolanda. I'm only thirty-eight."

She grinned. Her eyes twinkled.

Shyly, "Okay." Then seriously,

"Do you think you can sell the Temujin for two-million euros?"

"That's easy. I will get more than that for it. I want a piece of it for you and your daughter. If it hadn't been for you and Giuseppe…" I watched for a reaction. None.

"…none of this would be possible, the museum, the convent, God's work would be stuck in neutral." She smiled again.

"You think Mother Sister wanted the larger amount all along?"

"Yes."

"I did, too." She gave a soft, mellow laugh.

She was hesitating to say something. "What is it, Jolanda?"

"I was thinking about what I almost asked you before we went to the convent."

"When I asked you if you were seeing someone? You said no."

"Yes, then, when you asked me."

"You wanted to know if I was seeing someone."

She looked directly at me. There was no shyness this time.

"Yes."

"For about two years I have…"

She put her hand on top of mine. I stopped my sentence. Slowly I turned my hand over and she ran her fingers between mine. We looked at each other and let our hands gradually tighten. We kissed carefully, not sure; then I put my hand behind her head and pulled her mouth into mine.

"Hank, Gina and Margherita are at her school now." I put a five euro on the table and we walked silently to her apartment with an arm around each other's waist. We went upstairs to her bedroom. She let the loose hanging dress fall to the floor. It was as I knew: a sculptured figure of feminine beauty. It had been a while for me. She whispered it had been much longer for her.

My departing words to Jolanda weren't an expression of love or even a plan for another meeting. I said only that I would call her as soon as I had something to say. She nodded. It was spontaneous combustion. Hers was purging once again from her mind what had to be a dreadful existence; and a deep gratitude for what I was promising for her daughter. For me, she was a soft and beautiful woman who needed something at that time, and the outlet I needed for my uncertain future with Carol. Neither of us saw any harm. My feelings for Carol were fundamentally the same: a mix of love and fear of a child. Jolanda had affirmed her femininity, her reason for leaving the convent she had just revisited.

I was approaching the Danieli when my cell phone pinged. It was 8:00 a.m. in New York. Lydia said,

"Hank, Phillip Santori called. He says you skipped out of London and he needs to know where you are. To be accurate he said 'Where in hell are you?' If I could, should I tell him?"

"Yeah. He knows you can't reach him. He'll call back. Tell him to use country code thirty-nine, city code zero four one. I'll wait for his call. He won't give me his number or his whereabouts."

"He's a ghost, Hank. I don't believe he exists. That's why he won't say where he is or give his number. He doesn't want to be traced. He's his twin brother."

We now had two-thirds of the firm believing that. The remaining third wasn't sure. It felt right and didn't feel right. Feelings can be perceptive. They can also mislead. Stick to the head when you want to be sure, major premise, minor premise, conclusion.

I wandered a bit off course, purposely, on the way back to the hotel. I needed to think of a way to Bouchard without Tresser knowing about it. More important, I wondered how to tell Tresser the Hun that the Temujin was available only if it went into a museum. That would not sit well; no, sir, that would not sit well.

I wandered south through the piazza of San Marco to the Grand Canal and turned left onto the Riva degli Schiavoni, the six-hundred-year-old walkway between the buildings and the Grand Canal, then onto the footbridge Ponte degli Schiavoni. At the top of it, I looked up the narrow canal that ran under the bridge into the Grand Canal. There was Venice's famous Bridge of Sighs through which hapless prisoners, mostly men who didn't pay their taxes, were taken into the old prisons from their trials in the Doge's Palace.

The Doge's Palace. It was right in front of me, where Tresser said Bouchard was curator. Bouchard could be only feet from where I stood. I went inside and found an official looking man standing near the entrance.

"I have an appointment with Mr. Bouchard. Can you tell me what floor he is on?"

"He's on this floor, sir. Go down the hall to your right. His office is the one at the end."

CHAPTER 21

Il Gazzattino's afternoon edition carried the murder on page 2.

Man Found Stabbed

Carmino Boccio, a licensed gondola driver, was found murdered early this morning in the doorway of 21 Della Marino. His body was discovered by a private investigator from New York who is vacationing in Venice. The investigator, Mr. Arnold Macgregor, said he was returning to his hotel and became lost in the winding streets of the City's residential area. He was questioned by the police and released.

A police officer who requested anonymity told a reporter that Mr. Boccio had known acquaintances in the underworld, but his police record showed only minor infractions. Mr. Boccio is survived by a wife and teenage son, both of whom live in Venice and have been informed.

The paper was laying on a table in Bouchard's vast reception room. I wasn't the only one who learned about it. I took a call and got a large, excited male on the other end. I went to the receptionist,

"Signora, I have an emergency call I will take outside. Please don't put anyone in front of me to see Mr. Bouchard. I will only be gone a few minutes."

"Si, signore. I will keep your place."

I stepped out of the reception room into the long, high-ceiling corridor. "Hello, Phillip."

"Tower, you work for me and I have to keep finding you. I'm in London, alone with my thoughts. No Tower, no Macgregor. Where are these investigators I paid to work for me? I find they're in Venice. How nice. Did they tell me they were going to Venice? No, I had to find out…"

"Hold on, Phillip. You'll pop the buttons off your shirt. Let me brief you…"

"Brief away."

"Your loving twin Paul is onto a thing he plans to sell for millions. He knows where it is, but he hasn't gotten possession of it. Also, there has been a murder here, a guy who was staking out a person someone else thought could lead him to the thing worth millions so he could buy it at a cheap price. Now…"

"Wait a minute, for Christ sake! I'm a simple man, not some chess champion. Straighten all that out for me. Make it two-plus-two."

"More than one person is chasing what your brother came to Venice for."

"How many are chasing it?"

"A man named von Tresser, another man named Bouchard, probably a man named Alistair Baker, your brother and me."

"You?"

"It's a bit tricky to explain."

"Tricky? It's insane. I'm coming to Venice today. Tower, I am interested in one thing – my stolen seven-hundred-and-fifty. If you're playing with millions, peel off seven-fifty for me and we can say bye-bye."

"Phillip, I have a feeling this is coming to a head. If I can pull off what I have in mind, you will get your seven-fifty."

"I'm coming to Venice. Where are you staying?" I said the Danieli.

"Jesus! Not on my bill!"

"It's not. Let me know where you are when you're settled."

"I'll call you."

I hung up and left a briefing for Arnie on his voice mail. If the other two-thirds of my corporation were correct, I just gave Paul Santori a briefing as well. Perhaps it was best, even if Paul and Phillip are the one and same. If will force an outcome.

"Signore Bouchard will see you, Mr. Tower."

I thanked her and stepped inside perhaps the largest office I've ever seen: marble columns in intervals around its perimeter, large, high windows draped with long, elegant fabrics of dark blues, bright reds, greens, each cinched with a gold tie, chairs alongside the walls with golden lion arms, a dome acrobats could perform in, and sitting rear-center amid all this splendor was Carlton Bouchard behind a desk large enough to play ping-pong on. He rose.

"Welcome, Mr. Tower. Please have a seat." It would have been a trip to reach him for a handshake. "My assistant says you have news of something called the Temujin."

Something called the Temujin, my ass. My bet is you would pay a hundred million for something called the Temujin. What a money-making attraction it would be in this palace.

"Mr. Bouchard, I know where it is, but I need your confidence."

He sat back in his high-back, golden-rimmed chair. He couldn't hide it. His inner lights were blinking like a slot machine that had just hit three bars.

With restraint he says, "I see."

"Do you want it?"

The man was in pain deciding whether to play it close or show his hand. He showed it.

"I want it desperately, Mr. Tower. It belongs here in Venice, in this Palace where Pietro Ziani fashioned it. It saved our city. I get stomach cramps when I think of it anywhere else. I thought it was lost forever until a friend said he was fairly certain he knew where…"

"Alistair Baker."

"Yes. He's an art dealer in London."

"Did you know his companion Jerome Manchester was murdered?'

"Good Lord, no. I was incommunicado in Moscow fro three days. My God, how…"

"Strangled. You see why I am concerned? The Temujin is taking lives. I must have your complete confidence, Mr. Bouchard. Without it you put my life in danger."

He nodded slowly. I continued. "Sums of money are being discussed that are far above what men kill for. The murder you may have seen in this afternoon's paper is another killing directly connected to the Temujin. Unless I have your word, I can't continue."

"Mr. Tower, you have my word nothing we say will leave this room."

"I am breaching the contract I have with my employer, Carl von…"

"…Carl von Tresser, an Austrian, wealthy and cunning. He wants it, doesn't he?"

"Yes, and he may be willing to pay up to a hundred-million euros for it. I don't want him to have it. I want it to be a permanent fixture in the Doge's Palace, but I want to stay alive. If he found out I was…"

"I understand, Mr. Tower, I understand completely."

"I have only one idea that would satisfy all the customers involved in this – for you and him to engage in a bidding war that you win. After he bows out, the Temujin would come to you for far less."

"You say you know where it is."

"Yes, I do. And I know the price I can get if for."

"How much?"

"It's well below the number I just mentioned.'

"Two or three million below?"

"More than that."

"What if I had a duplicate made. For two or three million I could do it, if I had the real one to copy, then I win the real one; Tresser gets the duplicate."

"He'd know it was a fake. Carbon testing would reveal the age of the fake."

"It's supposedly made of gold and jewels. They're all the same age."

"He'd certainly know there was one on display in this Palace. Say he has a private showing of his prize and is mocked. 'How do we know yours is the real one, Carl.' That would blow his ego to pieces. There would be repercussions."

Carlton Bouchard rubbed his chin. I said,

"He says he always wins, always."

"Yes, yes." He went into a deep concentration, rose and walked around his desk and returned to his seat.

"I need your confidence, too, Mr. Tower. I can match, even exceed the hundred million you mention, but I have no way of knowing how far I would have to go. Tresser is known to, how do you say? pull out the stops when he's obsessed."

"Do you know how he makes his money?"

"Oil and gas, I believe."

"Do you know much about his art works?"

"Yes. He buys most of it himself. I understand he has several Impressionists, some old Masters, some Rodin statuary. I have helped a dealer I know in Vienna sell him a few pieces."

"The dealer owes you."

"Yes, I suppose so. He hasn't sold him many, but he's made good money off the works he has."

"He knows what those works are, of course."

"Yes."

"What if that dealer circulated a rumor that the pieces of art Tresser bought on his own were fakes, that it was whispered among the cognoscenti that Tresser was a terrible judge of genuine art, that he was simply a *nouveau riche* trying to impress and had fallen easy prey to the dark side of the art world?"

"Kill his reputation so no one would believe the Temujin was real, if he showed it."

"There are four driving forces in Man, Mr. Bouchard: sex, money, eternal life and recognition. If he isn't recognized as a legitimate art connoisseur, why should he buy art? He would be shunned when he wanted to show it off. Owning the Temujin and bragging about the price he paid for it would only prove he's a super fool. Why would he take that chance? We need to discredit him."

"Do you really think he is a killer?"

"I don't want to find out the hard way."

"Hmm, yes. Your idea suggests we take the bidding-war course. Once he's worried about his reputation, the less he will want to raise his bids."

"How long would it take for such a rumor to spread?"

He laughed. "About ten minutes. Gossip is the bread of life in our rarified world."

"I have to tell him that there is another buyer in the game for the Temujin. The low price I mentioned to him is no longer available. I'll say the buyer has bid fifty-million euros for it. Are you okay with that?"

"Yes."

"He will know the buyer is you."

"Yes, but this is different from your situation. Bidding is a game Tresser is familiar with. It's rough, but it's aboveboard. If something happened to me, the entire art world would know he was behind it. He knows that. I am not in the danger you are." He paused and said,

"Why are you doing this almost saintly thing, Mr. Tower?"

"I'm no saint. I probably have a streak in me that says some things shouldn't be owned and shut up. They should be seen by everyone – the Magna Carta, our Constitution and Declaration of Independence, the Mona Lisa…"

"..and now, the Temujin."

"Yes. Now to my needs."

"I am listening."

"The keeper of the Temujin gets two-million euros, a separate trust fund is set up for another two-million euros, a check will be written for seven-hundred-and-fifty-thousand dollars and another check for two-hundred-thousand dollars. Names will be provided when needed."

His eyes widened to saucers. "You're saying that I can acquire the Temujin for four-million, nine-hundred-and-fifty-thousand euros?"

"The Doge's Palace can acquire it for that, yes."

He sat back in his royal chair. "My God in Heaven. If this works, Mr. Tower, I will have you sculpted and placed in the hall with the Doges."

"No. I would be a permanent finger in Tressor's eye. I'm sure he has a long memory. If we pull it off, we'll have a glass or two of expensive cognac."

"Incredible." He put his hands behind his head and grinned, "Unbelievable. Our nemesis is about to be – what would you say?"

"Bushwhacked, comes to mind."

"Good morning, Alistair," said Paul Santori, trying to appear calm. "Are you staying here?"

"Yes. I thought we needed to be together, Paul. Two heads are better than one, as the old saw goes. Consummating this deal of ours is important to both of us. It would be negligent if we didn't maximize our chances of success. On the surface it appears very simple – you have a product and I have a buyer for it: but, alas, the world is not simple. One must often rely on the help of another to avoid its pitfalls. Don't you agree?"

Paul thought another head was a head best twisted off and thrown in the sea. He could do quite nicely with one head.

He sat his huge body across from Alistair and stared at him. Getting rid of this worm dominated his mind. Alistair sensed soothing words were called for.

"I believe I can get as much as one-hundred-million euros for the Temujin, Paul. Sixty-percent of that is a handsome sum."

Forty-percent for doing nothing is a disgustingly handsome sum. I don't need your buyer, little man. I have my own in Vienna. He held back the words and continued to stare at Alistair, who was getting jumpy looking at him. The man looked like Satan deciding what floor to assign him in Hell. Jerome wanted the Temujin; Jerome is dead; I want part of the Temujin…I am…He ended the thought.

"Do you have the product, Paul?"

Paul saw his silent, expressionless stare was getting under the foppish Englishman's skin and continued it at full glare.

"My buyer is able to close a purchase in a day. All he needs are the bank numbers you and I want to use for the transfer of funds."

Paul continued his silent stare and thought. I could set him up for a close then stiff him, but he could have a deal in place with his buyer for the forty-percent. Finally, Paul spoke.

"Alistair, I have to make a phone call to my banker. I'm going up to my room."

He lifted his bulk slowly from the chair with his eyes on a straight line to Alistair's. He turned his huge back on him and went out the door. Alistair thought again, Jerome wanted the Temujin; Jerome is dead; I want part of the Temujin...I am...He ended his thought calculating a third of the selling price, rather than forty-percent.

Paul noticed the Message light was blinking on his room phone. He listened to the voice mail and froze. It was Mother Sister Michelle. She wanted to talk to him as soon as his schedule allowed.

In the residential part of Venice on the street where Carmino Boccio was murdered, Long Finger was writing down the addresses of each apartment to check against a phone book in the hotel where he was staying.

In his grand Doge's Palace office, Carlton Bouchard was speaking to his contact in Vienna about a rumor he had heard that the art Carl von Tresser had been buying on his own was fake. They both agreed it was possible. Buying and selling art was quite risky and should be left to professionals like themselves. The friend said he would ask other dealers in Vienna if they were aware that some of Tresser's art might not be genuine. The man in Vienna said, "There was that Degas he bought privately that we all thought was fake…"

CHAPTER 22

The Danieli is next door to the Doge's Palace and consists of three former palaces, one of which goes back to the fourteenth century and was the residence of the Doge Dandolo and his family. The Doges spanned a thousand years before their inevitable decline The staircase in the restored Dandolo palace, now the Danieli's lobby, is worthy of a descent of angels. Descending it now, however, was a less noble creature of the Deity's making, Carl von Tresser. We saw each other and he waved to a couple chairs in a private corner of the lobby. We sat.

"Carl, there's a development. My hope of delivering the Temujin to you for as little as four or five million has evaporated."

I didn't expect a smile at the news, but I didn't expect a death mask either. Always to the point,

"How much more?"

"Somehow another bidder has gotten in the act…"

"How much?"

"The bid is fifty million."

He stopped a waiter passing by. "Two cognacs – XO."

Philosophically, "One learns not to trust what sounds too good. Who's the bidder?"

"I don't know. The keeper of the goods refuses to say."

"The keeper of the goods."

"Yeah. If I reveal that, I might get killed. You, too."

He gave a twisted grin. "It's Bouchard. He's found out about it. He wants it for the Doge's Palace."

"I don't know." I let it settle, then asked, "Do you want to make a counter?"

He looked away. "Crap."

"That would be rejected. You said early on that you would pay fifty million for it in a blink."

The cognacs arrived. We sipped.

"You should learn the difference between bravado and reality, Tower." He looked away and uttered a similar four-letter word.

"I'm at your disposal, boss."

"Have you seen the Temujin?"

"No."

There was no indication if that was a good or bad answer.

I sipped again, slowly. He said,

"Sixty million."

"Sixty it is. I'll deliver the news in the morning. There's no rush. I said you would counter. Carl, don't have me followed."

He sipped his cognac and looked across the lobby at a magnificent, ornate fireplace, as if I were no longer present. Something bigger was on his mind. Could Bouchard's rumor mill be working its mischief already? A half-hour ago he joked it would take ten minutes for something that juicy to proliferate in his clubby world.

With today's communications it might take only five. "Have you heard? A large part of Tresser's collection might be bogus." It would be difficult for a gossipy dealer to keep news like that to himself or herself, especially if Tresser had previously snubbed his or hers assistance and bought a piece direct. It would also be a chance to insert a long needle into the arrogant Austrian, "I'm hearing that some of your art…"

I stood up and downed the remainder of my drink. "I'll have an answer by nine-o'clock tomorrow, boss."

I called Arnie on the house phone and told him tonight looked like open time, as the tour companies say. "Take a look around the place, but take my tail when I leave tomorrow for the convent. I can think of several people that might follow me, not just my psycho friend."

"Aye, 'ank. That's why I'm here," which was true.

I freshened up, put on some clothes that had just arrived from the hotel's cleaning service with a price close to their original cost. I was starting to feel a little guilty about spending Tresser's money, but as Arnie observed, his personality provided relief. More important, I still wasn't sure he didn't have Jerome murdered. That "Someone beat me to it" was too glib. Nevertheless, I intended today to be the demarcation line regarding Arnie's and my expenses. I would reimburse Tresser for whatever we spent after I made the deal with Bouchard; except the dry cleaning. That was ordered before Bouchard and I met.

It was noon in New York. Carol might still be in her office. I picked up the phone to call and it vibrated in my hand.

"Hello, Mr. Tow…Hank."

A low charge raced down my spine.

"Hello, Jolanda."

"I was hoping I could hide my call behind a report from Mother Sister, but she never called."

She paused. Her uneasiness was palpable. "It's all right. You can call me when you want. We're working together on this."

"Does…does…well, does…"

"Does having a tea together qualify as working?"

"Yes. Thank you for helping me."

"Absolutely. Would you like to have it here…" I killed that immediately. "No, not here."

Where? She was subject to kidnap alone on the street and she would certainly be followed by some new minion of Tresser's and/or Long Finger, if she came here.

"I'm not sure it's safe, Jolanda. I don't want to put you in danger. If you were kidnapped…"

"What if you never left your hotel and I never left home?"

"How…"

"I will have a close friend come to my apartment. She loves spending time with Margherita. I'll switch into her clothes and enter the hotel through the service entrance. An ex-sister runs the laundry there. She'll let me in. I can take the service elevator to your floor and leave the same way."

The electrons in my spine were spinning. I shouldn't. I won't. I don't want to hurt her. I can handle it. It's just a drink. She's the key to my case. She may know something. I can handle it. It's just a drink. No, it isn't. Yes it is. "Yes, it is" won the round.

"It's room three-twelve. Have you eaten?"

"Well, no, but I don't want to…I just meant to have a…"

"Fish, you must like fish."

"Oh, yes, but Mr. Tow…Hank. I don't…I feel like I am…"

"Try for seven o'clock when there's a mix of glow and night lights. The view is spectacular. Be sure to match your friend's hair and shoes."

'She has a cap I can wear and plain black shoes. I won't be very dressed up. She's a maid in the Bauer hotel."

"Wonderful." Imagining a dress or pants or habit that would make her unattractive was impossible.

Paul left Alistair in the tea room wondering what was going on behind Paul's silent stare. Paul's "Please call me" message from Mother Sister Michelle had him on edge more than the demands of the foppish art dealer and his tea cup. As long as he had the Temujin, he held all the spades in the deck. How to handle his "partner" downstairs would come to him when action was necessary. But did he still have a deal on the Temujin?

He stared at the phone with its various service buttons as if it were a terrorist bomb. Was there someone else in the game? Would a nun stiff him?

Yeah, if she had a higher bid. Low money has a way of trumping high ideals when those professing them are about to sink into the sea. He had another two-hundred-thousand in the bank, but he had the feeling the game was now in the millions. If so, he would need the proceeds from the sale of his co-op which would take at least another week to close. Maybe even that wasn't enough for the sisters. If more than ten million was needed, he would have to go directly to Tresser and ask for an advance against his selling price. His bona fides were certainly superior to Giuseppe's. If that failed and he couldn't handle the good sister's price himself, he would have to involve Alistair and his client, whoever it was.

Finally, he picked up the terrorist's bomb and pushed some of its buttons. Mother Sister Michelle answered herself.

"Is this Mr. Santori?"

"Yes, Mother Sister. I am retuning your call. Is there something I can do?"

"Thank you for calling so promptly, Mr. Santori. If you were surprised I knew it was you, well, my telephone doesn't ring more than three or four times a week. We are purposely isolated here in the convent. Most of our time is spent in prayer and washing and cleaning and ironing. It is our chosen life." She stopped, then resumed with the voice of someone digressing from the main topic.

"Occasionally, I venture out of our prayer books and hymn books and read secular authors. I even have a book of John Paul Sartre's on my desk that I brought with me from the Sorbonne in Paris. Have you read him, Mr. Santori?"

John Paul Sartre? Was he an admiral in the Revolution?

"No Mother Sister, I have not."

"I see. Well, if you have the time, I recommend it highly. It's titled *Being and Nothingness*. I quite disagree with its theme and suggest you read it for general knowledge and not be converted to his thinking. Mr. Sartre is persuasive. He does know his business."

Paul had gone from apprehension to fidgeting with a note pad. In his experience when someone started out a conversation as far off Job One as this one had gone it meant the deal was in trouble.

She went on.

"Now, I am sure you have read Mark Twain, Mr. Santori."

Paul answered, "Yes, but it has been a long time, Mother Sister."

"A very astute observer of our nature. He formulated many maxims about it. One is quite famous. Perhaps you have heard of it?"

"What is it, Mother Sister?"

"It was meant to be funny, most likely, but there is much truth hidden in it. It says 'When in doubt, tell the truth.' Do you see the wisdom of it?"

Paul saw the wisdom. He also saw the deal he had committed so much of himself to coming apart.

"I am in doubt that you intend to place the Temujin somewhere for everyone to see, as you promised me when we met, so in respect to the maxim I will tell you the truth. Someone has pledged to buy the Temujin and place it publicly. Having the Temujin on public display is a criterion for our selling it."

Paul was flummoxed. Tresser just went out the window. There was no way he would put it on public display. He wanted it for his private collection. If Alistair's buyer intends to put it in a museum, then despite the forty-percent, Alistair was essential to a deal; but if he didn't have the product…It was confession time.

"Mother Sister, I did plan to sell it to a private collector. I offer my apology as sincerely as I can. If you refuse to accept it, I will understand."

"Our faith is built on contrition, Mr. Santori. I accept your apology."

"If you have not sold the Temujin yet, I would like to re-bid on it with the guarantee that it will be placed in a museum or some other public place for all to see."

The table had turned on her. Mother Sister Michelle now had to decide if she would honor the arrangement she made with Mr. Tower and former Sister Jolanda or entertain another offer from Mr. Santori. Mr. Tower had said the piece was worth far more than the half-million euros Mr. Santori offered her. How much more was it worth? Mr. Tower's two million was a great deal of money, more than anything the convent could possibly contemplate as a charitable gift. Was more than that necessary? Was the Devil tempting her? Two-million euros seemed adequate to repair the convent and provide basics for the sisters for decades to come; but how could she be sure? Was Greed tempting her? She had read about evil coming from too much money. Would more money help the sisters or would it cripple them? She needed contemplation and prayer.

"Mr. Santori, I cannot answer that."

Paul took that as a life. "I understand, Mother Sister. May I call you later today? Is that enough time for you to consider hearing a new offer?"

She hesitated. Something said the Devil was standing behind her, that he wanted the convent to have too much money, that he knew it would destroy them. She held the phone aside and opened the ledger on her desk with her other hand. On the far right was the balance column. She ran her finger down the entries to the last one. It showed a bank balance of seventy-nine euros, about three euros per sister. She gathered strength and said,

"Yes, but please call before ten o'clock."

Tresser took the call from Jon, his number-one man in Vienna. Tresser asked,

"Is it true?"

"Carl, I've gotten two calls, one from the art editor of *Der Standard* and one from an influential dealer in Paris. They are hearing that you bought fakes for your collection. The editor wants comments; the dealer wants to know if it's true."

"Of course it's not true. I bought most of those paintings myself…"

"That's what's behind it. The callers say that they heard you were taken, that you didn't know they were fakes. The Degas, the Picasso, the Rodin., the Titian, the…"

"Okay!"

"Carl, what they cite totals nearly three-hundred-million euros. What do you want me to do?"

Tresser wanted to tell him to shoot everyone of the bastards in the head, but held back. Something's going on here.

"I smell a rat, Jon."

"So do I. You've had most of the pieces I've heard about so far for years. Why now?"

"I'll tell you why. Because a certain curator in Venice wants to discredit me as a judge of art so I can't brag about the Temujin. It would be seen as a fake. Are there rumors about the pieces I bought through dealers?"

"No, just those you bought direct."

"They're getting even because I cut them out. Bastards."

"What can I do, Carl?"

"Tell the editor that what he is hearing is false and slanderous, that I intend to take legal action when I trace the source of these despicable rumors and drown their lying asses in the Danube. I want his paper to print all that in big letters."

"I might edit it."

"Not too much of it. I want these dandies to know I'm steaming."

"When are you coming back to Vienna?"

"As soon as I tell the certain curator I mentioned that he's out of bounds and retracts what he started. Then I will have a talk with him."

Jon knew what that meant. "Be careful, Carl. Be careful."

Tresser ended the call and put on his suit coat jacket. The Doge's Palace was next door to the hotel, there was no need for a topcoat. He stepped out onto the quay and walked toward Bouchard's office. Behind him was an ordinary-looking man, alone, taking in the sights, clean shaven, hatless and neatly coiffed. He pulled up his coat collar and quickly returned his right hand to his coat's side pocket in an unusual way. His thumb and three fingers were showing outside its rim, the fifth finger was inside it. He followed Tresser as closely as he could without being noticed until he was certain where Tresser was going.

CHAPTER 23

Tresser marched into Bouchard's vast reception room the same way Phillip Santori had marched into Hank Tower's much smaller reception room in Manhattan. He thundered past the receptionist and burst directly into Bouchard's cathedral-size office. Bouchard was speaking to a man sitting at the side of his desk. Bouchard had never met Tresser, but he knew of him and his personality, and that he was in Venice. Bouchard nodded to his visitor who politely left the room. Tresser watched him close the door, then turned to Bouchard.

"I am going to nail your ass to the courthouse door – after you make a retraction to every art dealer in every major city of Europe."

Unruffled and seated. "You must be Carl von Tresser. Mr. Tresser, I heard you were in Venice. I have some pieces of art that I am sure will interest you…"

"Bouchard, pick up your phone and call whoever it was you told I bought fake art. You're going to say how wrong you were and how sorry you are that you suggested such a thing."

Perplexed. "I'm sorry. I'm not sure what you are…are you saying you bought fake art? I hope not. That can be very costly."

"I'm saying you said I bought fake art, and you're going to retract it. I'm not a fool, Carlton. I'm also not easy to deal with when I am angry and I'm damned angry. Sometimes I lose it and do bad things. Do you understand?"

"Carl, may I call you Carl? Please have a seat. I truly do not know what you are upset about. I intended to reach you when I heard you were in Venice…"

"Bullshit! Hear me clearly, Bouchard. If you don't pull back your dirty rumor scheme, you're in danger. You'll wish for a court solution. Do you understand?"

"Please, Herr Tresser, explain what this is all about."

Tresser didn't like "Herr" and Bouchard knew he wouldn't. It's the equivalent of Mister in German, where Von is the same as Sir in Britain.

"You know damned well what it's about. It's about the Temujin."

"The Temujin? Surely you don't believe in that old story, Carl."

Tresser didn't expect that. It cost him a second or two before he answered, a pause Bouchard noticed.

"Yes, I believe in it. And I believe it's in Venice, but I don't know where." He was calming." I know you've made a bid of fifty-million euros for it."

"Carl, you must be…that's ridiculous. Fifty million for an item that doesn't exist…"

"Fifty million. You're the only one with that kind of money – and you want it. So do I. How far are you willing to go to get it?"

"Willing to go? For a ghost? Is this a game?"

"How far?"

"My dear fellow, if you want to play a game, I suppose there's no harm. If the Temujin existed and was available and someone was willing to pay fifty-million euros for it, I would pay more to have it in the Doge's Palace."

"How much more?"

"Probably sixty million."

"And if I said seventy?"

"Then I would most likely up my bid to eighty. Really, Carl…"

"And if I went to ninety?"

"Well, I would say you wanted it very badly, but then I would ask if you were sure you wanted to invest such a large sum of money in it. After all, there's this rumor you bring up. Wouldn't that taint the Temujin's authenticity, if you put it in your collection? I have so many legitimate pieces I can offer you…"

Tresser went blood red from neck to forehead. Bouchard had not only thrown his filthy conspiracy directly in his face, he had the balls to offer him art! As often happens when men reach a level of anger so fierce they find it beyond their ability to cope with it, they go quiet; and so it was now with Tresser. He stared at Bouchard with fire, but he said nothing. The plot against him was clear; he was trapped. And he knew the price he'd have to pay to get out of it. Bow out of the Temujin game and the rumors will be retracted. The value of the pieces you bought directly will be restored to their original value without the necessity of having them appraised, and the risk of finding that one or two really are fakes. That *ff* be devastating. He sat and fumed, but there was nothing he could say. He rose and walked out of the room. All that was left was revenge.

The faint knock on the door was barely audible. I opened it and into my room stepped perhaps the most attractive maid a man may encounter in his life. Her cap was pulled tight to contain her hair and her black shoes looked like what a beat cop would wear; but neither they nor the frumpy gray and white striped dress could hide the diamond within.

"Hello, Hank."

I grinned at her and shut the door. "Jolanda you look ravishing. The cap, the dress. Those shoes are the next new thing. I can see them gracing the red carpet at the Academy Awards."

"I feel silly, but I am sure I wasn't followed. Why would anyone follow a maid? May I take off my hat and shoes?"

"Of course, but keep on the lovely dress." She gave a blushing grin and laid aside the cap, letting her dark hair fall across her shoulders, then removed the shoes. She was sockless and barelegged. Round two was going to be tough.

"I haven't ordered dinner yet. I thought you would like to see the menu."

"All right, but not yet. I want to see the view you mentioned."

"It's chilly on the terrace. I don't see a coat."

"I left it with my sister-friend. I didn't want to be seen wearing it in the hotel."

"Here." I pulled a soft blanket off the foot of the bed and draped it over her shoulders. I opened the French doors to the small terrace and we stepped out three floors above where the Grand Canal begins. It's the main artery of car-less Venice and it winds its way alongside the city's grand palaces and under its bridges like a backward "S." The last glow of the sun was reflecting off the dome of San Giorgio Maggiore across the city's harbor. The tower of St. Mark's was to our right. It was about as romantic a setting as a romantic could imagine. Browning, Keats, Wordsworth and Shelley, working as a foursome, might come close to a worthy description, but they would have to put their shoulders to it. Now add a beautiful woman barefoot in a maid's dress wrapped in a blanket and… and you have something that you should have thought through more thoroughly.

She went to the railing. "Oh, Hank. All my life in Venice I've never seen anything like this. All I had was the convent, then Switzerland, then Giuseppe, then Margherita, then…" She paused. "All those years I was confined or too busy working to see where I lived. This is beautiful."

She pulled close to my side. I turned to face her, intending to speak the big brother sermon and explain that she will find someone for herself and Margherita, that I was not the one, that she was young and beautiful and could look forward to a happy life, that I was only a passing ship, that Life had so much waiting for her, that she was reacting to long deprivations, that I would be leaving, let's have dinner when she opened the blanket, pulled me inside it and pressed herself against me. With her lips close to mine she said,

"Hank, I know you are going to leave…and that we will not see each other again…I want to…to cherish this time with you as much as I can. Please understand." I didn't know what to say. She said "Take me to bed with you."

Please understand. Please understand. She was asking me to please understand her desire when it would take most of the Arctic Ocean to cool my own. I didn't make it to round three. With a cuddling, forty-five degree breeze coming through the terrace doors and a mango colored sky hanging over perhaps the world's most beautiful city – the Queen of Cities – Jolanda Marcelli and I made love knowing it was the last time.

Alistair was still sitting in the tea room feeling numb. Paul's Svengali stare had unnerved him. What did he know about the man? Only that he was pursuing the Temujin. Maybe he's a killer, maybe he saw Jerome's fanaticism and killed him or had him killed. Maybe I pushed him too far, he thought. Maybe he will kill me to keep one-hundred percent of a sale. But he doesn't know Bouchard. Does he know someone else? Not likely since he made a sweetheart deal with me. Could he reason that the Doge's Palace was a logical place for the relic and then find out who was in charge of acquiring such things? The demons were working their picks in Alistair's brain again. He finished his tea and was getting ready to go upstairs when Paul reappeared at the small room's door.

"I want to talk to you." The big man easily moved a large wing chair to Alistair's side. He's strong as a bull, he thought. He could have strangled Jerome despite his wonderfully fit body. He remained quiet while Santori gave him a piercing look, then after a sufficient dosage, the big man said,

"I want to change the deal we have."

Alistair in his mind had already accepted a two-thirds, one-third arrangement to appease his wrath. Now, he thought the wise course was to concede a bit more to him. He said,

"I know you have been unsure about it, Paul, and, frankly, so have I. Forty percent is more than the normal commission art dealers receive for placing a seller with a buyer. I find it is even more out of place in our agreement since I have no overhead to cover. These thoughts have been on my mind. I have always dealt fairly in my profession…"

"What is your proposal?"

"Well, I think a three-fourths, one-fourth arrangement is fairer."

Gruffly, "Eighty-twenty."

"Well, that's a bit…"

"Eighty-twenty."

"All right. But do you have the product?"

"Yes, but I don't have the money to buy it."

"I see. Well, if I have to find the purchase money, we should reconsider the original deal…"

With evil in his eyes, "Eighty-twenty, you skinny bastard, or I'll rip your head off."

Alistair recoiled. Maybe this man did kill Jerome. He's dangerous, unpredictable. Take the twenty percent and get him out of your life, said a shaken Alistair to himself.

"As you wish, Paul. There's no need for that kind of talk. I will keep my word to you. Now, tell me what we have to do."

"We'll need your buyer to advance three-million euros. He can deduct it from our selling price."

"He will want security of some sort."

"Does he trust you?"

"Yes, we have known each other for many years."

"Have him deposit the money in your bank and give me a bank check for the three million payable to me. I will endorse it over to my seller. Once we have the product, our client subtracts three million from our selling price and makes out two checks, one for eighty percent and one for twenty percent."

"I will speak to him."

"I recommend you do that now. I need to strike before the iron cools."

"Iron?"

"It's a saying, idiot. Make the call to the buyer now and have the check for three-million euros here at the desk. I'll pick it up and get the product."

"Not from here. I'll call from another place. I don't want you listening and I don't want you following me. I mean that, Paul. After I make the call, I will find another hotel so we're separated."

Paul went to the door, turned toward the registration desk and disappeared.

Alistair wanted the removal of Paul Santori from his life to begin immediately. If he got Bouchard's approval – and Santori got the Temujin – Bouchard would give the twenty-percent check to him and that would be the end of his relationship with this large and fearful American. He gave his room key to the clerk and went outside. He was walking toward the Doge's Palace when he called Bouchard.

"Carlton, it's Alistair. I need to see you right away. Are you in your office?"

"Yes, I was just about to leave for a cocktail…"

"Please wait for me. I'm only twenty minutes away. It's important."

"All right. Can you tell me…"

"No. Please wait. I'm on my way."

Paul left the hotel a few minutes after Alistair and started walking to the convent. He wanted to see if anyone entered it before Mother Sister's deadline of 10:00. There was still a dim light, thank God. How could anyone find their way around this tangle of streets at night? You need a sugar trail to trace your route back from wherever you go, assuming you get there in the first place.

He had memorized a few buildings when he returned earlier from the convent to the hotel and was having an easy time of it, but then something didn't look right. Did the church he had noted have two or three columns? This one had two and the square looked smaller than the one with the church he thought he had memorized. He backtracked to where the streets forked and where he had turned to the left. It must be down the other street, he thought; but it didn't look exactly right either. The higher buildings along its sides were blocking the last light from reaching the bottom of the narrow canyon. The only light was a dim glow across the top of the buildings on one side and near darkness on the other side. He noticed a wooden sign hanging from a pole over a closed shop. "Silver and Glassware", it said. He'd seen that before, but had he seen it somewhere else? He couldn't be sure. The small-church route was clearly a dead end; this must be the correct way.

He stepped forward, avoiding the dark side of the alley-like street. There were no other pedestrians to be seen and that made him uneasy, but then it was nearly 8:00. All the day-trippers to Venice from the mainland had returned, and those who lived here were in their homes dining most likely. He heard a small rock rolling across the cobblestones behind him and turned to look. The street was empty. The light on the wall to his left had already inched higher. It would be dark in a few minutes, maybe he should go back to the hotel. He heard another rock.

He turned more quickly this time, alert, but there was only the empty passageway. He stepped up his pace. A rock banged against a metal drain pipe. He started and stepped toward the middle of the street to get a better look into the dark side of it. A cat sauntered out of the shadow. He smiled and bent to pet it and felt a sharp blade pierce his right side an inch above the belt. He staggered. It was removed and plunged back into him a little higher and again a little higher and again... He fell on his face coughing blood. The blade went across the front of his neck. He was silent.

The cat looked at the large man lying on the stone street and meowed its concern to the man standing over him. It was reassured with a soft stroke across its back and side by an abnormally long finger.

CHAPTER 24

Alistair Baker huffed and puffed past the front of the Cathedral of St. Mark's, through the eternal gaggle of dirty pigeons that live off the tourists in San Marco piazza, then onto the Riva degli Schiavoni and into the Doge's Palace. He went directly to Bouchard's office. He caught his breath and announced himself to the receptionist in reserved British.

"He's expecting you, Mr. Baker. Please go in."

Alistair opened one of the massive two doors and stepped into Bouchard's mini-cathedral. He had always thought Bouchard should hire a couple of bishops to walk about the place with their staffs and red hats – or did Cardinals where red hats? Cardinals would be more fitting. Why scrimp? Bouchard's office clearly didn't go far enough in the pomp business. The curator rose from his high-back chair.

"Alistair Baker. When was the last time we were together? Ah, the Napoleonic Wars. We won those, you know." It was a French needle to the stuffy Briton.

"Not quite that long ago, Carlton. I believe it was just after Waterloo."

Bouchard chuckled at the one-up as he came from behind his desk. The two men shook hands.

"It has been too long, Alistair. I have been traveling the world for art's sake and enjoying the hell out of it; but I find myself going east instead of west to London, Paris and New York. There are mountains of money in Russia and its neighbors, billions of BTUs of it."

"Yes, I know, Carlton. May I get to my purpose and then ask you to join me in a drink afterwards to catch up? I'm under a deadline."

"I sensed that."

"It concerns the Temujin." Bouchard tensed up. *Decades go by and there's never a syllable spoken about it; now, in a matter of hours two well-connected men bring it up in my office.* He kept a poker face.

"The legend lives on, eh?"

"Yes. I have an associate who claims he knows where it is, and can deliver it. I know you want it here in the Doge's Palace."

"Desperately."

"Here's the delicate part, Carlton. Would you advance part of its purchase price to me?"

"So you can buy it for me?"

"Yes. It's that simple."

Bouchard's brain was whirling. *Was Tresser behind this? Was this a ruse of his? If so, how would he gain?* Bouchard was at a loss to know how he would. Tower's scheme had Tresser boxed. He was out of the game; but Bouchard knew von Tresser was never out of a game he had entered to win.

"Do you know where it is, Alistair?"

"No, only that it's in Venice."

"What price are you and your associate looking for?"

"A hundred million." Alistair didn't need to justify the price. Recent art sales did it for him. Bouchard knew "The Scream" recently went for more than that price, and there was more than one version of the painting. There was only one Temujin.

"Alistair, of course, I'm interested. It belongs in the Palace, no where else. But is there some flexibility on the price?"

Alistair suddenly realized that something very critical had escaped Paul and him. Once he asked for the advance against their selling price, he would reveal what they were paying for the Temujin. The absurdity of it hit him like a hammer. He was about to ask for a three-million-euro advance from Bouchard to buy something he would turn around and sell to him for one-hundred million. Not only was that an offense to the man's intelligence, it was something Alistair would never live down. His reputation in the art world would crumble, if even the attempt at such a rip off were ever exposed. Those hectares in the Loire Valley were shrinking.

And they were becoming less important to him. His ethical side was asserting itself. My business isn't angel pure, he thought, but it's not satanically immoral either. The deal he was about to propose, if not satanic, was blatant – and transparent – thievery. There was deeper thinking to it as well. His resentment of Paul Santori's treatment of him on top of his suspicion that he killed Jerome were firing a hatred for the large American. He wanted rid of him.

The whole damned thing was wrong. Bouchard was an honest dealer, a friend and a responsible curator who wanted the relic placed where it belonged, where it was born, in the Doge's Palace. But Alistair Baker didn't make quick decisions, even when he was sure he knew what his decision was going to be. He liked every beak and tail of his ducks in perfect alignment before he committed himself. He said,

"Yes, there is flexibility, Carlton. Let me speak to my associate and I will call you."

"If someone else bids on it, Alistair, let me counter."

"I will, Carlton, I will. Let me arrange my drink with you at a different time. I want to talk with you badly, but I can't until I…"

"I understand, Alistair. I'll be here. You do what you have to do. We go back a long way. Maybe not to the Napoleonic Wars, but…"

"But far enough, Carlton, to know when a deal is right or wrong."

Bouchard looked at him curiously and nodded his head. The scene had a Tresser smell to it, thought Bouchard. Alistair wouldn't work with Tresser, would he? No, but Tresser would squeeze Alistair without a blink, if he could get a use out of him. Did he have something on Alistair? Bouchard decided to table the speculation and wait to hear from Alistair.

Jolanda and Hank were in sumptuous white robes eating mahi-mahi filets sautéed in an unforgettable sauce. The French doors to the terrace were closed and the sun had set. The impending break-up hung over their dinner like a rain cloud.

"It's probably the best dinner I've ever had, Hank." She left out "…and the last one we'll have."

Tower was struggling for something appropriate to say. The usual "You're a very special person," or, "I'll never forget you," or any twist or turn on the theme fell flat before it reached his tongue. So he simply smiled at her enjoying the meal. It's been noted by minor scholars that women are better at these kind of scenes than men are. Perhaps men feel guilty for "taking," whereas women experience the far superior feeling of giving. Whatever drives the dynamic, Jolanda was the one who finally broke the tension in her soft voice.

"Hank, remember what I said. I know you're leaving as soon as we arrange for the Temujin to go to the Palace. I have no regrets about what we have enjoyed. I hope you have none."

"No, Jolanda, I have none, only very good memories…"

"It was I who caused it. There is no reason for you to feel guilty about leaving." She went silent for a few seconds and looked directly at Tower.

"Hank, don't tell her about this. It will hurt unnecessarily." Her eyes betrayed what she said next.

"Don't think I have fallen in love with you."

Tower knew eyes. Seeing behind them was part of his business. If he could have seen behind his, he would have seen what he saw in hers, and what he saw in hers didn't match her words. He refrained from saying anything further. He was looking at the soft, flawless skin showing through the open neck of her robe. He wanted her again. Any moment he might go to her chair and pick her up and…

He stood behind his chair, holding the top of it in a death grip, and said,

"Jolanda, it's almost ten. If you don't leave, I'm going to toss your robe in the Canal and you on the bed."

He said it without a smile, but she smiled back so knowingly Tower almost did pick her up.

"I will come to your apartment tomorrow morning. Together we'll see Mother Sister. After that…"

She came around the table and kissed him hard on the lips, then with her head on his chest said,

"…after that we will part."

Arnie called me shortly after Jolanda left.

" 'ank, there's been a murder. Paul Santori. Knifed several times, throat cut on a side street. A young woman found 'im looking for 'er cat. Very messy. I got the news from a patrolman I was killing time with. 'e got it on 'is radio. We went to the scene together."

"Paul Santori? Arnie, maybe it was Phillip. He said he was coming to Venice from London."

"No. I checked for the neck mole. There wasn't any."

"There was a mole on Phillip's neck."

" 'e showed it to ye, right? Are ye familiar with moles?"

"No. It looked real."

"'ave ye ever been to a costume shop? They can give you warts and crooked teeth, funny eyes. Why not moles?"

"Right. You still believe there's only one Santori, not two, like Lydia."

"Aye. No one 'as ever seen the two of 'em at the same time, at their office or anywhere else I've checked."

"Lydia was going to look for a birth certificate…"

"None in New York or nearby states, for Phillip or Paul."

"Are you sure he's dead?"

"By the God in Heaven, 'e's dead, all right."

"Then if we get a call from Phillip…"

"Aye, but my sense is we won't."

"Where was Paul staying?"

"We traced 'im from 'is pockets to a small 'otel near the Rialto bridge. I'm going there now with two officers."

Arnie had gone from a murder suspect to part of the Venice police force. The bond transcends oceans.

"Call me when you've had a chance to investigate."

I tossed my robe onto a chair next to hers and climbed in the bed. I could smell her sweetness and feel the warmth of the sheet where she had laid next to me. Jesus!

Oh, what a tangled web we weave when first we practice to conceive, to paraphrase Sir Walter Scott's insight on lying. I was holding the phone to call Carol when Jolanda called. That's how close I came to, maybe, having the strength to sidestep that tangled web; but I didn't. And it didn't "just happen," and I didn't just let it happen. No, I wanted her. I wanted her. Jesus, I wanted her.

My phone vibrated. I tensed. Was it Jolanda? No, it was Arnie.

"We 'ave a Brit 'ere at Paul Santori's 'otel who wants to talk to ye, 'ank. 'e's a bit shakey. 'e's name's Alistair Baker. 'ere 'e is."

"Mr. Tower, I'm afraid for my life. I want to hire you for protection. I need you near me until I can get out of Venice."

This was a nice twist. I might have lost one client only moments ago and already another one is at my door. If business had been this good back in New York days ago, I wouldn't be in this British, Austrian, Italian mess. Carol and I would be in the Caribbean on a beach, drinking rum and tickling each other in a hammock…and

Jolanda's scent wouldn't be…

I explained my fee to him. "Fine, fine whatever it is, I'll pay it. I want out of this hotel and I'm afraid to go out into the streets alone…I asked the police for an escort, but was told they don't do that. I'm at a loss…"

"Give the phone to Arnie."

"Aye, 'ank."

"Take him under your wing and bring him here to the Daneili. Set him up in a cheap room, if there is one, and tell him to chain-lock his door until you or I call him in the morning. Then get some sleep, as I plan to. I have a feeling tomorrow is going to be eventful. Pump out his story so we can go over it before breakfast. I'm getting an appointment at the convent as early as I can."

"'ank. One thing. "'e mentioned the Temujin in 'is fever."

"Good Lord! I'm starting to believe the whole world wants the Temujin. It reminds me of an old vaudeville entertainer who got rid of hecklers by shutting them up with 'Everybody wants in the act.' Jimmy something. We'll talk at seven-thirty."

As if my feelings needed more proof of their tangled state, I forgot to ask Jolanda to get an appointment time tomorrow with Mother Sister. She forgot, too. I called her at home and told her to call me with the time and that I would pick her up twenty minutes earlier; and not to go out until I arrived.

I got in bed and fought six exhausting rounds with the pillows before falling asleep.

Carl von Tresser had the temper of a wild horse trapped in a corral, but he wouldn't be worth billions of euros, if he didn't know how to channel his anger. His temper was still snorting and kicking when he left Bouchard's office, but his mind was already racing for a way to get even with the pompous s. o. b. He was so absorbed in his vengeance he almost missed the calm voice behind him ask,

"May I have a word with you?"

Tresser turned. It was an ordinary man neatly dressed and coiffed who kept his right hand in his coat pocket. A bystander watching the short conversation that followed would assume that the one who stopped the other was probably asking for directions. Neither gave an indication they had ever met before.

The man told Tresser that he had been following several people moving about in Venice, including an overweight American staying at a hotel near the Rialto bridge. He wasn't sure what the American was doing in Venice, but he suspected there was a large amount of money involved since others in Venice "including you" also seemed involved in what the large one was pursuing. He went on to say that he, too, had an interest in the item under pursuit, and to that end said he followed the man from his hotel to a convent. The man stayed inside it for about a half hour and came out quite elated.

Tresser's temper cooled to subzero. Convent. Elated. Bouchard. His mind connected the dots with the speed of light. The big American had found the Temujin and was going to sell it to Bouchard. That's why Bouchard was so sure of himself; that's why he wanted me out of the game. Well, the game is still afoot, Carlton; yes, it is still very much afoot. He asked a few questions of the stranger, and they parted. His mind was processing now.

There is perhaps another prerequisite to earning billions – paranoia. One must trust no one, not friends, family, employees, church, state, press, God, and in this case, Hank Tower and his red-haired giant. He sensed Tower had just enough goody-goody and smarts in him to finagle the Temujin into Bouchard's Palace

"Where everyone can see it." How nice.

Giuseppe, you gigolo ass, if you had control over your sex glands all this could have been avoided.

He went into the Danieli and Googled "convents" in Venice. There it was. The Convent of Mary Magdalene, as the man had said. There was a phone number. He dialed it and waited.

"Hello, this is Mother Sister Michelle."

"Mother Superior…"

"I prefer Mother Sister. Superior sounds authoritative and unequal."

"Of course, Mother Sister. Are you the person in charge of the convent?" The Austrian couldn't imagine someone eschewing authority.

"Yes, I am in charge."

"I would like to meet with you tomorrow morning regarding an artifact you may have. Is eight-thirty all right?"

Mother Sister wanted to say no, but the force she was struggling to overcome won the match again. She made the appointment at 8:30 with Mr. Tresser. Later she made one at 9:30 with Sister Jolanda and Mr. Tower. Mr. Santori had another half-hour before his deadline expired. I hope he doesn't call, she thought. It will make all this easier for me.

CHAPTER 25

"Mr. Tower, I want out of this imbroglio. My companion was strangled and now this man Santori is butchered like an animal. The Temujin belongs in the Doge's Palace under my friend Carlton Bouchard's supervision. If I can help you or anyone else achieve that end from the safety of England, I will; but I am retuning to London today."

Thus spoke Alistair Baker to Arnie and me over breakfast in the Danieli hotel. I refrained from adding the third murder connected to the Temujin – the late Carmino Boccio, Tresser's hired shadow. Two seemed quite enough for Alistair Baker's sensitivities. I said,

"I understand, Mr. Baker. I believe the relic belongs in the Doge's Palace as well, but there is at least one person who sees it differently…"

"Von Tresser."

"Yes, how did you know?"

"The art world is too small not to. He has the cash and the obsession. I have gotten calls from him over the years seeking exotic artifacts. It would never enter my mind that he would have people killed to satisfy his insane fixations. Now…"

"Do you think he had your partner and Santori killed?"

"I don't know. I don't even want to think about the possibility. I want to be back in England where I can focus on my business, and arrange a sale of my penthouse. Every time I go to the door I'll see Jerome lying dead on the floor with his eyes staring…" I broke in.

"Do you know if Santori knew where the Temujin is?"

"I am sure of it. He not only knew where it was, he had a deal arranged to buy it. He said he thought his bid to the person who has it was final, then someone bid higher. The second bid was too high for him to match it. I was just as greedy as Santori. After seeing Carlton, I thought of going back to Santori and saying we should reduce our profit to a level in keeping with the standard commissions in the business, but I knew he wouldn't hear of it. Besides, he was dead before I had a chance to suggest it.

"This is important, Mr. Baker. Think hard before answering. Has Tresser found out where the Temujin is?"

"There's no way for me to know. Santori knew where it was – as I said, I am certain of that – but he never revealed who the owner was. It was his leverage in our arrangement. Mine was the secrecy of the buyer. Now, there's this gruesome murder. Mr. Tower, can your assistant Mr. Macgregor accompany me back to London?"

"No. I need Arnie here, but I will arrange an escort for you."

"I am enormously grateful, Mr. Tower, enormously. I will add a bonus to your regular fee."

I smiled. People grateful for relief from an overpowering problem frequently express their gratitude by promising extra remuneration, but I find that the intensity of the largess invariably decreases in a straight line from promise to check.

"May I ask you to call me on this number, Mr. Baker, if something, anything, comes your way regarding the Temujin?"

"Of course, of course. I want this resolved quickly. I've never been closer to a murder than pictures in the tabloids. I want no part of it, none at all." He paused.

"One more question, please, then I'll arrange an escort back to London."

"Yes, of course."

"Did Paul Santori ever mention a brother?"

"No. He was a man of minimal words."

"I see. Thank you." I left for Jolanda's apartment.

Mother Sister Michelle, linguist, leader, manager and front-woman for twenty-four cloistered nuns asked her charges for special prayers at their usual 5:00 a.m. assembly. She was tortured, but she didn't reveal the cause of her torment to the twenty-four souls she was responsible for. She only asked that they pray deeply that she would make the right decision on a matter that concerned the convent and the many lives that were devoted to it now and in the future.

There was no "Can I help, Mother Sister?" It would have been an encroachment on her authority. She had been chosen to represent them because she was the most educated and the one most likely to know the ways of the outside world. She was the most suitable to protect and sustain their chosen life from the vagaries of the secular world. It was rare that she asked for their prayers, so they prayed intensely and again after breakfast.

Mother Sister took special notice of the breakfast that morning. There was less bread than yesterday. The spoonfuls of scrambled eggs were smaller – a single egg for each sister had ended weeks ago. Now, the scrambled eggs were enhanced with milk. Tea bags were shared. A stroke of anger went through her, but she quickly subdued it as sinful. Only she knew the state of their finances.

She welcomed the absence of a call from Mr. Santori. If he had made a bid higher than the one she had from Mr. Tower, as he said he would do, she would have been in a quandary. The whispers of conscience would return. Still, how could she know if Mr. Tower's bid was sufficient to repair and sustain the convent into the future? Were the whispers reminders of her responsibility to protect the sisters, or were they temptations from Satan that would destroy the convent? Thankfully, Mr. Santori never called.

But Mr. von Tresser did. He was the reason for the special prayers. She knew he would surpass the bid Mr. Tower made, so why did she permit him to come to the convent? Could she retract her permission to come? It was too late. At 8:30 sharp she heard the convent's doorbell ring. Moments later the convent's loyal and aged servant Gregory was announcing Mr. Carl von Tresser to her.

Tresser stumbled his opening. Perhaps his memory suffered from his passion to stiff Bouchard with a high selling price for the Temujin. He entered the room and said,

"Mother Superior, thank you for…"

"Mother Sister, Herr Tresser."

"I am sorry. My Catholic youth got the best of my memory. I apologize, Mother Sister."

In German, "Please have a seat. Our quarters are not what they once were, but they are adequate for our needs."

Tresser wasn't impressed by her switch to his language. It put him on guard. Her German revealed that she knew the difference between Von and Herr and had used the latter in retaliation for his faux pas. This was not going to be the in-and-out transaction he foresaw. Still, money was power.

"Mother Sister, I would like to talk to you about…"

Mother Sister said with steely eyes,

"You say 'Your Catholic youth,' Mr. Tresser. Are you no longer a Catholic?"

Tresser hadn't prepared for this. He was ready to bargain, yes, but answering a question about his religion, of which he had none, wasn't on his list of talking points. He chose to lie.

"Yes, I am still a Catholic, Mother Sister. Austria is a Catholic country."

"Yes, it is, but so many of its people have chosen to leave the faith. I am glad to hear you are still among us."

Tresser's trained ear heard trouble in the response. Maybe one throwaway line, then quickly to business…

"I am proud to say I am not one of those who have left the faith. What I would like to talk about, Mother Sister…"

"Then you must go to mass every Sunday. What church do you belong to?"

Jesus, woman, let's get on with it! But he didn't say that. Instead he defaulted to the church every man, woman, child, tourist and bat knew about in Vienna, St. Stephen's cathedral. But he didn't escape her.

"Oh, yes. I have seen it, an absolutely magnificent structure. It goes back to the fourth century. It's the mother church of the Archdiocese of Vienna, but, of course, you know that. How lucky for you to attend it every Sunday. The monthly newsletter I get from Rome – it's my only window to the outside – said Cardinal Beckman was still the Archbishop of the diocese. Have you met him?"

The billionaire in Tresser saw the set up. He had no idea who was the Cardinal of St. Stephen's, which he thought was an architectural monstrosity, and didn't care if he went to his grave ignorant of who ran the ugly pile of stones. But this black widow knew who ran it and it was his bet that the reigning boss of St. Stephen's cathedral was not a Beckman.

"No, I haven't, Mother Sister. I'm afraid my visits are too short and the Cardinal's schedule is too busy."

But Mother Sister noted that he failed to correct the Cardinal's name, which was not Beckman.

"And I am sure you are a busy man, too, Mr. Tresser. I won't gossip anymore. It's my lack of outside contact our chosen life demands, but sometimes I fall prey to temptation and take advantage of visitors. Forgive me. Now, please tell me how I can help you."

Tresser was relieved, but only partially. He had to watch every step he took.

"Mother Sister, I have learned that the convent has been housing an artifact called the Temujin for centuries. I..." He started to say "I am an art collector" and instinctively refrained. "...would like to buy it from the convent. I believe the value I can give you for it would help you restore your home and provide you and the others who live here with a modest income for many decades."

"I see. Yes, the artifact you mention has been under the convent's care for centuries. I assume you know its history."

"Yes, I do."

"I know that is what makes it so valuable. But I must be honest with you, Mr. Tresser, another person has offered to purchase it."

Tresser knew damned well who that person was, and who he planned to give it to.

"It doesn't surprise me, Mother Sister. I only learned of it being in Venice. I am sure others were aware of it before me. Would you share with me the price the other person has promised to pay, assuming you haven't committed to it, of course?"

That was a mistake. It went to the very spot of Mother Sister's soul where her torment was the rawest. She had made a commitment to a former Sister of hers and a man who pledged to put the Temujin in the Doge's Palace. Before she could respond to Tresser he said.

"I can offer you ten-million euros for it, Mother Sister."

The wheel on the rack stretching her conscience turned its ropes tauter. She was on the edge of being ripped apart. In two days the value of an item that had sat unknown and undisturbed for centuries had gone from a half-million to two million to ten million. There was no question that ten-million euros would accomplish what the convent needed, now and for many decades to come. Then why the warning whisper? And what was its source?

Tresser saw her uneasiness and misinterpreted it. "Mother Sister, I can increase…"

She held up her hand. He stopped immediately. Something else was going on here, he thought. Was the old bag wrestling with the moral side of her commitment? Christ! If people were only guided by money and pitched the other stuff…

She closed her eyes to avoid seeing his face and to intensify her hearing. She asked,

"Do you plan to put the Temujin in the Doge's Palace, Mr. Tresser?"

The question struck at Tresser's latent temper. He had heard too damn much about an obligation to show the Temujin to the public. What the hell has the public done to be so privileged? The heat rose. I'll put it where I damned well choose to put it. I own it! What do these people think I am, a charity? He was able to tamp it down, but not enough for a cloistered nun whose eyes were closed to his pleasant face and whose ears were as open as a NSA spy dish.

"I will certainly consider that very seriously, Mother Sister. I believe it belongs there."

A sensation of relief passed over her body and soul like a warm shower.

She looked hard at him with his "...consider that very seriously..." still ringing in her ear. Her dilemma was solved. After politely turning him down and escorting him to the door, she said a second before closing it,

"By the way, Mr. Tresser, the Cardinal of Vienna is Christoph Shorborn."

Outside, Tresser looked hard and long at the convent. He memorized its iron gate and fence, the building's entrance and windows and the slant of its roof. He similarly inspected the building only five feet from it on its right ride. It housed several ateliers. The sign in the top floor window read in Italian, *Belts, Jackets, Hats*.

He arrived back at the hotel at the same time Hank Tower arrived at Jolanda's apartment to escort her to their meeting with Mother Sister Michelle at 9:30.

CHAPTER 26

The "Be Careful" bell was ringing in my brain on my walk to Jolanda's apartment. The ring stems from my discovery of an increase in vulnerability when you think a danger has passed and what remains is a cinch. I recall as a youngster being driven up Pike's Peak in Colorado. The road is scary, but the driver said virtually all the car accidents occur on the last section of the return trip, where the road is nearly normal.

"People are glad to have the worst part of the drive behind them and forget to take precautions near the end," he said. I have found that to be true in my work as well; but anticipating a final end to the Temujin story was dulling the "Be Careful" bell.

Jolanda was also dulling the bell. I had thought of calling Carol several times, but always hesitated long enough for something to interfere before hitting the button. It wasn't concern about Tresser or the fifteen-percent psycho nut on the bridge or Bouchard or Paul Santori or the murders at the Plaza that got in the way. It was Jolanda's breath and voice and eyes and legs and breasts and skin and hair and every other part of her that kept my finger off the button.

Her apartment door opened after one push on the bell.

"I'm ready, Hank. We have plenty of time to get to the convent by nine-thirty."

She started to close the door behind her, then stopped. "Mammina!" came from the foot of the staircase just inside the apartment door, then at the open door came "Mamm..." It was accompanied by two big, brown eyes staring at me from the face of what had to be the prettiest three-year-old in Italy, and why not? I saw her father with Eleanor just before they went to room 716. He was one of the *crème de la crème* from a country with a high percentage of the world's handsomest men. Now, add in a mother who couldn't hide her beauty in a maid's uniform…

"This is Mr. Tower, Margherita."

"Ciao, signore."

"In English, Margherita."

"I am glad to meet you, Mr. Tower."

"We are going out for a while, then mommy has to go to work, but I'll be home tonight. You do what Gina tells you to do."

The child was standing about four feet from me with her eyes still fixed on mine. She stepped forward and offered her hand and said again "Mr. Tower," as if she wanted to remember the name. I took her small hand and said,

"Margherita, you are a very lovely little girl. Your mother has told me that you are very curious about things."

"Yes. I like the stars."

My repertoire with three-year-olds is non-existent. I tried to think of something pithy to say about stars and came out with, "They are always there every night."

"That's what mommy said. Did she tell you that?"

I grabbed it. "Yes, she did."

"Okay, Margherita. Back inside. We have to go."

"Will Mr. Tower be with you when you come home tonight?"

We both froze on that one. Neither of us knew where I would be tonight. Jolanda came to the rescue. "Inside. Upstairs. Right now. I'll see you tonight. Gina!"

The aunt appeared and closed the door.

We walked side-by-side quietly, then Jolanda took my hand and smiled at me. With a squeeze, "Relax, Mr. Tower."

Ten minutes later Gregory was escorting us into Mother Sister's small, drab office.

"Only outside access," my ass. The old hag didn't learn her techniques from reading some religious newsletter from Rome, thought Tresser. She studied trickery between her prayers. I will not be beaten here, not by some Machiavellian nun or pompous ex-Frenchie posing as the keeper of Italy's treasures, or a smart-ass detective from New York.

Tresser was hot, but not irrational. It was clear the Doge's Palace crowd had won the day with Mother Sister. But a deal isn't done until the goods pass. When that would take place was unknown, but having dealt with her he believed the good Sister would most likely insist the money be in her bank account before releasing the Temujin. That would take at least a day…and a night.

He ordered breakfast and made a call to his trusted right arm in Vienna.

"Jon, I need two of the best burglars in Venice by six tonight. The target is believed to be about two-feet long and three-feet high, maybe less, and probably weights about sixty pounds, maybe more. I need stealth and strength."

"Jesus, Carl. You want to steal the Temujin! Let it go, for Christ's sake! The police will know who did it and search your home.

You'll wind up in jail. You've got other things to worry about – like a big energy company. I just got a call from the Kiev office. The oil leases are being held up for…"

"Do as I say, Jon, or you'll be working for a small energy company. Call Ericsson. Get his two best. Have them meet me on the Riva degli Schiavoni in front of the La Pieta church. Pack night gear."

"Carl, please listen to me. I'm over three-hundred miles away and I can feel the bad vibes on this…"

"Part of being the big boss, Jon, is never giving up. I'm aware of your concern, but I'm not bringing it home. I'm selling it."

"What? You're selling stolen goods?"

"See, there's another mistake. Words matter, Jon. I'm merely relocating it before delivering it to the person who wants to buy it very badly. I am merely a middle man."

"But, Carl, if you get caught…"

"Tell Ericsson to recruit from Venice or nearby. No Vienna boys. The terms are the same. Total denial, if something goes wrong."

"Carl…"

"Do it, Jon."

Silence. "When will you be back?"

"As soon as I make my sale."

Resignedly, "Any special instructions?"

"Yeah. Tell the boys not to shoot any nuns. Bad press. Anything that looks like a New York detective is open season."

"I'll pass it on to Ericsson." My god, he's breaking and entering a convent, thought Jon. I work for a maniac.

"Please come in, children. Thank you, Gregory." Gregory closed the door and Jolanda and I took a seat in front of Mother Sister Michelle's dilapidated desk. She seemed more chipper than during our last visit.

"I must tell you," she said, "that there have been two other offers for the Temujin since we first met. I am very confident the convent will survive. At breakfast this morning I thought…" She stopped. The observation was a private one.

I was a bit uneasy with the two-offer news. "Mother Sister, are you entertaining one of those offers?"

"No, I am not, but I will share one of them with you. It was ten-million dollars."

"Was it from Carl von Tresser?"

"Why, yes, it was. Do you know him?"

"Mother Sister, he is a dangerous man. Whatever he promised you he will not keep. You were wise in refusing to sell the Temujin to him."

"Yes, I sensed that, Mr. Tower. How are you today, Jolanda Marcelli?" She looked at Jolanda, then at me. She sees it.

"I am fine, Mother Sister. May I say that you look fine, too?"

"Yes, you may, and thank you; but before we conclude what has brought Mr. Tower here, may I express something that is nettling me." I nodded.

"The Temujin is the convent's last chance to survive, Mr. Tower. I am loath to say that, but it is true and I am in charge. If we don't restore the building and provide somehow for the food and clothes of the sisters, well, centuries of history will end. I just don't know if the two-million euros you promise for the Temujin is enough to do both of those things. I am not a finance person. My experience goes no further than buying the simple things we need."

"Mother Sister, I am certain I can increase the amount to three million euros. I think there is little question that would be enough to shore up the foundation of the building and leave enough for the convent to earn a hundred-thousand euros a year in interest. Would that provide adequately for the sisters?"

Her eyes were wide. "Oh, yes, Mr. Tower, most adequately. Oh, yes. We could even…" She stopped. Apparently whatever indulgence entered her mind was just too sinful to entertain.

"All right, then we are agreed. Now, Mother Sister, von Tresser is a dangerous man. What kind of security do you have here in the convent?"

"Security? Well, we lock the front door at night."

"I thought so. Von Tresser will not use the front door to steal the Temujin…"

Jolanda, "Hank, do you think he would do such a …"

Mother Sister Michelle, "Mr. Tower, surely he would not break into the convent!"

"Mother Sister, I would not only say yes he would, I will give odds he will. It won't be him. It will be people who work for him. He must. Once the Temujin is in the Doge's Palace it is lost to him forever. Today, probably tonight, is his last chance."

"What can I do?"

"Move it today, but not until the three million is in your bank. Does the convent have a checking account?"

"Yes, but there is only a few euro…"

"Doesn't matter. Give me the numbers at the bottom of one of your checks. I am going to have the three million transferred today. You and Jolanda get the Temujin and bring it downstairs. Keep it out of sight. Is it too heavy for you?"

The two looked at each other and smiled. "We carried it upstairs to escape the flood."

"Good. The numbers, Mother Sister."'

"Oh, yes. All this is happening so fast."

"I'll call you, Jolanda, regarding the pickup time. I want to be here with Arnie when they arrive." She gave me a hero smile and I went outside to call Bouchard.

"Bouchard."

"Carlton, we have a deal no other curator on earth can come close to, but it has to be done fast. Can you get a trustworthy team to pick up the Temujin and take it to the Palace?"

"My God, Tower, you have it?

"I have it, but Tresser's sharpening his knives. We have to get it into the Palace immediately. I had to go to three-million euros from the two we discussed. No change on the other terms, two million into trust, seven-hundred-and-fifty and two-hundred-thousand in checks. Say yes."

"Yes, yes, good Lord, yes."

"Good, now I'm going to read you some bank transfer numbers.

Tell whoever your banker is that if he doesn't transfer the three million by two p.m., he's lost your account. Got a pencil? Okay. Here they are...I will pick up the bank checks I mentioned.

"Five-million, nine-hundred-and-fifty-thousand euros. Does it sound better that one hundred million?"

"Tower, Jesus. I don't know what to say..."

"Don't say, transfer and write checks, then get your team. Three men should do. Who do you know on the force?"

"The force?"

"The police force. This needs an armed escort."

"I know the Commandant."

"Ask him for his best four men and get them to the Convent of Mary Magdalene immediately. Have them stand in front and on the side between the convent and the building to its right. It's an easy jump from there to the roof of the convent. Tell them to be as visible as possible."

"The Convent of Mary Magdalene?"

"The Temujin has been in God's care for centuries."

"My God, I'm getting a dream price and donating to good works on top of it. Who is Jolanda Marcelli? Don't tell me, she's feeding the poor in Africa."

"No, she's the mother of a three-year old. The money goes into trust for her education."

"And the seven-fifty?"

"To a client that might not exist."

"You lead an interesting life, Mr. Tower."

"See you in two hours."

I called Jolanda. "Jolanda, tell Mother Sister that four policemen will arrive at the front of the convent within an hour. Don't be alarmed. They're there to keep out von Tresser. Shortly after that three men will come to take the Temujin to the Doge's Palace. Arnie and I will be there before they arrive. I will also have a bank check for two-million euros payable to you. A man named Carlton Bouchard will advise you on setting up a trust for Margherita."

"Hank, I have to see you. I can't let you go away…"

"I know." Then the mischief side of me erupted.

"Have you ever made love in a convent?"

I expected a rebuke, but instead I got, "There's a place in the rear of the first floor I used to escape to. It's where the laundry is piled up. My sister friend…"

"The one who let you in the Danieli."

"Yes."

"Do you know the term 'turn on'?"

"No."

"If there's a chance, I'll show you what it means."

After a short pause, "I think I know."

Tower turned away from the convent and started walking toward the Danieli. Tresser would be there and Tresser was cor-

253

nered. All men are dangerous when cornered; rich men obsessed with an object they must have and might lose are exceptionally dangerous. Would Tresser do something foolish? He knows I have a gun, thought Tower. Arnie has a gun, too. Tower called Arnie to brief him.

The man standing within eyeshot of the convent had witnessed the rush of calls Tower made from in front of the building. He was now convinced that whatever was inside that four-story vault was the answer to the puzzle he was trying to solve. He had seen Santori go in and concluded that he was the one who would provide the answer, but that was not to be.

Then he thought Tresser was his ticket to the fifteen percent, but he watched Tresser leave the building fuming in a display of anger that was clearly the result of whatever had transpired inside the building. Now, his surveillance told him that Tower had the best claim on the thing or person that was worth so much to everyone. He fell in behind Tower on his way to the Danieli.

CHAPTER 27

"Arnie, have you seen Tresser?' I had just entered the lobby of the Danieli.

"Aye, I saw 'im come in. 'e's steaming. "e went up the staircase in a few steps and is up there somewhere. I've been watching for 'im from the elevator and the staircase."

"I'm convinced he's going to break into the convent for the Temujin. Bouchard is arranging a police guard."

"Any calls from Phillip Santori, 'ank?"

"No. It seems he died with Paul."

"Aye. I called Lydia. She still 'asn't found a birth certificate for either a Paul or a Phillip Santori. Do ye think they were born outside the U. S. or they're false names?"

"If so, he or they are traveling on another country's passport. I want you to go to the convent and watch it. There's a building on the right with easy access to the roof. I can't imagine he would have his minions storm the place in daylight, but he might do it because he thought no one thought he would. I am going next door to the Doge's Palace to pick up three checks that are supposed to be ready at two – an hour from now."

"Aye, 'ank. I'm on my way."

"Be careful. Arnie."

"It's in me genes."

I went to the registration desk and had all of Arnie's and my charges from my cut-off time switched to my bill. I also took up watch for Tresser, not to protect the convent from him – he would have others do that job – to protect myself. He hired me to find the Temujin, which I did. He didn't hire me to broker its sale to him, which I didn't; but I'm not sure he would make the distinction.

I left a message for Lydia to tell me if the bill she e-mailed to his Vienna office was paid. If it wasn't, there was zero chance it would be. I took a seat with a view of the stairs and elevators and called Bouchard.

"Hello, Mr. Tower."

"Carlton, I'm at the Danieli. I'm coming over to pick up three checks and a wire transfer confirmation. I'm also watching for Tresser. He's boiling and dangerous. Where are you on three men to pick up the Temujin?"

"They're standing in front of me."

"Trusted?

"Impeccably."

"Wait until the police arrive before you send them. How are they carrying the Temujin?"

"In a large wooden box."

"Have the police accompany them to the Palace. People will think it's an important corpse. It will help clear a path walking to the Palace. How are you guarding it?"

"Relax, Hank. We have that covered. The place is full of valuables."

"But Tresser only cares about one of them."

"We have it handled."

"Okay. I'll be there at two."

"The transfer's already made to the sisters."

"The bank must think your account is worth keeping."

"It does."

I hit Jolanda's number.

"Are the police outside?"

"No, not yet."

"Christ!...sorry. They should be and that makes me nervous. Arnie, my associate, will be there in ten minutes. Don't open the door for anybody. Is the Temujin ready to travel?"

"Yes. It's on the first floor. Gregory is sitting on its steel case."

"Good. Now, I don't care if someone leaves a wailing baby at the door, don't open it."

"I won't. ...Hank?"

"Yes?"

"My whole body is tingling. All that's happening...the danger... the money for Margherita...I want you close to me...I..."

"I feel it, too. We are only hours away from ending this mad chase. I won't leave without seeing you. I promise."

"And then...oh, no, don't listen to that. I know what lies ahead..."

Then too quick to filter, "It's a small world, Jolanda."

"Carl, Ericsson has two Venetians on the job. They're ready to go when you give the word."

"In daylight? I hadn't thought of that. Why not? Waiting until night leaves room for chance. Yes, the sooner the better."

"They'll be seen, Carl. They may not want that risk. The law is very clear, I believe, about robbing a house, even in Italy."

"You see, Jon, this is why you need me. One must look beyond these small impediments. Houses in Venice sit on petrified trees that were submerged eons ago by the sea. Tell them to come in from below."

"From below?"

"There's a narrow canal behind the convent. Use a gondola, then go underwater and through the foundation pillars and up through the floor. The building looks decrepit enough to fall into the sea. There has to be a way through the floor from below."

"Hold on. I'm calling Ericsson."

The guy might be mad, but he's inventive, thought Jon.

"He says that will double the cost."

"Pay it."

An hour later two men tied what looked like a long Viking canoe to the backside of the four-floor convent and took off their gondolier coats. They slipped quietly into the chilly water and swam underwater through what used to be a door before the rising sea permanently submerged the upper half of it. Inside, with tiny halogen lights beaming from their caps, they inflated a small rubber boat and guided it through the maze of pilings that supported the convent's floor. There was only three feet of air space between the water level and the floor above them. They found a weak area in the planking near the front of the building that revealed a dim light peeking through the separations. They dimmed their own lights and found a plank loose enough to remove quickly and wide enough to climb through and point a gun at whoever might be in the room. They secured the inflatable near the break-in point and holding onto a pillar applied two crowbars to break through the floor.

"Arnie, are they there yet?"

"Not yet, 'ank. I 'ave a good view of both buildings. Nothing."

"What's with the Italian police? I'm calling Bouchard."

Bouchard, "Hank, there's a boat parade on the Grand Canal. The Commandant has to find men he can pull off it. Crowd control, he says. I can't push him too hard. We use the police at the Palace."

"Do you have the checks?"

"Yes, I do."

"I'm coming over to get them, then I'm going to the convent. Every bone in my body says Tresser…"

"Hank, what would he do with it? We have him boxed. No one will believe it's authentic?"

"Think, Carlton, think. You have five seconds before the buzzer…"

"He'll sell it to me."

"Right, and it won't be at the price you're paying now. I'm on my way."

I bounded out of the Danieli onto the Riva degli Schiavoni and straight into the Doge's Palace. Bouchard was behind his monster desk holding an envelope with the three bank checks in it.

"Thank you, Carlton. If I seem anxious about the money, please understand I hate working for nothing."

"I understand the two checks made out to Cash, but the large one to Jolanda Marcelli? I sense *amore*. Has Venice worked her romance on you?"

I grunted. "Jolanda will come to you for advice regarding the money. Set up a trust for a top education for the three-year-old and let her handle the rest herself."

"My, my, I never thought of Americans as altruistic. All that rugged individualism stuff we read about."

"Please handle it for her."

With a grin, "I shall, for her...and for you."

Fifteen minutes later I was at the convent.

"Still no police, 'ank."

"They're watching a boat parade." I called Jolanda inside.

"Arnie and I are outside within earshot of the front door. The police aren't here yet...the Palace delivery boys will be here in twenty minutes, three of them. Where are you?"

"With Mother Sister in her office."

"And Gregory is babysitting the Temujin in the foyer?"

"Yes. So is Mary Magdalene."

"Eh?"

"The steel container is on the floor right in front of her statue."

I almost said, "That's comforting," but refrained.

"When the carriers come I will call you. Come down to the foyer and wait for a one, one-two, one-two-three knocks on the door. Okay?"

"Okay."

"How far is the laundry room from the foyer?"

I could imagine the pink rise and fade in her cheeks. "It's complicated. I'll take you to it."

I grinned. "Now, we wait for the three from the Doge's Palace and hopefully at least two policemen."

Gregory sat on the steel container with his back to the statue of Mary Magdalene not sure of what else to do. Twenty steps above him on the second floor was the chapel and Mother Sister's office where she and former Sister Jolanda waited tensely for events to play out. On the third floor were the dining room, kitchen, a reading room and library. The sleeping quarters were on the top floor. The nuns had been instructed to keep the windows on all floors locked.

Gregory could hear water below the floor lapping against the foundation. Unusual, he thought, perhaps an exceptionally high tide was washing it. He looked at the floor and thought he saw a dim light through the cracks between the boards, some of which were a half-inch wide. Silver fish? With the tide? He was told to report anything he thought was unordinary, so he went up the stairs and relayed what he had heard and seen. Mother Sister took out her tide table – a must tool in oft-flooded Venice.

"It's near low tide, Gregory. Are you sure you heard water?"

"Yes, Mother Sister, and I saw a dim light coming through the cracks."

"I'm going down with you."

"No, Mother Sister. Please stay here where the sisters know you are. I'll go with Gregory."

"All right, dear, but let me know what you find."

Jolanda and Gregory descended the twenty steps to the foyer. They both went quiet.

"Listen, Sister Jolanda."

"Yes, there is something going on…"

Two black crowbars exploded through both sides of a large plank and with their hooks ripped it down into the water below. Jolanda jumped as if two snakes had struck at her. A head wearing a pullover cap with a small light attached to it and a ski mask covering its face came through the floor and looked directly at Gregory. The head was followed by a shoulder then a hand holding a gun pointing straight up. The breakthrough was only two feet from the edge of the steel container holding the Temujin. The other hand appeared holding a rope.

"Oh God, Sister! What shall we do?"

The gun was lowered at Gregory while the other hand reached to thread the rope through a circular ring on the end of the container. He's going to pull it through the hole, thought Jolanda. She pulled off her wool skirt and wound it into a thread small enough to run through the ring on the other side of the container. The strip stunned the concentration of the man trying to thread his rope. She had nothing on but panties and leaning forward to run her skirt though the ring exposed the smooth skin of her inner thighs. His eyes were fixed on her nakedness long enough for her to thread the ring. Now, she was pulling the container away from the hole in the floor. Gregory had stepped back away from the match, too numb to act. The tug of war was at a standstill, then the man pointed his gun directly at Jolanda's head. She would have been shot but for the weight of the statute of Mary Magdalene. It was too heavy for the damaged floor in front of it to support. The hole was only inches from its thick base. Its six-feet of marble tipped forward and fell into the hole, taking the man holding the gun with it in a gruesome cry. Jolanda went to the door and yelled for Hank. He and Arnie came rushing in guns out, but the invaders were not to be seen. The statue had buried them in the dark water below.

I stepped near the hole in the floor and was yelled back by Jolanda, who was still tugging the steel container to safely. I took the makeshift rope from her and pulled it into a solid corner of the room, then handed her skirt to her. Gregory was in a semi-trance, staring into near space. Mother Sister was at the top of the stairs asking in a controlled scream what had happened, was everyone all right? Outside the three men from the Palace arrived with what looked like a small coffin, and coming around a corner from a different direction were two policemen. Jolanda looked at me and started to shake.

"Arnie, call your guy on the Venice force and have them fish out whoever is down there. Then accompany the three Palace men and the two cops with the Temujin to the Doge's Palace. Tresser had his shot and lost."

I called Bouchard and told him he had the prize of his career, that the procession delivering it would leave the convent in about five minutes.

She was still shaking. "Hank…ank…I have to show you…"

"Arnie, there's a special part of the convent Jolanda has wanted to show me since we met. I'll meet you at the Danieli in about an hour."

"Aye, 'ank. I'll handle this. Is it a secret chapel? These old buildings always had one. I'll tell Mother Sister the two of you will be back to see her later today."

"Thanks, Arnie."

Jolanda turned to Arnie, "It's where the oldest ceremony of all is performed."

It's said that surviving danger can heighten sexual pleasure. Perhaps the need to reproduce is triggered after a close call with death. Whatever the cause, the saying is true.

CHAPTER 28

Tower and his assistant's dash for the building's door, the arrival of three men with what resembled a child's coffin, two policemen making a last minute run to the scene…it all told Long Finger that whatever was taken out in that box, thing or person, it was the treasure so many people were pursuing. Now that it was no longer available to any of them, Tower and the big guy would be going home. He did not want to be seen on the same plane with them.

Two hours later he was on a taxi boat to the Marco Polo airport for a non-stop, Delta flight to JFK and a cab to his one-room apartment on Manhattan's Lower East Side. He hadn't spoken to his homing pigeons in their loft on the roof for nearly a week; or fed them the sweet hummingbird feed that made them so strong; or let Boomerang perch on his long finger while he stroked him. He had timed Boomerang, his prize athlete, at 120 mph in a hundred-mile race he won handily.

The contents of the box must be worth in the millions to justify all the excitement, he thought. Being a fair man in these matters, he would use three million as his appraised value. Whatever was in the box might be worth more, but a commission of four-hundred-and-fifty thousand would be adequate compensation for his follow-up fee and the extra work it required. He had taken moderate stances in the past when the value of an item transferred as a result of his killing was difficult to determine. Yes, three million would suffice. He would call for it when the time was opportune; first, the pigeons.

The three delivery boys and two policemen arrived at

Bouchard's office with a wooden box and expanded chests. Arnie walked in behind them and stood back. It was curtain time.

One of Bouchard's men pulled out the temporary nails securing the top and with another's help set the wooden box on the front edge of Bouchard's expansive desk. There was only a weak clasp on the metal container inside. One of the three delivery men bowed as a signal for Bouchard to come around and do the honors. He approached it as one might approach a loved one deathly ill in her sick bed with eyes closed. Was she alive or dead? Was the treasure inside or not? He removed the top.

There it was: a small golden ship with as many as twenty golden oars protruding from each side angled down as if they were propelling the ship. The hull, the sides, the main deck, the angled roof were all gold. On the prow high above the deck was an empty, golden throne sitting atop a pod of leaping dolphins lined with emeralds and dotted with diamond eyes. Bouchard and one of his men carefully lifted the small ship from the container and set it on his desk. On the starboard and port side in letters composed of alternating diamonds and rubies was written "Temujin." Curved beneath the throne on the prow in a language only Bouchard knew was inscribed in a series of similar precious stones, "A Universal Ruler must reign over sea and land."

The miniature ship was two feet long, two feet high to the tip of its golden throne. There were no sails to power it, only the delicate, golden oars extending from each side. It sat on a golden cradle also decorated with diamond-eyed dolphins. The six men, including Arnie, simply stared at it, as if words would demean the moment. Finally, Arnie broke the silence with a hushed, "Aye, 'tis a beauty to see." Bouchard said,

"Mr. Macgregor, yes it is. There must be a thousand precious stones along its sides. It's interesting that the throne is empty. The Doge must have wanted to imply that the Great Khan would occupy it and be the senior partner in their mutual rule of the world. I plan to display the Temujin as the Brits display their Crown Jewels. There will be a small fee to see it and a short film of its history and purpose. The Temujin is not only a piece of art of the highest order, its play to the Khan's pride delayed the Horde's advance on the west. It probably saved our civilization.

"Its beauty and history will make enough money for the Doge's Palace to maintain the treasures it has and acquire more. To think another person wanted it only for himself; well, that's over. It saved Venice and now it's in Venice for the world to see. My office owes you and your associate a great deal, Mr. Macgregor."

"I believe 'ank is still at the convent, if you want to call 'im to see it."

"I'll do that right now, Mr. Macgregor."

Something's wrong, surmised Carl von Tresser, sitting in the lobby of the Danieli hotel. Through a wall of stained glass he was watching the shadows of people walking by outside. He saw them as devils mocking him.

Ericsson's men were trained to report events immediately. He called Jon in Vienna. He reported,

"Ericsson has nothing. No report, no call, zero. It's a flop, Carl. Get a boat to the airport and get on the Gulfstream now. You need to get out of Venice fast. There is a crisis here on the leases…"

"Not until I find out. Tell Ericsson to call me with what happened in the next ten minutes or he's blackballed across Europe. Call me back."

"Roger."

Tresser called Tower's room. Voice mail. Ditto Arnie's room. If I've been had, he thought, both of these bastards are going to pay.

Ten minutes later, Jon, "Ericsson got to the police through a sergeant that moonlights for him. Both hires are in custody. One has a crushed cheekbone and broken nose. A statue fell on him trying to nab the box you wanted. Get out, Carl. Get out now! This is blowing up."

'Goddam it! I'm not going to…"

"Carl, you're my boss. I work for you. I know you. There will be other deals. Get on your plane. Whatever it was you were after is now under police guard in the Doge's Palace. Do you want to break into…"

"All right, damn it. All right. I'm leaving now. I'll be back in Vienna by five, then…then I'm taking a trip to New York. Get me where a guy named Hank Tower lives or works. He's a private detective."

"Think about New York later after you've calmed down. Please, get on the Gulfstream. I need your Rolex mind on these leases. I'll tell Josef to have his twins from Odessa waiting in your apartment. You need therapy."

Unhearing, "Yes, yes, then I'm going to New York."

"I won't see you again, will I?"

I rolled over on my back. We were dressed in warm towels fresh from the large dryer, lying atop a pile of clean laundry bags full of sheets, nuns' habits and God-knows what else.

"Jolanda, I can't envision that."

"There is your woman…I have hurt her…I…"

I rolled back on my side to see her. Her face, her beautiful face and her soft lips were only inches from mine.

"No, none of that. I'm over twenty-one. I w anted you passionately. I still do now and I will tomorrow, but I have to return to New York."

"When you leave we will part. I have known that since the moment I took your hand in mine. I wanted you more than you wanted me. Since Giuseppe…since Giuseppe there has been no one, just Margherita and Gina and my work. Then you…I am…I am going to miss…"

She stopped. There were no tears of relief and there were no wise thoughts of comfort I could think of for her or for my messed up head. We automatically put an arm around each other and pulled our bare chests tightly together before an act of lovemaking that was perhaps the truest of my life. We were water in water.

We dressed and silently made our way up the stairs to Mother Sister's office and stood in front of her desk. The shrewd old bird saw through us as if we were open windows. I took the lead.

"Mother Sister, the Temujin has paid its rent for the convent's safe-keeping for so many centuries. It's now in the Doge's Palace, with some help from Mary Magdalene."

"I have been informed, Mr. Tower. One of the policemen said he will have the statue recovered today. The Doge's Palace is where the Temujin belongs. That is good. The convent owes you and Jolanda a great debt. We are financially secure and can stay where we are. I have feared for years that this crumbling building would evict us. There was no money to go anywhere else. The Temujin saved us."

"Sister, to accept your compliment would be false. I have been paid handsomely for what I have done. I am only an adventurous capitalist."

"The Good Lord will decide that in due course, Mr. Tower."

Then with the confidence of a trial attorney asking a witness a question he knows the answer to, she said,

"Perhaps He has already paid you His compliment?"

Jolanda shifted weight from one foot to the other. I retuned the nun's smile.

"Mother Sister, Venice ranks number one as the world's most romantic city. Even a capitalist's heart is not immune to its charm."

She smiled and said, "A Mr. Bouchard called a moment ago and asked if you were here. He has opened the Temujin and would like you and Jolanda to see it."

She walked around from her desk and extended her frail and wrinkled hands to Jolanda and me and said,

"Remember us. God be with you both."

We walked without words to the Doge's Palace. I didn't ask what was on her mind, but I felt like I had just been married. Jolanda knew some short cuts through the complex system of streets and canals that have evolved over centuries. You rarely see a tourist without a map in his or her hand, scrutinizing its cat's cradle of multi-colored lines. A visiting city planner would probably never sleep peacefully again.

Bouchard's receptionist announced us and the doors swung open to his basilica-size office. The small object on his desk dominated the vast expanse like a candle in a dark room. So here was what saved Vienna, Venice and perhaps much more from the Mongol Horde, what monks and nuns had been hiding from pillagers for roughly nine-hundred years, what the rich would pay tens of millions for, what people had been murdered for. I ran my finger over its golden roof in respect.

"It's here for good, Mr. Tower. It will be guarded like the British crown jewels. I cannot say I have seen anything more beautiful."

I looked at Jolanda. "You should know, Carlton, that this woman saved it from Tresser's men in a most creative way, I might add."

"I was told. What do you think of it?"

She looked at the Temujin and then at him and said very seriously,

"It has brought me the happiest day of my life and the saddest."

Bouchard said with a fatherly tone, "You are young. You will remember the happiest day much longer."

We left for her apartment. At the door I held her and said,

"I have to return, Jolanda, but not until tomorrow. Come to the Danieli and stay with me tonight. There is no danger. Tresser's probably as hot as Satan's pitchfork, but he wants me, not you. The same is true of another interested party I met on a bridge in London."

"I'll be there at seven for a cocktail. But don't let me have more than one. I don't want to dull any of my...my..."

"Neither do I, Jolanda, neither do I."

We kissed hard and I took a slow, lumbering pace back to the hotel. Christ! I'd rather knife-fight a mad Turk than deal with this heart stuff. I shuffled along trying to empty my head. No use. Finally I mumbled to myself, Carol, I know all the considerations… a Venice romance, the bonding danger creates, a lonely, love-starved ex-nun, a twelve-year age difference, a three-year-old daughter of a gigolo father; yet I don't know what to do, Carol. I don't know what the hell to do. I don't know what to tell you. She's in my head, my gut, my bones, and yet I can see you lying next to me and desire you…Jesus!

"I've booked a reservation for us on a late afternoon flight through London to New York, 'ank. It will be good to get 'ome and see the girls and my lass."

"Do it, Arnie, but I'm staying overnight. I'll get the twelve-thirty tomorrow."

"Aye, 'ank. Are ye fine? Can I do ye a favor?"

"I'm fine." I wasn't sure about the truth of what I said next, but it was cover for the conflict Arnie was picking up.

"I'm still worried about Tresser. The man's the most dangerous kind of fruitcake, a rich one. He's been beaten by people he hired to help him which will piss him off triple time. I want you to take these two checks and tell Lydia to deposit them first chance. They total nine-hundred-and-fifty thousand. We may need part of it for the psycho on the bridge in London. I prefer killing him, but he might not give us that option. Stay on high alert. He kills like we swat flies."

"Aye, 'ank. Take a rest. I'm off to pack. I'll see ye in the office."

I smiled at the big Scot. He knew why I was staying, but it wasn't his business.

"In the office, Arnie."

The six-hour difference meant it was noon in New York when she called. I was in my hotel suite undoing the .38 from the small of my back.

"Mr. Tower, am I disturbing you?"

"No, Edna. I'm just brushing up for dinner."

"I tried to time my call to the most convenient time for you. Forgive me, if I have disturbed you, but when my woman and professional instincts combine I am nearly powerless to defend myself from them."

I took a seat. "Has something happened?"

"I have the feeling something has. The more I thought about the case during your absence, the more I thought someone would be killed."

"Three people have been killed, an art dealer in London, a person hired to follow the person who knew the location of a very valuable artifact and the Paul half of the Santori twins, two by a professional killer. We don't know who killed the art dealer yet."

"Is the professional killer still at large?"

"Yes. I suspect he is on his way back to New York."

"I see. Is he planning to kill you?"

"Probably not, if I comply with his fifteen-percent fee."

"Is he the same man who killed the two people in the Plaza?"

"I am certain he is."

"Has he seen you?"

"Yes, and I have seen him. We had a discussion on a bridge in London."

Silence. "You are in grave danger, Mr. Tower."

"I'll handle it, but…"

"But what?"

"Nothing. I'm returning to New York tomorrow…"

"And you would like to talk to me about something other than the case."

I wished for a mad Turk with a knife, then plunged.

"Yes."

"Of course we can talk, but let me ask about the other twin. Where is he?"

"It's possible he doesn't exist. My associates think the murdered one, Paul, was playing both sides of the twin game. *Why* is an open question. I'm not sure he was, but their case is strong."

"I am aware of twins using their similarities to their advantage, but someone posing as his twin is inventive. With nearly fifty years in the field, I haven't come across it. If the other twin – Phillip, wasn't it? – is still alive, does he pose another danger to you?"

"I don't think so. If he's alive, he's still my client. Do twins murder one another?"

"Mr. Tower, the mind is capable of anything."

"I'm staying another day. I'll be back tomorrow."

"Mr. Tower, keep guilt out of your considerations. It can cause bad decisions."

I did a mild jump. From 4,153 air miles away, she knew why I wanted to talk.

CHAPTER 29

Jolanda was sipping a chardonnay; I had a pinot noir, slightly chilled. Beneath us, again, alive with activity, was the large Venetian basin where the Grand Canal empties into a much wider channel. From the fifth-floor terrace of the Danieli, we were watching the various boats of this car-less city going this way and that way, as if they were looking for something. The sight is romantic, captivating, hypnotic, calming, pleasing, unique and magnificent. I had my arm around her waist snuggling her close to me. If Venice is the "Best in Class" in the world's list of romantic cities, then we were standing in Cupid's pulpit.

We had planned to have dinner inside the rooftop restaurant behind us, but...

With her warm breath on my cheek, "Hank, I had a snack around five. I'm not hungry. Besides, dinner must be very expensive here. Why don't we skip it and have a big breakfast."

Moments later we were in bed in my suite.

We talked, but avoided the obvious. If we got too carried away with our happiness, or too forgetful of our situation, Separation would drop its gavel as a reminder. She kept looking at the clock on my side of the bed, so I turned it aside. We finally fell asleep about midnight, at least I did. At 7:00 we were awake, but remained in bed until 8:00.

Breakfast was served in the room, but there was no appetite, despite the lack of dinner. We picked at the fruit and nibbled the croissants silently. My 10:00 boat to the airport was looming over us like a death-row priest. Finally, we went downstairs to the small canal on the side of the Danieli where boats pick up and deliver guests. I handed my bag to the driver and we stepped a few feet down the narrow landing. This time there was a tear.

"I hope she is a good woman for you, Hank. It's right that you go back to her. I...I will be all right. If you ever come back to..."

"Jolanda, let's leave it as we remember it. If circumstances change..."

I didn't finish. She kissed me hard on the mouth, turned quickly and disappeared into the hotel. I stood there staring for a moment while the driver waited. Finally, he helped me into the boat and backed it out of the narrow canal into the main channel where he turned the bow toward the airport and revved the engine. I didn't look back from the boat or the airplane.

Von Tresser woke early, dismissed the twin entertainers from his bed and freshened himself with a shave and cold shower. The romp had cleared his thinking on how to handle the oil-lease problem, but it did not lessen his determination to avenge the loss of the Temujin to two amateurs from New York. He arranged for the Gulfstream to fly him to Shannon Airport where he would fly commercially to JFK in New York.

He had Tower's East Fifty-sixth Street address in his pocket and from Ericsson he had instructions on how to contact a freelance killer who lived in Manhattan. It was a departure from the distance he usually insisted on in these matters, but this time he wanted in on the kill, both of them. He figured the six-hour flight from Shannon to JFK and the six-hour gain in time zones should get him to the Ritz Carlton on Central Park South early afternoon today, New York time. Once there, he would contact Ericsson's man.

The twins showered separately and were slipping on their panties when Tresser emerged refreshed and naked from his private bath. He growled like a beast, picked up one of them and dropped her on his massive bed. The other twin giggled and jumped in the game, rolling her sister playfully off of Tresser and smothering him with her own nakedness. The imminent killing of Tower and Macgregor had Tresser's libido at full staff.

A half hour later he dismissed them again, dressed and went to the Vienna airport where his Gulfstream G550 was waiting for him. He would breakfast in the air.

Long Finger always let his phone ring four times before answering it. If it stopped at four, then rang three times and stopped, then two times, then one, he would answer it immediately, which he did now. He gave his code name and got confirmation.

"This is Herbert."

"Herbert the Second?"

"Yes."

"I'll be watching the first horse carriage in the line on Central Park South across from the Ritz Carlton. I'll be there in an hour. Pet the horse's right cheek, then get in the carriage. I'll join you."

"I'll be there." Long Finger was standing inside the large loft where he kept his homing pigeons. He pocketed the phone and sprinkled more hummingbird seed into a large dish on top of an old kitchen table. Two of his five pigeons immediately started pecking at it. He carefully moved them away and invited Boomerang to feed.

"The Captain always eats first. Mark and John always remember that, why can't the two of you?" he asked, referring to the pair of pigeons sitting obediently on top of the small cage he used for racing events. The bad-mannered Luke and Matthew backed off reluctantly, letting their leader have first go at the delicious seeds.

"Next week we race from Boston back here, one-hundred-and-ninety miles." Stroking Boomerang's back, "You did it in ninety-one minutes last time. This time you'll do better."

The other four were perched side by side on top of the travel cage. "Yes, this time we'll set a new record." He gently lifted Boomerang on his long finger and the other four arrived at table with a single flap of their wings.

Long Finger exited the cab and walked to the line of horse carriages waiting for customers along Central Park South. He stroked the first horse's right cheek, paid the driver and stepped up into the seat. A winter blanket was folded next to him. He told the driver another person was joining him.

Three minutes later Tresser stepped up into the carriage and froze at the sight of the man who stopped him on the walkway in front of the Danieli hotel in Venice. The two stared at each other. Long Finger had his hand under his jacket on his nine-millimeter. Tresser quickly held out his hand. "Wait! We need to talk."

Long Finger kept his hand in place and moved as far to the edge of the two-seater as he could, keeping his eyes on Tresser. Tresser sat on the blanket and said in a low, hurried voice,

"I'm surprised, too. I didn't expect it to be you. We have a mutual interest. Let me explain." He motioned the driver to begin and the carriage jerked forward. Under the noise of the traffic and the clopping of the horse's feet on the hard pavement, Tresser said,

"I will pay you a half-million dollars, one-third immediately and the rest when it's done." Long Finger waited. "I want you to kill Hank Tower and Arnold Macgregor. Nod yes or no." Long Finger's cold eyes remained fixed on Tresser's, his hand still on his gun.

It was four o'clock and starting to get dark.

Part way into Central Park Tresser left Long Finger alone in the carriage. The killer had neither nodded nor shaken his head. He simply handed Tresser a small piece of paper with bank numbers on it, to which Tresser nodded his understanding and said he would execute the transfer immediately. He walked briskly back to his suite in the Ritz Carlton satisfied that he had not been seen or heard by anyone.

The man never said a word, thought Tresser. Was that unusual among hired killers? He would ask Ericsson. But something else was eating at him. He could understand silence and freezing stares, but he detected something else in the man's frozen face. Calculation, he thought. He's a negotiator. Tresser didn't doubt he was a killer. His instincts said so, and Ericsson wouldn't err in that regard. But this one was an electronic calculator as well. Would he take the down payment and disappear? Tresser doubted that. Ericsson would cut him off his list. Would he take a better deal? That was the rub. Tresser couldn't decide. His private phone rang. It was Jon.

"Carl, the deal's off. Centurion doubled our bid. I told you we were too low! These guys aren't patsies. Boss, get back here in Vienna. Please! They won't listen to me. They don't believe we're serious unless you're across the table from them. If we don't get the leases, the stock will plunge. The press has hyped it for us…you could lose…"

"I know how much I could lose. I'll call you back."

Tresser knew his company's stock price reflected the oil leases being a sure thing. He certainly paid the reporters plenty to say so in their columns. If Centurion prevailed, the stock could be cut in half. He would lose on paper nearly a billion dollars. He thought of letting it happen and buying the rest of the shares at the basement price, but what if missing this deal meant he couldn't get any new leases? That would send the stock to the center of the earth. The risk was too great. He called Jon.

"Go ten percent above Centurion."

"It won't fly, boss. They want you and your signature. We have one more bid. If they think it's too low or a head fake, they go with Centurion. They say they have heard discomforting rumors about our breakdown record."

"Shit to that! Have the Gulfstream at Shannon. I'll be on the next non-stop from New York."

"Jesus, Carl, is that where you are? My God, take a cold shower. Forget it, for your company and yourself, forget it, forget it, forget it. Your fortune and many others are at stake here. Get the goddam art thing out of your head. What do they say about cutting off one's nose to spit the face? It applies here."

"Another lecture like that and you'll have a nose-less face. Get me a first-class ticket. I'll pick it up at the counter. God damn it!"

But Carl von Tresser would not leave unfulfilled. He had one-hundred-and-sixty-seven-thousand dollars transferred to the numbers the iceman gave him in the horse-drawn buggy.

The six-hour time difference had me home in our apartment at 3:00 in the afternoon. With a short nap, a shave and shower and a shot of Remy XO I would be back on all cylinders, physically. Seeing the apartment, the furniture, the bed was not as easy to handle. I was away only a few days, a short time measured by most of my excursions, but looking around our home everything seemed a year old. Carol wouldn't be home until 7:00, most likely, so I wrote a note saying I was back sans bullet holes and cuts and needed some time at the office. Don't do dinner for me. I softened that to "I'll pick up a sandwich at the office."

I tossed my coat on a chair, put the airline gun box in the closet and sat for a moment in a chair across from the couch. The lightheadedness from the long plane ride had me seeing Carol lying on the couch naked under one of my white shirts. Her hair was hanging loose over her shoulders and a long shapely leg dangled over the side. It was the position I found her in when I entered the apartment over a year ago. We were silently deciding whether to move in together and if we did, which apartment would we occupy. Hers was clearly the better one, but I loved mine. Abandoning a good apartment is not an easy decision to make in Manhattan. People hunt the obituaries for first shot at a good one. She was reading something, I recalled, oblivious to the heart-stopping picture she posed. I remember saying to myself, looking at her, "You're a dead duck, Tower. Welcome to your new home." Now, now I...

I had no intention of telling Carol about Jolanda, but there's a truism buried somewhere in the Aeneid I remember from way back. It says you can't deceive a lover. Dido knew from Aeneas's behavior that he was leaving her before he knew himself. Carol was not only bright; she was every piece a woman with all the instincts and sensitivities that come with the gender. Unless I shook Jolanda from my mind, Carol would know and, God, I didn't want to hurt her.

I flopped on the bed and forced a two-hour nap. After a fresh up and a shot of Remy, I was in the office at 6:30. Lydia was gone and Arnie wasn't due until the morning. I was taking off my suit coat, looking at the deposit receipts Lydia had put on my desk for the two checks I gave Arnie, when I heard the door to the outer office opened slowly. The amounts were almost one-million, two-hundred-thousand dollars, not nine-hundred-and-fifty thousand; then I remembered the checks were in euros, a twenty-five-percent bonus.

I started to loosen the .38 in the small of my back when a large man with a pepperoni face bundled for Siberia stepped inside, smiling.

"Damn, is it always hot in here? Let's have a talk, Tower," said Phillip Santori, shedding his massive fur coat and Cassock hat.

CHAPTER 30

"Isn't Venice a wonderful place, Tower? I'm surprised Janet never hauled me off to it. Lord knows, it meets her top criteria – expensive. Did you enjoy it?" He was working his mass into the chair in front of my desk.

"That Italian girl. A real knockout. I'd take her over Eleanor any day."

That caught my attention. "What do you mean you would take her over Eleanor any day?" I maneuvered in my chair to free the .38 in my back. This surprise visit could be going places unforeseen.

"Tower, surely you have put your mind to that aspect of my doings, but then again, there was that Italian girl. Can't blame you. Beauty distracts."

"You were having an affair with Eleanor?"

"A torrid affair. No, make that a hellfire affair – for me." He scanned the room. "You have a recorder in here?"

"No, go on."

"Well, at first it was a gag. I played Paul and got her in bed one afternoon. Damn, it was good, so good I repeated the performance a few times with an afternoon 'Surprise, it's me!' He caught on, of course, and a rather nasty exchange followed between us. By this time I was as hot as a sire horse with a mare. I was going mad because of her, so…"

"So you had her killed?"

"It was the only way to get her out of my life. Paul told her to look for the mole…" He pulled back his collar, showing me the one on his neck "…and that was that. No more goodies for Phillip. Only mockery. She was a triple-crown bitch, Tower. The world will not miss her, Paul certainly won't."

"You had your twin killed?"

"No, no, I could never do that. I actually felt sorry for him. The guy really loved the whore. Me, I saw her for what she was. I wanted the sex. A very dangerous game, Tower. I recommend against it. Sex, good sex, the kind that sends you crashing through the Pearly Gates, gets a hold on you. God, it was good. You sure you don't have a recorder in here. I'll bust your gut, if you do."

"I don't, but right now I wish I did. So who killed Paul?"

"The pro I hired to put Eleanor out of my life. It's the only explanation I can come up with. He thought Paul was me. I met him face to face. Not good, Tower. I recommend against that, too. If you need a professional killer and you want to meet him, tell him to wear a ski mask. You do not want to know what he looks like. Anonymity is essential to his trade. If you come across the one I used, tell him to wear mittens, too. He has a grotesque finger that sticks in your memory like a spear, and he knows it does. He was tracking me for elimination and saw me go into Paul's hotel near the Rialto bridge - and Paul come out on his way to the convent."

"You knew about the Temujin?"

"Is that the thing? Like I said, I only knew there was a hot item in play and I wanted a piece of it, so, again, the old substitution game. Paul and this British dandy were talking about it in an area off his hotel's lobby, a conversation I overheard. I saw Paul leave and go up to his room. I waited a few moments and came back into the room pretending to be Paul returning. The pansy spilled all the details to me. I actually had a shot at a three-million euro check, but being a fair man, I would only demand my seven-fifty as soon as Paul had the money from the sale of the thing-a-ma-jig everyone was sexed up about. When Paul was murdered, I took the next boat to the airport. I knew the killer thought Paul was me."

"Then if the killer spots you in New York, he'll see his mistake and…'

"Not a particularly brilliant insight, but accurate. That's why I'm going to earth. I need the seven-fifty I hired you to get back for me to finance my new life."

"Not yet, Phillip. There's another murder to account for, the one in London. You were in London…"

"So was the guy with the finger. I saw him there and split for Venice. That's where Paul went and where the thing he was after was located. Want my theory?"

I leaned forward with a speak-goddamn-it face.

"I take that for a yes. Do you want an infomercial or a one-minute spot?"

"Jesus, Phillip!"

"Ah, you prefer brevity. I ask you this. If one twin can hire a killer, can the other one?"

I thought back to Edna's fantastic story of the identical twins separated at birth, and found to be indistinguishable in their appearance and traits decades later. It's a strong match.

"I would have to say yes."

"And that is my theory. Paul saw a threat in this art guy and somehow hired my finger guy to knock him off. I don't know how that happened. Maybe the killer found Paul, thinking he was me

– not to knock me off, to get more money, then knock me off. Paul realizes he's a pro and hires him to get rid of his London problem. Now the psycho has two reasons to knock me off, if he finds me.

"I repeat. The seven-fifty, Tower. I need to travel. Have you ever been to the Brazilian jungle? No, probably not. I hear it's hot as Hades, but the women are quite accommodating. I read they like kooky stuff."

If he was right about Long Finger not allowing anyone to know his face or finger, I was in trouble as well. We were face-to-face on that bridge in London.

"So you think Paul had Jerome Manchester killed to keep him from messing up his big score with the Temujin."

"Yeah."

"Phillip, you are an accessory to murder. Two murders, Eleanor and Giuseppe."

"One. Giuseppe belongs to the killer. That was his decision."

"One is enough for life imprisonment." Then with an angry voice, I said,

"And me! What about me? You sent me into a killing den. You were setting me up to get killed, and you want money?"

"Yes to the money part; no to the set-up part. I had no idea the finger guy would work that fast, or work at all. I was new to the hired-gun game. My wise-guy source had never met him or seen him. He only had a phone number and a code to follow.

"I truly wanted pictures of her in bed with someone. I didn't know if the killer would perform or would simply take my down payment and disappear. If he did that, I would still have pictures to show Paul and other suckers she would try to work after Paul pitched her. Hell's fury isn't exclusively female, Tower. My mistake was misjudging you. You were smarter that you were supposed to be. Insufficient research. It always comes back at you. Now, the seven-fifty."

"Phillip, I don't keep more than five-hundred dollars in the office. The money is in the bank."

"What bank?"

I told him.

"Go on line to your account. I have my bank numbers." Along with that instruction came a gun, a small caliber, shiny, three-shot that looked ridiculous in his catcher-mitt hand. It was easy to hide and deadly at close range.

"I've only used it once. I missed the target twice, but got it right on the third shot. There's a two in three chance I'll miss you. Want to chance it?"

"Phillip, I…"

My sentence ended abruptly, as did Phillip's life. Standing at the door was Long Finger holding a nine-millimeter with a silencer that had just put a bullet into Phillip's skull. He slumped forward, stuck in the chair, dead. I started to reach for my .38…

He pointed the gun at me. "Don't. I want you alive."

He stepped forward and took the gun from Phillip's hand and put it in a side pocket of his jacket. With his gun still pointed at my head, he said,

"Don't be foolish. Put your gun on the desk where I can see it. Hold it by the butt with two fingers."

There were no two chances in three this shooter would miss. I obeyed. He pulled a chair from the side of the room and took a seat alongside the slumped over corpse. He said righteously,

"I executed him." A man who had committed two murders in New York, one in London and two more in Venice and probably countless others seemed proud of his public service. Why he wanted me alive was a welcomed mystery. Did he want his fifteen-percent, follow-up commission, and then a permanent bye-bye to Tower?

It was a commission deal all right, but not the kind I expected.

"Push your gun a little closer to me. Good. Now, let me explain why he is dead and you are not. I want you as one of my silent partners."

He waited for a reaction. There was none. How in hell do you react to that?

"Mr. Tower, there are six-thousand murders that go unsolved every year in the U. S., one-hundred-and-eighty thousand over the last thirty years. Some are drug related, but many are transactions for clients by people in my business. My problem is sitting next to me. He insisted we meet. That means I can't let him live. Seeing this man in New York means killing his twin in Venice was a fortuitous transaction. He might have gone free and identified me. I just wasted a bullet because this fool wanted direct contact. This is no way to do business.

"So I use intermediaries. Very few of them see me. I pay a thirty-percent commission."

"You want me to recommend killings to you?"

"Transactions. I have read newspaper articles about you. I watched you perform in London and Venice. You advertise, you attract a lot of customers. I am sure some of your prospective clients, like this one sitting next to me, want an irrevocable solution to their problem. If he had contacted me through you, the bullet wouldn't have been necessary."

The only thought in my head was staying alive as long as possible and hope the cavalry would arrive. He went on in the sincere and assuring tone of a mutual fund salesman.

"I've been in the business about fifteen years, but sales are down from twenty to ten a year. If we team up, that could go to thirty. If you have moral problems, consider that six-hundred-thousand figure and people who steal lifetime savings. It's not a perfect world. If you have a moral problem, let me know."

I knew what that meant and was about to disown the penal code, the tax code, the Ten Commandments...any rule I could think of. But from the outer room came not the sound of the cavalry's bugle, but a sound that sent terror through me...

"Hank, are you in there? I was in P.J. Clark's with Didi and saw the light." It was Carol.

"Keep her out or I have to kill her."

I jumped from my chair to the door and quickly closed it behind me.

"Carol, my God, honey, please leave..." I did rapid thumbs down on what was in the other side of the door.

"Please, I'll be home in an hour, but leave now..." More thumbs down. She got the message, but "Why?" was written all over her face.

"Please, Carol..."

The door opened two inches and she saw the muzzle of a silencer peek through.

I yelled "Stop! She's leaving!"

The door opened another two inches. He was going to kill her. I threw my weight against it, pinning the gun's silencer for a moment, then jerked it open and bowled into him like a hunched over fullback. I knocked him back, but not down. He still had the gun and was getting his balance. I grabbed my .38 off the desk by the barrel and whacked him in the forehead with the butt. It was a glancing blow, but enough to keep him off balance and keep him from aiming the gun; but he still had control of it. The silencer was coming up at me. I reversed the .38 in my hand – almost dropping it – and fired two shots into his chest. He went back from the impact, still alive, eyes wide open, with a Satanic grin at Carol who was standing frozen behind me. The gun was still in his hand. I fired a third round into his forehead, then a fourth in his right eye. It was over.

Carol had her hands over her face, screaming in fright. I pulled her close to me. She was trembling uncontrollably. I held her as close to my body as I could without breaking her ribs. I wanted to put another bullet in the psycho's head – the son of a bitch almost killed my woman! – but stayed with her, holding her tightly to my chest.

I led her to the couch in the outer office and closed the door on the two bodies. All I could do was absorb her violent shaking and hope it would subside. She wouldn't have heard a word I said had I known what to say and tried to say it. Finally, she put her arms around me and returned my tight hold. Her head was down in my chest when she said, "My God, Hank, this is madness."

And it was. And I was responsible. And this was wrong, wrong, wrong. And this…and this…and this could never happen again…and…

Captain Tom Holden of the Seventeenth got Hank Tower's call

and sent officers and a Medical Examiner immediately to the scene. The M. E. gave Carol a sedative and after promising Holden a complete statement, Tower took her home in a cab. She was groggy from the medication, but it's doubtful anything would have been said between them had she been fully alert. He took her into the bedroom of their apartment in Greenwich Village, helped her undress and stretch out on the bed. He set the M. E.'s remaining capsules and a glass of water on the bedside table. She went quickly from wooziness to sleep.

Tower stood over her thinking how close death had come, to him as well, but her death was the one weighing on his mind. He wondered how deep the mental scar would go and how long it would last. He tried to dismiss the latter with a "Time cures all" palliative, but he knew that has always been false. Time doesn't cure trauma...it merely hides it under subsequent events. Dreams never forget.

She was beautiful. Lying there drugged and helpless, he wanted to protect her, to kill mercilessly anyone who would harm her. A surge of self-anger went though him. Protect her? How laughable was that?

He recalled the spark the first time they saw each other in the Plaza hotel's lobby bar. Their coming together was as natural as a summer breeze. They would go on to kid each other with impunity, laugh together at something when others were just too square to see how funny something was. Making love always washed away the tensions that arose between them occasionally. In the simplest of terms, they were happy. Could they be happy again? Could he be happy again?

He went into the living room with a blanket and slept fitfully on the couch. The dreams came and went. There was the Temujin with a locomotive facing the wrong way on its deck; Jolanda kissing someone else while he tried to find her in the mishmash of Venice's streets and canals; Carol in dressage riding a horse in a jumping contest. Then came a silent, terrifying, bodiless force that wanted to crush him. He shook himself awake and fell back asleep dreamless.

Carol called in sick and I lingered over breakfast. We said nothing until I mumbled that I had to give a formal statement and rose from the table. She remained seated. I put my hands on her shoulders and squeezed gently. I said,

"I'll be back around three." She nodded.

I told Lydia to take the day off and after I briefed Arnie he said he would clean up the office. The statement took about an hour with a woman lieutenant and a stenographer in the Seventeenth Precinct's chilly headquarters. I signed it and went to Edna's apartment in the East Seventies. She was holding a half-hour open for me.

"...and that is how it ended," I said, proud of my ten-minute summation of events since we last talked. She was sitting in an old leather chair across from me with her eyes fixed on mine. I noticed a box of tissues on the table next to me.

She continued the silence and the staring. Was this some kind of cat and mouse game? Finally,

"Has it ended?"

"The case is over. The police have the guy's prints and ..."

"Mr. Tower, you know that's not what I mean."

I did, of course, but I didn't have an answer.

"I'm not sure Carol and I can make it after what happened."

"I see. Why did you set up such a generous trust fund for Jolanda's daughter? You could have kept all or part of it for yourself."

I squirmed a bit. "If you could have seen her…"

"Yes?"

"She was beautiful and bright. It would have been a waste for her not to have the best education possible."

"I see."

"You think I saw my own daughter in her."

"Did you?"

I looked out the window. "I'm over here, Mr. Tower."

"Yeah." I looked back at her prying eyes. "Maybe I did."

"I see. And Jolanda. Did you see her as your wife?"

Spontaneously, "No, I…"

"You saw her as what?"

"A beautiful woman, sensuous, caring, soft, intelligent."

"I see."

Something cleared. I had just described perhaps the perfect woman, yet I didn't see her as my wife. I had to think about that.

Edna kept her twin x-rays on me. "Do you see Carol as your wife?"

"Yes, I do, but I don't want to…"

"…to have a child."

"No. It's too much responsibility."

"I see."

"Edna, if you say that one more time I'll draw my gun."

She smiled. "Carol seems to accept your line of work and I doubt the trauma will change that. It will remain with her, but a child to care for would overpower it. May I suggest you speak to others whose work includes danger. Would you like to speak again?"

I dropped my chin for a moment then raised my eyes directly into her line of fire.

"Yes, I would."

EPILOGUE

Long Finger's name was Francis Clarke. He hailed from a small town in Kansas and had served a short spell in its state prison for car theft. Tom Holden told me that it would be unlikely they could connect him to any unsolved murders. His quarters on the Lower East Side were eventually found with the help of Carol's web site, solve-it-ny.com, where his reconstructed picture was posted. A few books on homing pigeons and a framed, close-up picture of a husky pigeon with "Boomerang" written underneath it were found on top of scratched chest-of-drawers, but nothing concerning his trade was discovered.

A death certificate for a Homer Santori dated 1999 was found in Paul's effects and was presumed to be his and Phillip's father. The search for the twin's birth certificates continues.

Alistair Baker was of no interest to me, nor was I of any interest to him.

Two months after Venice, Jolanda sent me a post card with a "Take care, Hank" sign off. I sensed a beau.

Bouchard sent me a "Come on back" note with a ten-thousand euro guest card for the Bauer hotel, the most expensive in Venice, and a letter entitling me to free bottles of wine from any of his many wine stores with a prudent "Good for a year, up to one-thousand euro" printed across the bottom.

Tresser?

Tresser worries me.

AUTHOR'S NOTE

I would like to point out a few historical truths in the novel. First, Temujin was indeed Genghis Khan's real name. Genghis Khan means Universal Ruler. The extraordinary number of the Khan's living male ancestors is also true; largely because he and his descendents murdered the males they conquered and seeded the females. It is also true that the Mongol Horde was at Vienna's doorstep in the early 1200's; but it wasn't the fictitious golden Temujin that delayed its march on Europe. More likely, according to historians, the Khan had to return to headquarters to settle political problems among his generals. His absence and death in 1227 allowed Europe and the Turks in the south enough time to fashion defenses against the Horde's advance. The ruling Doge at this time was, in truth, Pietro Ziani; but it's permissible to doubt his role in the story.

The fearsomeness of the Horde is accurate. For an understanding of its methods and the terror they struck in men and women, read an extraordinary piece in the April 25, 2005 issue of *The New Yorker* magazine by Ian Frazier entitled *The Invaders*.

Charlie Horn

ABOUT THE AUTHOR

Born and educated in St. Louis, Missouri, Charlie Horn was a Naval Officer, a corporate "Mad Man" in New York, a writer of numerous successful "How to" financial books, a Registered Investment Advisor, publisher of an investment newsletter subscribed to by thirty-thousand people, and one of the top direct-response copywriters in the country. His DR ads sold $200,000,000 worth of products. Now, he is an accomplished writer of crime fiction.

His Hank Tower PI series includes a variety of human insights in the fast-moving world of who-dun-its. His fresh style moves a reader smoothly from page to page.

Horn targets two Hank Tower novels a year. Currently available on e-books and in printed form from amazon.com are:

WALL STREET KILLERS
THE BENNINGTON MURDERS
THE DEATH CHIP

Horn lives with his wife in Connecticut and has a daughter, son-in-law and three young grandchildren.

ACKNOWLEDGEMENTS

To Barbara for her professional critiques and advice.

To Al and Matt and Lynne and many other heavy readers of the genre for their positive playback.

To Linda for her wifely overview.

To Doug for his cover design and formatting patience.

To the web for its boundless supply of information.

Made in the USA
San Bernardino, CA
22 March 2013